praise for _Cigarettes_

"In _Cigarettes_, Mathews takes us more interestingly than ever into that unfinished work of art, the self, exposing powerful dependencies and subtleties in a cast of characters distinct and poised yet half-groping toward others and themselves. The plot, the tale, the laying bare, are intriguingly staged and timed in a novel as imaginative as it is disturbing."—Joseph McElroy

"Harry Mathews is the only American author I know whose utter originality does not erode his heart and his content. _Cigarettes_ is odd, skillful, touching, wide, cultured, and engrossing."—Ned Rorem

"_Cigarettes_ has the delicate yet rigorous architecture of latticework: if we concentrate on the light streaming through its apertures we are still attentive to its carpentry; if we focus on its geometry the light is, of needs, a constant presence. It is a triumph of the imagination."—Gilbert Sorrentino

"Wonderfully fresh and inventive."—David Lehman, _Newsweek_

"A very complex, original, unusual, provocative work. . . . A tight, intriguing modern novel that deserves wide attention."—_Library Journal_

"Mathews has perfected a witty, supple, and aphoristic style, capable of many effects. . . . An odd and gratifying novel."—_New York Review of Books_

"There is a relentless quality of incident, but Mathews runs the whole sequence without a hiccough of implausibility or forced conjunction."
—_Times Literary Supplement_

"A brain-teasing game that is both absorbing and exhilarating. . . . As a stylist, Mathews manages to tinge familiar objects and places, such as New York, with a delectable strangeness."—_Publishers Weekly_

"Like a clever gamester, Mathews teases the reader with plot twists and jokes as he subtly but seriously examines the nature of perception."—_Booklist_

"A brilliant and unsettling book. . . . Mathews weaves into each of his several story-threads more unexpected twists than you'll find in the average multi-volume Victorian novel."—Tom Clark, _Los Angeles Times Book Review_

"_Cigarettes_ is Harry Mathews at his most brilliant and passionate, a tour de force by one of the most remarkable prose stylists presently writing in English."
—_San Francisco Chronicle_

"Brilliant . . . highly original, a tour de force. . . . On the basis of _Cigarettes_ alone, Harry Mathews has few, if any, equals in modern fiction."
—_San Diego Union_

D1225034

"Like Roubaud and Perec, Mathews engineers a funhouse labyrinth in which guise disfigures guise and the logic that reigns is that of representation."
—*Voice Literary Supplement*

"*Cigarettes* provides enough plot for a season of mini-series."
—*New York Times Book Review*

"A brilliant Jane Austen-like social comedy on the unfathomable nature of human relationships."—Lanie Goodman, *Washington Post Book World*

works by Harry Mathews

FICTION

The Conversions
Tlooth
Country Cooking and Other Stories
The Sinking of the Odradek Stadium
Cigarettes
The American Experience
Singular Pleasures
The Journalist

POETRY

The Ring
The Planisphere
Trial Impressions
Le Savior des rois
Armenian Papers: Poems 1954-1984
Out of Bounds
A Mid-Season Sky: Poems 1954-1991

MISCELLANIES

Selected Declarations of Dependence
The Way Home
Ecrits Français

NONFICTION AND CRITICISM

The Orchard
20 Lines a Day
Immeasurable Distances: The Collected Essays
Giandomenico Tiepolo

Cigarettes
Harry Mathews

Dalkey Archive Press

Portions of this novel first appeared in *Conjunctions* and the *Review of Contemporary Fiction.*

Library of Congress Cataloging-in-Publication Data:

Mathews, Harry, 1930-
   Cigarettes : a novel / by Harry Mathews. — 1st Dalkey Archive ed.
     p. cm.
   ISBN 1-56478-203-4 (pbk. : alk. paper)
   1. Interpersonal relations—New York (State)—New York—Fiction.
   2. City and town life—New York (State)—New York—Fiction.
   I. Title.
   PS3563.A8359C5 1998
   813'.54—dc21   98-23363
                    CIP

Grateful acknowledgment is made for the following:

Excerpt from *Two Serious Ladies* by Jane Bowles. Copyright © 1966 by Jane Bowles. Reprinted by permission of Farrar, Straus & Giroux, Inc.

Excerpt from *Parade's End* by Ford Madox Ford. Copyright © 1950 by Alfred A. Knopf, Inc. Copyright renewed 1978. Reprinted by permission of the publisher.

Excerpt from *The Big Sleep* by Raymond Chandler. Copyright © 1939 by Raymond Chandler. Copyright renewed 1967 by Mrs. Helga Greene. Reprinted by permission of Alfred A. Knopf, Inc.

I'VE NEVER BEEN IN LOVE BEFORE by Frank Loesser from "Guys and Dolls." Copyright © 1950 by Frank Music Corp. Copyright renewed 1978 by Frank Music Corp. International Copyright Secured. All Rights Reserved. Used by permission.

TAKE HIM by Richard & Lorenz Hart. Copyright © 1951, 1952 by Chappell & Co., Inc. Copyright renewed. International Copyright Secured. All Rights Reserved. Used by Permission.

This publication is partially supported by grants from the Illinois Arts Council, a state agency.

Dalkey Archive Press
Illinois State University
Campus Box 4241
Normal, IL 61790-4241

visit our website: www.cas.ilstu.edu/english/dalkey/dalkey.html

In Memory of Georges Perec

Contents

Allan and Elizabeth *3*

Oliver and Elizabeth *16*

Oliver and Pauline *30*

Owen and Phoebe: I *42*

Owen and Phoebe: II *74*

Allan and Owen *111*

Lewis and Morris *133*

Lewis and Walter *155*

Louisa and Lewis *171*

Irene and Walter *185*

Priscilla and Walter *200*

Irene and Morris *216*

Pauline and Maud *227*

Maud and Priscilla *238*

Maud and Elizabeth *249*

"Let me tell you a story on the subject," said the Linnet.

"Is the story about me?" asked the Water-rat. "If so, I will listen to it, for I am extremely fond of fiction."

Oscar Wilde, "The Devoted Friend"

Cigarettes

Allan and Elizabeth

JULY 1963

"WHAT'S HE MEAN, 'I SUPPOSE YOU WANT AN EXPLANA-tion'? He doesn't explain anything."

The gabled house loomed over us like a buzzard stuffed in mid flight. People were still arriving. Through the lilac hedge came the rustle of gravel smoothly compressed, and swinging streaks of light that flashed beyond us along a pale bank of Japanese dogwood, where a man in a white dinner jacket stood inspecting Allan's letter with a penlight.

He passed the letter around. When it was my turn I read, in another revolution of headlights, ". . . the state I was in—barely seeing you when they were taking me away . . . Darkness, blinding light . . . I couldn't manage a squeak." I too was confused. Even dazzled by Elizabeth, could this be Allan?

I wanted to understand. I planned someday to write a book about these people. I wanted the whole story.

After an absence of many years Elizabeth that day had come

3

back to town. A little after midnight she went to the "casino," as the last private gambling club was called. Allan was leaving. Having drunk too much and started a noisy argument, he was being politely bounced. He passed Elizabeth in the glare of the lobby. At the door he was told, "Next time, Mr. Ludlam, please keep it down. And watch yourself on the road."

"Thank you. Who *is* she?"

"Beats me."

Outside, the night was hot and starry. Allan started driving home, stopping on the way at the Spa City Diner. Maud would have long been asleep.

He had two cups of coffee, chatting with late-night customers. He wished he could visualize Elizabeth exactly. (He remembered the sparse whiteness of her clothes, the flurry of her red-gold hair.) He knew she had seen him; her ready acceptance of him in those circumstances made him wince.

Allan had cleverness, if not wisdom, and he prized it. He held the world and himself in contempt. Recently he had shown kindness to me when few others had. My best friend had died, and gossips had cruelly blamed me for it. "You're lucky," Allan told me, "learning young what bastards people are. 'People,' " he added, "includes me." He meant that befriending me made him no better than the others, only smarter. He mistrusted his own decency.

On his way home, passing the Adelphi, he saw a red-haired figure in white crossing the faintly lighted porch. He braked. Perhaps a minute passed while he recollected that he was a local worthy, that he had already demeaned himself, that he was still drunk. He parked his car and went into the hotel. On night duty he found Wally, who had known him for thirty years. Allan asked if it was too late for a nightcap. Wally said, hold the fort, he wouldn't be a minute.

The lobby looked empty. Allan stepped behind the front desk to examine in the open register the arrivals on this first day of

July. He stopped at a familiar name: Elizabeth H., the woman in the portrait Maud had just bought. He had met her once or twice, long ago. She might have been the one at the casino. Perhaps he had unconsciously recognized her—that would explain her effect on him. Hearing Wally returning, he noted her room number.

After a minute spent sipping his highball, Allan said he was going to the john. Out of sight, he entered the honeyed glow of the carpeted stair. On the third floor he turned right. He had no plans.

Behind one wall a pipe produced a spasmodic whine. Unless, Allan thought, a chipmunk was trapped in the old timbers; the sound struck him as animal. He counted door numbers until he reached Elizabeth's.

The whine was coming through that door. He pressed his ear to the wood. The voice was not a chipmunk's. Allan dropped to one knee and set his eye to the keyhole: Yale. The edges of the door lay snug in their jambs.

The high voice sang waveringly on, needling Allan like a stuck car horn. He tried the doors of the adjacent rooms. The one on the right opened, and he entered a dark bedroom where light from the street revealed an empty bed. Crossing the room, Allan raised the window and leaned out. A ledge a foot wide ran across the building at floor level. From the window at his left faint light was shining. Gripping the window frame, Allan lowered both feet onto the ledge and slid along it. Reaching the light, he was confronted by backlighted blue shepherdesses strutting in a monotony of willows. The curtains allowed his sight no chink. Again he heard the voice sustaining its reedy cantillation. In the lobby, when the woman had looked at him and then looked away, from the unbuttoned top of her dress one unhaltered breast had slipped and been tucked back smoothly into place. He had conceived her nakedness under the white cotton and the cinched broad belt buckled with golden snakes.

He looked down at the street—anyone there could see him—
and began retracing his path. Downstairs, Wally waved him out
into the fervent night. Allan was so astonished that if Maud had
woken up when he came home, he might have told her everything that he had done.

In his letter, Allan wrote Elizabeth, "I kept wondering, was
it really your room? Your voice? Who was with you? What
exactly was he or she or they doing to you? I didn't want
answers—I wanted *you*. I felt *deprived.*"

Finding Elizabeth took him a week. He had many friends in
that little town: some of them said they knew her; one of them
had been asked to a party where she was expected. Allan went
too.

The party was being given at a large house on Clinton Street,
near the edge of town. Allan pointed out the woman from the
casino across the lawn, and his friend confirmed his hunch: she
was Elizabeth. Allan peremptorily declined to be introduced to
her. Twenty minutes later he regretted his refusal. He had
hoped to catch Elizabeth's attention; she had not even looked
at him. He derided himself as foolish and incompetent. Two
waterless drinks aggravated his helplessness.

Turning away from the crowded bar, where he had gone for
a third helping, Allan found Elizabeth waiting behind him. He
looked into her eyes as hard as he could. She did not recognize
him. He was comforted that she hadn't remembered his disgrace, discouraged at having made no impression on her. He
hoped, absurdly, that she would see at once that she already
obsessed him. She smiled: "You look lost."

"I was. You're the reason I'm here." He had lost all assurance, so that what might have sounded impudent rang true.

Elizabeth slipped her arm into his. "Tell me what's up."

They moved out of the crowd. Hardly knowing what to say,
he confessed his expulsion from the casino and his having seen
her there, in some disarray. Elizabeth laughed: "At least *you*

noticed." Allan's embarrassment attracted her more than the usual urbanities. "And now?"

Allan thought of the voice in the hotel and blushed again. "How about dinner? At the casino? You'll put me back in good standing."

"OK. But if we play, you'll have to stake me. I've got barely enough for bed and breakfast."

At the casino, after reserving a table, Allan bought five hundred dollars' worth of chips and gave half to Elizabeth, for which she kissed him on the cheek. They agreed on roulette.

Leaning over the seated players, Elizabeth bet all her chips on the first turn: a hundred and fifty dollars on black, the rest on 17. "Pure superstition," she told Allan. "It *never* comes up."

Quinze, impair, noir, et manque were announced. ("Close, at least," remarked Elizabeth.) A man yielded his seat. The croupier slid a hundred and fifty dollars towards her, neatly stacked.

Allan sat down across the table. He felt mildly irritated. He decided to ignore Elizabeth's play and concentrate on his own. Before betting, he kibbitzed a list of recent turns from a neighbor and watched six more himself. Allan liked roulette. It tested his self-control: he made himself bet at foreordained intervals and on numbers he had chosen statistically. He scored early that evening with a 6 *en plein* that put him ahead two hundred dollars. (He glanced at Elizabeth's chips: worth a thousand at least.)

He won another two hundred during the next half hour. He had more than doubled his stake, and their table was waiting: time to quit. An old man was sitting in Elizabeth's seat.

"Nice going."

As he turned, his nose grazed her breasts. "And you?"

"It was extremely exciting—close to two thou at one point. Shit!" She pointed to the wheel, where the white pellet was cruising in 17.

Allan's irritation returned. He was irritated with himself. He knew that Elizabeth would have played no differently with her own money; and she had cost him nothing, since he had made good her loss with his winnings. She was looking at him without remorse, almost with contentment. She did not care whether she lost or won, and that made him jealous. He hated losing. He could not help thinking of Maud. Elizabeth was beginning to frighten him.

She told him later, after slapping him hard in the face, "You bastard, stop holding back!" One of her legs was hooked behind his knees, the other encircled his hips.

In love, too, Allan exercised self-control. He took care to please first. Elizabeth preferred abandon—no "mine" or "yours," certainly no yours and then mine. For Allan, a woman's pleasure guaranteed his own. It was money in the bank.

Elizabeth nailed him: "I love the things you do to me, but let's not spend all night paying our dues. It's *you* I want." He started to explain. She laughed: "Look, I like being irresistible, too. Stop running things."

He agreed to try. Trying only discouraged him more and shriveled his purpose. Elizabeth understood how he felt. She began playing with him as with a child. In a while he somewhat forgot his predicament; and then when he too was playing she slapped him again, just hard enough to toughen his desire with sportive vindictiveness. He let go, and kept letting go, and as he did so, a high, eerie, familiar wail filled his head. He forgot himself, he forgot everything, except for one offstage, insidious question: Who's listening tonight?

The next day he wrote her a letter: "I suppose you want an explanation. . . ." He must by then have known that Elizabeth wasn't interested in explanations; he must have known that he had nothing to explain. He had urgently wanted to write her, and he had yielded to his impulse without realizing that it

sprang from something he hadn't told her and wished he had—
that he was married to Maud. He still did not mention Maud
in his letter. He told himself that a woman like Elizabeth
wouldn't care.

Elizabeth had learned about Maud with no help from Allan.
When he next saw her, she had changed. She had become more
interested in him, less so in "them." She had accepted her role
as a married man's lover.

They met late in the afternoon, two days after their first
encounter. When Allan acknowledged Maud's existence, Elizabeth insisted he talk about her. Once again he found himself
baffled. He berated himself for not admitting his marriage at
once. At their first meeting he had immediately suppressed the
urge—what was he to say, "You're the reason I'm here, and I'm
happily married"? At supper he had been afraid of displaying
his desire. He felt that warning Elizabeth about Maud would
seem as obvious as taking off his pants; and after that it was too
late.

In twenty-six years of marriage Allan had sometimes been
drawn to other women. He had never before loved two women
at the same time. He now felt compelled to keep them separate.
Telling Elizabeth about Maud, like the thought of telling Maud
about Elizabeth, made him afraid of losing one or even both of
them. Even in his private thoughts, pretending he had two
unconnected lives felt safer. (He was unexpectedly troubled by
the portrait Maud had bought: a painted "Elizabeth," chosen
and paid for by his wife, was waiting to be hung on a wall in
his house. Although Allan earned, as they say, "real money,"
he had always respected Maud's, augustly self-replenishing, as
the guarantor of their position. He did not love Maud for her
money; he had also never known her without it.)

He struggled with his novel passion. He could not understand Elizabeth's many kindnesses at their second meeting. She
struck him as all too obliging—eager for details about Maud,

fussing over a present ("My favorite demisemiprecious stone!"), agreeing to meet him whenever he could get free. Her docility suggested, illogically and inescapably, that he no longer mattered to her. If he had, she would have made more of a fuss. Had his silence concerning Maud brought this about? He must have disappointed her in other ways, too. When he asked her, she swore he hadn't.

They met several times during the rest of that week. To Allan's amazement, Maud made it easy for them. His stay-at-home wife started partying every day. Once he knew Maud's exact plans, he would notify Elizabeth and, later, drive to her hotel.

Sexual vacations begun in dalliance may become exhausting exercises in self-discovery or evasion. Allan had fallen in love, and hardly knew it, and labored vehemently to control what he refused to admit. Elizabeth did her best. Touched by his confusion, she wished he could like himself a little better, and she let her own liking for him express itself openly and attentively. Her compassion only put her further out of reach. Allan felt she was turning him into a fool. He had lost his script.

He had hoped that Elizabeth would fall desperately in love with him. That might restore his worth. He could then anticipate the pain of letting her go.

Allan consoled himself with their pleasure—hers, his—and resorted to it with growing fury. He grew pale beneath his tan. Elizabeth began to look at him with maternal concern.

A week passed. Their fifth meeting left him more disheartened than ever. He had gone to Elizabeth in unusually good humor. He had pleased himself by writing an effusive letter of thanks to a man who had helped him. He had reassured himself with propitiatory acts—changing into a striped mauve shirt she admired, going to the barber's, drinking only water at lunchtime.

He had hoped that when he entered her room she would fall into his arms. Instead, she gave him the quickest of kisses and a glance, not unkind, implying that men never looked more ridiculous than fresh from a barbershop. She sat him down on the couch to watch television: the sixth at Belmont. She followed the race like a child at a circus, with the kind of look he yearned to kindle in her eyes. At the finish she shrieked.

"You see," she explained, "he's a friend."

"The owner?"

"The horse." His name was Capital something. "I'm thirsty for gin-and-tonics."

They drank awhile, until Elizabeth at last embraced him. They undressed, bit by bit, caressingly; finally Allan went into her like a fist. She shrieked again, she started laughing, wrestling him like a happy ten-year-old grappling with a roommate. She pulled his hair and called him Capital something. She did nothing to conceal her happiness. He watched himself giving in, and gave in. Once again she was proving too good for him. More than good: the thing itself. Stratagem and skill would never get the better of her. She had nothing to lose. He lay under her feeling plundered.

She coddled him and kissed his mouth. He turned his head aside: "You don't know what I've been going through."

"I guess not. I've been having too much fun."

"You don't really care who I am. . . ."

"Let me think. This is Sunday, you must be—"

"You never even call me by my own name." The words shamed him. A nervous weariness was seeping through his body. Elizabeth looked down at him, perplexed. She felt motherly again—a step away from passion, as he might have noticed if he'd stayed awake.

They decided to take the next day off. Allan pleaded business; Elizabeth accepted his suggestion with an inward smile. She told him she would go riding at ten. He could reach her later if he wanted. She hugged him goodbye: "Goodbye, Allan—sweet Allan."

Allan hadn't lied. He had an appointment the following

morning, with a man whose trade was horses. They had a tricky deal to conclude, one that Allan expected would keep him late; but he was driving home before noon. Approaching his driveway, he stopped at the sight of a horse on the lawn, tethered to a birch tree and cropping the grass. He parked on the road and skirted the grounds to the back door of his house.

He let himself quietly into the pantry. From the front rooms came familiar voices: Maud's and Elizabeth's. Allan took off his shoes and tiptoed up the back stairs to his bedroom, where the voices did not carry. He thought: I'd better get this job finished. He picked up the phone to call the city. Through the dial tone he heard Maud speaking, her voice far away, then abruptly stilled. Someone else was using that particular downstairs extension.

He heard no click of a handset being replaced. Dialing his number, Allan said "I love you" into the speaker. His call was promptly answered.

Knowing that Elizabeth was listening, he felt a sickening need for her as he began stating his business. He wanted to be sick in her lap and be forgiven for it. After telling himself, hang up, go downstairs, talk to her, Maud or no Maud, he went on giving instructions.

He carefully repeated his words so that Elizabeth would remember them. He was making an arrangement that would reveal him as unscrupulous, even criminal. He wanted Elizabeth to understand that she did not know him at all, that he was more than the man she thought she knew. She would junk him for good, but with a certain astonishment, a certain respect.

He crept downstairs. The women's voices sounded louder. He listened from the hall:

". . . you still want that milktoast?"

"That's for me to decide!"

"It's him or the portrait. You can't have both!"

Each vehement declaration was followed by a silence as of

mythical personages raising high the boulders with which they would assail one another.

"You're disgusting!"

"It's my portrait, isn't it?"

"*Of* you—hardly yours!"

"Cut the crap, Mrs. Miniver. I need something to show for my week."

Allan gazed across the living hall to the front parlor. He stepped forward, then turned away, realizing how foolish he would look without his shoes. Elizabeth's words made him want to disembowel her, and at the same time want to cry. Through the library door he saw the still-unframed portrait resting against a wall. He remembered how light the painting had seemed for its size. Taking it from the library, he carried it out the back door.

Allan brought the portrait to the city that afternoon and stored it, wrapped in a sheet, in the back of his commuter's apartment. Leaving the house, he had planned to burn the painting; now he was unsure what to do with it. He did not know what to do with himself, either. He could not imagine speaking to Maud. The next morning, however, he felt a new concern for his wife, or at least for her opinion of him.

Allan's deal of the previous day required him to find supplementary insurance for a racehorse. The horse, a competent, veteran gelding, had come up lame after his last race. Because only one stablehand knew of this, the owner planned to subject the horse to a hard workout during which he would almost certainly break down. This would supply the pretext for destroying him. The owner aimed to collect all he could in insurance claims. He had been told that Allan might help.

As a partner in an established firm of insurance brokers, one that dealt chiefly with large businesses, Allan could not be expected to insure one horse. It might seem even less likely that he would help out a fraudulent small-town client. However,

Allan had already involved himself in much greater frauds than
this. For years he had periodically swindled the insurance companies he usually represented so well.

He would have found it hard to provide a sensible explanation for this clandestine activity. It had begun in the late summer of 1938, when the hurricane that ravaged the northeastern
United States swept through the site of an unfinished, under-
capitalized housing project in Rhode Island. Allan was approached by its developers and their contractors with a discreet
plea to rescue them from imminent bankruptcy. They suggested
that he arrange to have them reimbursed for the damages they
would have suffered if they had completed the project, as would
have been the case if the construction schedule had been met.
Allan realized that proving their claims unfounded would be a
hard task for the best of inspectors, given the devastation
wreaked by the hurricane in that part of the state. He found
himself tempted hardly at all by the ten-percent commission,
tempted considerably by outrageous wrongdoing: no one he
knew or worked with would dare contemplate such a risk. He
accepted it, got away with it, and became—like someone who
audaciously tries a cocktail for breakfast and soon finds himself
a chronic morning drinker—addicted to professional deceit.

Allan was now being asked to persuade a small insurance
company to offer preferential terms to the owner of the doomed
racehorse. This was why he had put through his call to the city.
He made it clear on the phone that his own commission had
been attended to.

The gelding was to be killed that week. Allan knew that in
such a small town, with her love of racing and horses, Elizabeth
was sure to hear of the event. She would then understand what
his phone call had signified. However, he had forgotten about
Maud. At the time it had not crossed his mind that in their
screaming match Elizabeth might tell Maud what she had
heard. Allan felt confident that after twenty-seven years Maud

would not abandon him because of a week's infidelity; but she
had no inkling of his other, devious business career, and this
sordid affair might disgust her. He couldn't blame her if it did.

Allan also craved to be forgiven. That next morning, he
called Maud a little before noon.

"A horse? Just a moment." Maud's voice faded: "Do you
know about Allan's insuring a horse?" She spoke again into the
phone: "We don't know a thing about it."

"We?"

"Elizabeth and I."

"Elizabeth . . . ?"

"Your Elizabeth."

"She's there?"

"I've invited her to stay." Allan kept silent. Maud added,
"Keep in touch. Someday I might invite you to stay, too."

Oliver and Elizabeth

SUMMER 1936

THE TOWN LIES ON A LOW PLATEAU OF SCARCELY RE-
lieved flatness; its humid climate swings from fierce cold in
winter to fierce heat in summer; yet visitors have been coming
here for generations, to "take the waters" of its saline springs,
to attend the fashionable August meet, and to observe each
other. Though remote, the town has seen even its year-round
population grow as its safety and amenity make it more and
more attractive to prosperous big-city families. A thriving black
community, established years ago by seasonal waiters and stable grooms who decided to settle here, has helped give this small
and sheltered place a cosmopolitan air.

Twenty-seven years before Elizabeth's return, the town had
been chosen as the seat of a July political convention. One
evening early in the month a garden party was given on the
grounds of one of the twenty-room "cottages" on North Broadway. More than two hundred guests attended, dressed in pale

summer colors, all too much alike for anyone's comfort but their own, clustering in groups as irresistibly as starlings. Among them, one young man stood conspicuously apart and alone. He hadn't come back to the town in twelve summers, since he was ten.

He had enjoyed watching the noisy throng (whom would he meet? like? love?); nevertheless he decided, after a second glass of champagne, that he should either mix or leave. He saw a face he knew—a young woman he had once been introduced to. He went up to her. She looked blank.

"You don't remember me? Sorry—I don't know a single soul . . ."

"Not even me!" she exclaimed. He named their mutual friend. "You're Oliver! I'm Elizabeth Hea—"

"I recognized *you.*"

"Terrific. Say, I don't know anybody either, at least that I'd want to. Let's team up and take our pick." Before Oliver could state his doubts, Elizabeth had imprisoned his left arm. "You go first. How about the lady in blue—pretty nifty, wouldn't you say? Not too old for you?"

"Not at all. I like older women." He was a year or two younger than Elizabeth—an abyss to one fresh out of college.

"I *see*—and she's so spry for twenty-six! Excuse me," Elizabeth said to their prey, "this delightful young man whom I've known for ages and can vouch for his adorably low intentions is nuts about you, and shy, so I thought I'd do you both a favor. This"—her hand clenched Oliver's shrinking elbow—"this is Oliver Pruell."

The name briefly drew Maud's gaze: "I thought I remembered all the Pruells. . . ." Because Oliver did not seize the opening, Maud turned back to Elizabeth. She made a distracting go-between.

Elizabeth kept Oliver continually off balance, introducing him with statements like "I can't imagine what he sees in you, but he's dying to meet you." He was soon relishing the game: he met two post-debs, the governor's wife, and a hooker of terrifying beauty, while introducing Elizabeth to the judge, author, and athletes of her choice.

He became rapidly obsessed by Elizabeth herself. Meeting the hooker may have predisposed him. Even then, he continued to think of Elizabeth as "older" and so "too old for him," until, as he was leading her towards some outlandish hunk of a half-back, she nudged him, with complicity more than intimacy: he was standing right behind her, and he felt her buttocks press against his thighs, soft and muscular as a tongue. Caught in midsentence, he could barely play out his part.

Near the end of the evening, Elizabeth was accosted by a pawy young man impervious to her evasive chatter. Allan, a little drunk, would forget the incident. Oliver stuck to Elizabeth's side, not letting the other man's back or elbow evict him, until he went away. A grateful Elizabeth asked Oliver to take her home.

She was staying with friends nearby. She didn't suggest going someplace else, or ask him in, or sit with him on the veranda. She only kissed him on the cheek, as if to say, I like you, I trust you. This was not what he was looking for, but he dreaded being clumsy. She *was* older. He needed an invitation.

On her way in she said, "I'm going to the Meville Baths tomorrow. Join me? I'll be at the pavilion at a quarter of ten. Ask for cell number eighteen. It's supposed to be the nicest on your side." Oliver went home content.

Next morning at Meville Baths, a private venture specializing in mud (it was dignified as *fango,* in a bow to Battaglia in the Euganean Hills), guided by a debonair Negro in seersucker uniform, Oliver found awaiting him in Room 18 a tub of what looked like steaming shit. He was issued a hooded terry-cloth robe and a pile of towels, given instruction in mud use, and left alone. He gazed dubiously into the tub. What good to him was this last resort of gnarled rheumatics? Having undressed and draped a towel around his hips, he slumped onto a stool, raising his eyes longingly to the frosted bluish skylight.

He heard a scrape of metal and, looking around, saw a door by the bathtub open slightly. A coral-nailed foot slid through the interstice. The door swung open to reveal Elizabeth. She kept one hand behind her back and with the other held to her throat an unvoluminous towel which, dangling as she stepped into the room, uncovered symmetrical fragments of still-unmuddied, clothesless skin. Because a lady was entering the room, Oliver of course stood up. Elizabeth asked, "Care to tango in the fango?"

Oliver felt his own towel slipping. As he grasped it with both hands, Elizabeth smoothly sidearmed from behind her back a mudball the size of a Hand melon. It caught him fair between the eyes.

He stood there blinded, suffocating, naked. Elizabeth's snicker reached him from a distance. She had withdrawn to her own room. She hadn't closed the door between. Oliver gouged the gunk from his eyes and mouth, scooped copious handfuls from the tub, and strode after her, set on revenge.

Now wrapped in a bathrobe, Elizabeth was standing in her room by the far door. As he advanced, she told him, "Wait," and he obeyed. She then emitted a shriek of heartrending terror. Another shriek followed; he still didn't understand. Someone was running down the corridor. Oliver raised one mud-filled hand. Elizabeth, still wailing, stepped away from the door, which opened to admit a sturdy matron whose apprehensive expression changed rapidly to one of bewilderment and then outrage. Oliver hurriedly turned back towards his own room, only to find that Elizabeth had slipped behind him. Whimpering disconsolately, she now barred his way.

The matron was moving towards the tub. Oliver saw the alarm button dimpling the wall above it. With the cunning of a beast at bay, he kept his mouth shut, slapped a fistful of mud over the button, and bolted out the door and down the corridor of the ladies' section.

Chronometrically his flight lasted twenty seconds. He passed one customer with her attendant; another, unaccompanied, who did not notice him; and a cleaning woman trundling a cart full of woolly sticks. In imagined time his course approached infinity, and during it he met other figures less palpable and far more real: his father jubilant at having his worst fears justified, his mother chalk-white on the sickbed to which his disgrace had brought her, the foul-mouthed trusty on his chain gang. He experienced terminal revelations about man's fate and the nature of reality. He recognized truth as both absolute and incommunicable, time itself as irreversible and irrelevant. He verged on a mystical understanding of *caritas*.

A racket of flapping feet—his own—recalled his circumstances. He then entertained the clever thought that the women's rooms might all have rooms for men next to them. Doors between bolted only on women's side? Why not? Women, women never molest men, ha ha, only men women. Togetherness possible if OK with girls? Baths big lovenest? He tried the next door: open, room empty. Unbolted party door: open, room empty. Opened door to far corridor—nobody there, all chasing maniac on other side! Lucky Oliver! He cantered back to Room 18, where, shutting himself in, he squatted breathless on his heels.

He'd better keep moving. Wash first. He stepped up to the basin. More luck: from the mirror glared a mud-masked face that might have belonged to Al Jolson, or anyone. He had remained anonymous. His still-gasping mouth was opening in a grin of chiaroscuro dazzle when, from under his raised arms, two sharp-fingered hands began curving around his chest to tweak his nipples. He started to giggle. She made him fuck her in the tub.

Over lunch he asked her: Why not last night?

"Where? Front porch? Back seat? No-luggage hotel? We still," she added, "need a place to go. I think I know where. Doesn't your skin feel *mad*?"

They drove out to the village called Lake George. At first Mrs. Quilty acted hostile. She had long ago worked for Oliver's mother, and she told him, "You're no Mr. Ratchett, you're Oliver Pruell. Master Oliver, what a thing to ask!" Oliver prepared to flee.

Elizabeth said, "All the more reason to help us, Mrs. Quilty. I've never talked about you with Mrs. Pruell, but I'm sure she has nothing but praise, and Frederick Stockton recommended you in glowing terms—"

"It's a difficult time we're living in, that's what I say," Mrs. Quilty interrupted. "Hard saving money, what with the government takes it all in taxes, even keeping the house in repair, you have to start paying city prices to people, and when all is said and done, there's no respect anymore, no respect from the young anymore, no respect at all—someone my age, used to be young men would tip their hats, now you're lucky if they nod." Mrs. Quilty barely paused. "It's eighteen-fifty a week, in advance, if you please."

Elizabeth made Oliver try out the room at once. His qualms were forgotten.

He asked her, "Who's Frederick Stockton?"

"Your father must know him. He had an arrangement with Mrs. Quilty. He also introduced her to other gentlemen. Hence the righteous indignation. She was quite an artist, it seems. That's how she paid for the house. You shouldn't have let her put you down."

"If she ever told my mother—"

"She doesn't give a hoot about your mother. She just knows you do."

"So why did she bother?"

"To show who's on top. You're too vulnerable, sweetie. Listen: you can be the way people want you, or they can be the way you want *them.*"

"OK." Oliver pondered: "Even my mother?"

Elizabeth smiled: "I see what you mean. . . . Does she still keep a time clock on you?"

"No. But she thinks a lot about me."

"Sure. She's a mother."

"I never know *what* she's thinking about me anymore. I'd rather have you to come home to."

"You'd like me for a mother?"

"You bet I would."

"Not a chance, baby." She sank three nails into his perineum. "Love you like a mother? Even Mrs. Quilty knows better than that."

Oliver reddened. "Love?" Elizabeth gave him a noisy kiss. She trapped him with her knees and elbows. "Hey!" he complained. "Am I supposed to love you?"

"What do you think's going on?"

"I don't think anything. I don't know. I've been having a terrific time. I love this. . . ."

Elizabeth let him creep his way to the next question, which he voiced a little high:

"Do you love me?"

Arching her brows preposterously, Elizabeth replied, "Dunno. Been having such a terrific time. . . . Dumbbell." She licked his lips.

Oliver felt towards Elizabeth an enthusiastic curiosity as to what she might do next, and not just in bed.

He had "written" in college; now he wrote her poems. They fell sneakily between the erotic and the obscene. She read each one slowly back to him, making him squirm, asking for more.

At the end of the third week in July, Oliver received a letter from Louisa, the friend who had originally introduced them.

She quoted what Elizabeth had written about him: "My Oliver! So elegant, so smart, and what of it? That's what trust funds are for. He has something else that may redeem the greed of his forebears and the repulsive expense of his education: enough talent to scram. He's just written a sonnet about my derriere that's so good that I swear to (a) get it published and (b) go riding every day to make sure it still means what it says. . . ." Reading this, Oliver told himself something like: She thinks, therefore I am.

Elizabeth's comments also dismayed him. Had he no worth except as a writer-to-be? Would he have to scram? Oliver liked his comforts. More immediately, he felt sick at the thought that, if his poems were published, his mother and father might read them—a ridiculous fear, and a real one.

On an afternoon in mid-August Elizabeth suggested they go fishing on Lake Luzerne.

"I hate fishing."

"At least you'll find out what might have been." He had an inkling of what she meant: his father cajoling a trout fly through forbidding foliage.

"What are we fishing for?" he asked as he pushed off their skiff.

"Who knows. Middlemouth bass?"

They took turns rowing. Twice Oliver pulled up a round-eyed, rough-scaled perch, which smacked the metal bucket for a while. In the middle of the lake Elizabeth racked the oars.

The afternoon was gray and placid. They lay in the bottom of the boat. Oliver rested his head against the cushioned plank at the stern, Elizabeth tucked herself against his side, a cheek in the crook of his shoulder, one hand inside his open shirt. The water slapped the slowly turning boat with varying briskness.

He watched the boat's slow gyrations, the little waves accumulating to slap it gently. Over the lake from reed-lined shores came a mulchy scent. Water and hills wavered in diffuse gray light. It was as if life had ended and he were dreaming a recollection. He could not tell what he was feeling. His feelings had turned into repetitions of waves and of the grayness that almost did not change, under the bright low sky.

He let the boat drift. He had no place to go. He did not think, except as part of the dreaming. Everything that had ever happened was only seeming, a seeming of having been dreamed, not mattering, without matter. The boat rocked sleepily, turning this way and that, providing his feelings, his thoughts, their objects. For one moment quickly gone he tried to say what was happening to him (maybe Hegel, maybe Heine; they didn't matter either). He had nothing to grasp. He was surrounded entirely by the dream of his being. He was surrounded by nothing. He did not need anything outside himself, outside this dream.

An hour passed. He gazed into the sky. The darkening grayness altered in the west. Above the silhouette of hills glowed low, scalloped reefs of emberish red. "Nothing outside us stays." Thought again subsided into the murk of woods and water, the clouds in their moment of fire and extinction looked to him like his own life being given shape, a hymn of pleasure and melancholy.

To the east the sky had assumed a darker and more soothing complexion: a slope of cool blue, or coal blue, the color that as a child he used to call policeman blue. He thought of the uncle the mention of whose name turned grown-ups silent, in disgrace, having squandered his money and his good marriage with other women. He was living in a suburb of Cleveland with a Mrs. Quilty. Blue, blue, policeman's blue. Oliver looked into the darkness and felt a shudder of power, realizing that his life belonged to him entirely, that there was no one else. He would never know such happiness again. When Elizabeth woke up, night had fallen.

Oliver's parents came back from Europe. He divided his time agreeably between Elizabeth and the family house.

On the morning of the last Wednesday in August, Elizabeth took Oliver to the track, leading him through the stable area to a particular stall, where a handsome bay stallion glared out at them.

"Assured, by Sure Thing out of Little Acorn. And look." Elizabeth pointed to the local listings in the *Morning Telegraph*: Assured had been entered in a thousand-dollar claiming race that afternoon. "They must be nuts. We can't not buy him. It's the best bargain since Louisiana." She wasn't kidding.

Oliver began arguing with her: something was wrong with the animal, where would they find a thousand dollars, what would they do with a racehorse? Elizabeth: she'd seen Assured work two days earlier, they'd raid his piggy bank, they'd buy another horse so it wouldn't be lonely. "You're right about one thing, though. It *is* fishy. Let's ask your father."

Mr. Pruell was a member of the Association, which at that time ran the track. Since Oliver's adolescence he had become a mystery to his son, who hoped he would remain one as long as possible. Oliver had a plan, kept secret even from himself: he would become so triumphantly successful that Mr. Pruell's dragonlike nature would be disarmed before he could unleash it. The summer had fostered Oliver's confidence. Elizabeth had authenticated him. She now threatened to mix up parts of his life that had remained comfortably distinct.

He implored her not to consult his father. Elizabeth knew he had no reason to worry and told him so. He refused to accompany her. This childish stubbornness offended her.

Elizabeth saw, perhaps too easily, that Mr. Pruell liked her and loved his son. She phoned him, he invited her for noontime cocktails and listened to her story.

"He can't really be claimed, you see—it's just a race to keep him fit. All the same, I'll check." He called up the owner, then told her, "Yup. The genteel fix is in. You understand—we all know each other here, and in cases like this, it's hands off. You'll have to look for another horse."

"Another dream gone! Mr. Pruell, this morning in the cafeteria, over at the track, I heard a man talking about Assured—that's how I knew he was running. I don't think he's heard about your arrangement."

Mr. Pruell made several more calls, the last one advising Assured's owner to scratch him. "Good girl. There's some fellow from out of town—Jersey, I hear—"

"Me too."

"Not Jersey *City*, surely? I should have been told. You deserve the Juliette Low medal," Mr. Pruell fondly added. "Now, you stay for lunch, and I'll take you to the track—the owner wants to thank you in person. Where's my little boy?"

Oliver went to bars. "How's Elizabeth?" he was asked. No one in town had ever seen him without her. He skipped lunch. He arrived at the track before two and stood in the infield with rented binoculars. He soon spotted her in the clubhouse with his father and some other men. One of them, lanky and young, stuck close to Elizabeth, staring at her, talking to her whenever he could. Elizabeth did not notice Oliver. Assured did not run. He went to Mrs. Quilty's: no message.

That evening Oliver drove out to Riley's Lake House, where a good band was playing. He stopped at the bar. A group of young people came in, some of whom he knew. He took a seat at their table, next to the lanky man he had seen at the track. Oliver began talking to him. His name was Walter Trale. How did he like it here? He had come here to work. To work—at his age? Yes, he was already earning his living, as an animal painter. Oliver said he liked the way animals looked unpainted. Walter laughed and explained that he did portraits of favorite animals. He had just painted Assured. He had made thousands of dollars since he was fifteen. He would go to college anyway, starting next month—gee, next week. "Unless I drop everything."

At this, Oliver felt delectable foreboding. He leaned invitingly towards his companion. Walter confided, "There are moments, you know, when the doors fly open—no, you see there aren't any doors at all."

"Holy smoke, Walter. Tell me more."

"Once I fell in love with a circus elephant."

"Walter, you can't expect me to believe that."

"You know how kids get crushes, don't you? I was eight. I wanted a picture of him, so my mother took some snapshots. He came out looking like a bag of fog."

"Mmm."

"One night I had a dream about my elephant. It was as if he was on a screen, but he didn't look like a bag of fog, he was all there. So next morning I drew him the way he looked in my dream. I had my love souvenir, and in one night I'd learned how to draw animals. They say it's natural talent, but the only natural thing is I was crazy about that elephant."

"You know, I wouldn't tell that story to everybody you happen to meet."

"I just love animals—I've loved all kinds of animals since then. The funny part is that I could never draw people."

"Why? Don't you love people?"

"I never felt as though I didn't. Still, you can imagine, getting so much attention and money, spending all this time with these rich old guys and their wives—I wondered, am I some kind of fruitcake? So today I met this person."

"You mean, a *woman?*"

"It wasn't so much that she was beautiful, it was the way she moved. Her fingers and knees moved the same way her face did, or maybe it's the other way around. You understand what I mean?"

"Boy, do I!"

"I couldn't take my eyes off her. She could see I was going crazy looking at her—" Walter broke off. Oliver asked him what had happened next. "She was really nice. She's coming to pose for me tomorrow. I can't believe it."

Oliver could. He was starting to say, "Well, I have to take

a shit something awful," when the band boomed into "Stompin'
at the Savoy." They gestured goodbye in the din.

Oliver went back to Mrs. Quilty's. No messages. He sat in
their room. He hadn't called either; but he was the one who had
been left out. Events had taken place where his presence had
not been missed. Elizabeth and his father, Elizabeth and Walter
(her business, of course)—Elizabeth had revealed herself as a
kind of person he hadn't suspected: a right bitch.

Unfair? Had she treated *him* fairly? His weeks with her had
exhausted him. She had demanded so much. She kept wanting
him to change. Like buying a horse. She was insane to think he
could write.

She had given him a wonderful vacation. Now vacation time
was ending. Next week came Labor Day, when he must go back
to the city and find a job. But why not get the jump on everybody and do it now?

He was discouraged at the prospect of staying alone in the
city, until he realized he could call his friend Louisa. He could
then be the first to explain what had happened. She must know
other girls.

Oliver left a letter for Elizabeth with Mrs. Quilty. In it he
blamed himself for the day's events, although he did mention
"others you have met." He said he was not surprised that she
was leaving him. "While I benefited from being your lover, I
don't think I benefited you, because my character is entirely
inadequate. I'd never be able to keep up with you. . . ." He
should have written "down with you"—Elizabeth had pulled
him earthwards. Oliver resembled a balloonist, unable to steer,
able only to rise or sink, and now he went up, up—firing the
air in his mind until he floated once again among comforting
coal-blue pinnacles.

He left the next day. Elizabeth never answered his letter. In
December he received the latest issue of *The Presidio Papers,*
a little review published in San Francisco, containing three of

his poems. Such a magazine, he told himself, would never come into his parents' hands. He was wrong. When his father died, years later, Oliver discovered that throughout his life he had collected erotica old and new. He found *The Presidio Papers* in his collection.

Oliver and Pauline

SUMMER 1938

T WO YEARS LATER, AFTER GRADUATING FROM COLLEGE, Pauline Dunlap came to stay with Maud Ludlam, her sister, and Allan, the husband Maud had taken the summer before. Maud, who was six years older than Pauline, had acted as a kind of foster mother to her ever since their father had become a widower.

Their father had died that March, leaving his entire estate to his daughters. The orphaned sisters learned, in the weeks following his death, that the conditions of their inheritance were known only to themselves and their father's lawyers. No one else seemed aware that Mr. Dunlap had amassed a great deal less than the many millions attributed to him, or that, as a believer in primogeniture, he had bequeathed nine-tenths of his fortune to his elder daughter. Since Maud was now married, the sisters decided to keep these facts to themselves: Pauline might benefit from appearing as a conspicuous heiress.

Oliver, who had known Pauline in boyhood, rediscovered her early that summer. He had come up on vacation from the city, where he now worked in his father's office. Both he and Pauline knew at once who the other "was" (a Pruell, a Dunlap), they enjoyed meeting once again, and when, later, during the party that had reunited them, a thunderstorm caught them out of doors together, a complicity emerged. They had taken refuge under an immense copper beech when lightning transsected the night and revealed Pauline picking her nose. Oliver couldn't pretend he hadn't noticed: "So that's how you spend your free time."

Pauline waited for the thunder to rumble away. "I couldn't wait. It *is* a basic pleasure."

The shower ended. They walked back to the lighted house. Merely sprinkled, Pauline's elegance had not been impaired. Had Mainbocher or perhaps Rochas, Oliver wondered, clothed that well-turned young body? She wore a dime-size yellow diamond on one hand, chunky green stones around a wrist; and at her throat, hung from a velvet band, a sumptuous tear of a pearl lay pink against her skin. Even after the rain, her hair kept the neatness of its image in rotogravure, combed sleekly back from her rounded forehead, the snug curls behind her ears starred with real, unwilted cornflowers. Eyes pure white and blue looked at Oliver with moist glitter as she implored, "You won't tell?"

"Never—provided you have supper with me tomorrow. Otherwise . . ." Oh, tomorrow was impossible. But not the evening after.

They dined. He liked her enough to take her out again. He liked her because she trusted him so readily. She liked him because he was easy to trust. He had a hold on himself, the know-how of someone who has not just been to schools.

She less liked his stopping at the politer kind of caress. Oliver could not have said what inspired his punctilious reticence. He simply felt that he could not take advantage of such candor. His decorum may have expressed a fear of seducing someone rich: among other things, "trust" meant taking good care of people's money.

At one roadhouse supper he watched her nimbly shattering a lamb chop with the stainless-steel chopsticks she always carried. Her one-handed performance undermined the known laws of physics. Oliver asked, "How do you manage? You're better than any Chink."

"Oh, don't use that word! Did you see the newsreels? Families bombed out of house and home! I *long* to go there, to do *something*. They need help so badly."

"Are you being serious?"

"As far as I can tell."

"Then go. Join the Red Cross. Volunteer with the Quakers."

"Oh, no. I have to see for myself. *I* want to be the one who decides what to do."

"You can still go there—"

"I can't afford it."

"You're *not* serious, you see? You could hock half your jewels and rebuild Nanking."

"They're not mine. Not yet," she quickly added. Leaning forward, she momentously confided, "Not only do I pick my nose, I'm on an allowance till I'm twenty-five."

"And by then your charge accounts will be surging through five figures. . . ."

"Oh, Maud buys me my clothes. But not China." She ate some more chop. In a most endearing way, she looked through his eyes, right into him: "Why won't you sleep with me? Is it me or is it you? Should I try Tabu? Lifebuoy?"

He hesitated: "It will be your first time out, won't it?"

"I'd start with the second if I could."

"You're as svelte as the *V* in Veedol, but—"

"Don't tell me! Just, please, give it sometime your most

earnest consideration." He promised to do that. Pauline continued, "Maud's a dream, but of course I'd love a little independence—you know, my own dough?" She added, "What's the fun of owning a horse if you can't pay for its oats?"

He explored legal possibilities with her, none of them very promising. "Try Lady Luck."

"Oh, I love to gamble. But how? The market's dead as a doormouse. Anyway, you still need capital to get started."

"You like horses—"

"Don't tempt me! My roommate did work out a terrific technique for betting."

"See? Your worries are over."

Oliver was joking; not Pauline. For the next week she was inaccessible before sundown. She spent her days in the Association library, which kept a complete set of the *Morning Telegraph*. She used the paper's charts to verify and improve her roommate's system.

The system decreed that, to be playable, a horse must have won its last start over a distance no shorter than that of its forthcoming race. To this requirement Pauline added certain strict indicators of the jockey's form. According to her research, when jockey and horse satisfied her conditions, which she cleverly reduced to three algebraic equations, she could pick a winner every third race.

Her method had one disadvantage. It eliminated so many entries that she could only bet on one race in twenty, and when she turned from theory to practice, a week at the local track gave her two chances at best to venture her five dollars. She lost once, and won once, at nine to two. While strengthening her confidence, the results also made clear that earning seventeen-fifty a week would not transform her life.

"I think I'll peddle my charms instead," she told Oliver, "something I may do anyway if you don't get off your fanny and into mine."

"Chopsticks, that's *not* your way to talk."

"Wrong nickname, toots. The point is, so far my system's no answer to a virgin's prayer. I suppose I could raise the ante."

"May I point out that Ma Bell and a good book can put every track in the land within your greedy reach? You'd have eighty races a day to pick from instead of eight."

"Terrific, but where does one find a bookmaker?"

"Just ask me."

"You do get around."

"In this town? There's one under every rainspout."

Oliver began taking her bets. Play increased dramatically. Pauline became even more infatuated with the lure of mastering risk, and her system at first worked better than Oliver had expected. But soon she grew impatient again. Her hopes had risen higher, and her rewards had remained slim: hours of calculation and a dozen bets for a profit of seventy dollars. She wanted China.

One day Oliver brought her bad news: their bookmaker had not appeared, and they had missed a winner. As he anticipated, Pauline responded with more fright than anger: "If I can't stick to the rules, I'll be wiped out for certain."

Oliver by now had become irrevocably involved. He did not know why—certainly not to help. (Scarcely a hundred dollars were at stake.) It felt to him more like a kind of seduction, one in which he was playing a spidery, rather feminine role. When he took her money, his skin would prickle electrically, as though he were masterminding a conspiracy.

"You're right," he replied. "You have no reserves, and at this rate you never will. I've got an idea."

"Oh, hurry."

"There's something called a martingale. When you lose, you double your bet, and you go on doubling till you win. Then you recoup all your losses *and* you get paid off on a bigger stake."

"OK. So I bet five dollars and lose, and next time I rebet that five plus another five makes ten"—she had her pad and pencil out—"and I lose and bet five plus the fifteen is twenty—right, doubles every time—and twenty at three to one is sixty instead of fifteen, so: I'm ahead forty-five dollars instead of . . . five? Why have you been hoarding this wisdom?" Before he could answer: "Wait! What if I lose? I'd be out, um, thirty-five instead of fifteen—couldn't that get expensive?"

"You bet the thirty-five with your next five and get it back—eventually you're bound to win. You say you never have runs of more than three or four losses."

"I showed you my tables. I ran into some bad streaks, but they were few and far between."

Oliver knew better. No matter what the game, losing streaks come as surely as nightfall; and sooner or later every gambler discovers the martingale. Oliver watched her charm herself with its promise.

He himself found charm in her growing dependence. He thought of repeating the drama of the unplaced bet in order to replenish her confusion but, instead, simply warned her once or twice that his bookmaker was out of town. "The powers that be always seem to do their being elsewhere," she cried. Her impatience made her the liveliest company. She almost succeeded in unbuttoning his deliberate propriety.

After a week, events of themselves produced a crisis: Pauline had seven straight losses. The last one cost her three hundred and twenty dollars. She dreaded putting up twice that amount, dreaded not betting. Oliver offered to stake her. She refused as vehemently as she could—not vehemently enough, she knew, although not insincerely. Oliver remarked, "You sound as though you'd be doing *me* a favor."

To Pauline, this suggested a way out: "I'll make a deal with you. If I can't pay you back, I'll bequeath you my maidenhead. And you *have* to accept it."

"Pauline, you're a babe in the wood."

"To hell with it. I'll ask Maud."

The prospect of having her in his debt excited Oliver. "I consent. But I insist on choosing the place and time."

"Maybe. I'll give you a week's leeway. While 'cherry-ripe themselves do cry. . . .' The horse is Disrespect. And he's going to win. Then I'll rent a real man, you churl."

This cunning insurance contented Pauline. She found fresh hope in her future. Disrespect finished out of the money, however, and with the loss her confidence shriveled.

Pauline was overcome with unexpected, unappeasable shame. Oliver's reassurances left her cold: "Even *if* the money didn't matter, *I* do. I won't let you let me off. I'm not a silly little girl."

"I know. We should have opened a joint account, then it wouldn't have mattered." Oliver did not know what he meant by this badinage.

In spite of their agreement, Pauline's remorse quenched any thought of not paying the debt in cash. She decided to earn the money. Oliver was surprised and not very concerned. Whether Pauline paid him back or not, he was becoming the center of her life. Never before had he so dominated anyone.

As for the money, Oliver had little faith in any gambling system, certainly not in Pauline's. He had laid off none of her bets; she had had no bookmaker except himself. She owed him nothing—he was holding six hundred and thirty-five dollars that belonged to her.

Pauline asked Maud to help her find a job. Maud, unaware of Oliver's importance in her life, suggested his father, a good friend who, at this time, was busily reorganizing the Association, of which he had been elected president. He might well think of something for her to do.

Disconcerted at first, Pauline quickly convinced herself that Oliver presented no obstacle to her approaching Mr. Pruell. She called on him the next day. They did not talk about jobs. He had noticed more than Maud, and he knew how his son spent his evenings. He liked Pauline. When he took her into his study, it was he who made an appeal: "Are you in love with Oliver? I hope so. I need help."

"Help with *Oliver?*"

"It seems to me he's turned into another person. Until a year or so ago, he used to treat me like an old fart. He knew what life was all about, and I was the slave to business. Now he not only respects and trusts me, he's actually gone to work for me. I'm worried."

"Don't you think he's happy the way he is?"

"How can he be? When I was twenty, I wanted to be a writer too. But I had no gift for it, so I went to work and made money instead. Listen, my dear, from the start I had a notion that if I made a fortune it would be so a child of mine could lead any kind of life he wanted. Why should Oliver do what I've done all over again? If he wants to write, he should write."

"Are you sure that's what he wants? He's never breathed a word—"

"He has real talent. You look skeptical. Well, I haven't much to show you since he left college, only some poetry, and that"— he took *The Presidio Papers* from a locked drawer—"extremely off-color. Still, you're a big girl." He handed Pauline the review.

She read about ten lines, after which, despite her host's warning, the volume tumbled to the floor. Pauline turned very pink, from more than embarrassment.

"I'm an idiot, forgive me." Tactfully, Mr. Pruell did not even smile at her predicament. "You'll have to take my word for it. You know, fathers usually discourage this sort of thing."

"Who was she?"

"And before it slips my mind, don't tell Oliver about the poems. I'm supposed not to know."

Pauline promised. She would have promised Oliver's father anything.

"Cherry-ripe, remember?" she chided Oliver that evening.

"How could I forget? *You* seemed to have." He kissed her in the mouth. "Let's meet at Meville Baths at eleven."

"In the *baths?* In the *morning?*"

"Ask for Room Thirty-two."

Oliver knew the time had come. Pauline's fresh fervor hardly surprised him; it confirmed his belief that power sticks to those who disdain it.

Oliver made exuberant love to Pauline—his poetry come to life. After the baths, he enjoyed her in other unlikely and even more public places: a treehouse, a moonlit green on the golf course in Geyser Park, the bottom of a rowboat on Lake Luzerne. They also used his room at Mrs. Quilty's, spending long afternoons there. He did things with his mouth she had never dared imagine. He invented the ways she felt.

His exuberance was not feigned. In reenacting the things that Elizabeth had taught him, he made them his own: they became proofs of his mastery. He watched Pauline fall in love with him with heartfelt joy.

He knew she would want to marry him. He let her broach the subject and told her, "You live in a style I won't afford for years."

"I'll eat cereal three times a day. I'll save the box tops."

"That's just what I mean."

"I only want to live with you forever. It can't cost that much." Oliver shrugged. "I'll get a job."

"My beloved, qualified *men* are unemployed these days."

"I tell you, I know people."

"You're a swell girl, Pauline, but you've been schooled for a life of idleness. What would our friends say if I let you work? I'd hold down two jobs myself if I could, but there aren't enough hours in the day."

"Oh, I don't want you to work *more,* I don't want you to have to work at all—not in an office."

"What do you suggest I do—make book?"

Pauline took this for a possible pun: "Ask your father to help. He thinks I'm good for you."

"He *is* helping. I'm on the payroll."

"I bet he'd set you up."

"If I were on my own, I'd like to show what I can do by myself, not with *his* money." Pauline smiled. Where Oliver meant starting his own business, she envisioned late nights over a typewriter.

"There must be something we can do—*I* can do. Oh, why am I such a twerp?" Oliver kept very still: as if, holding a sure hand in a game of chance, he were waiting for his adversary to plunge. "If only . . . ," Pauline was saying, and Oliver did not budge; did not light his next cigarette.

Pauline had decided not to tell Oliver about her true expectations. She honestly believed the matter irrelevant: she'd always had enough money, and they would have enough. She saw nevertheless that, to be convinced, Oliver needed tangible prospects.

Maud wanted her to marry well. Maud had money to spare. Would she spare it? Why not? Oliver never knew what bitterness then came between the two sisters. Pauline had only told him that she would ask Maud to advance the date of her inheritance. Oliver accepted the lie and discounted it—wills could not so easily be changed. He did not care. In his own way, he was as indifferent to money as she was. He was getting what he most wanted: Pauline was committing to him everything she had.

Two days later, Pauline told him what she had obtained from Maud: her spending money would be doubled, their father's house in the city would be put in her name. Oliver was impressed. He maintained a show of reluctance for a day, then yielded, all too content to declare to the world that this lively, beautiful, sought-after young woman had preferred him to all others.

Mr. Pruell gave a party to announce their engagement. Maud did not attend; she was traveling in Europe. She did not even get back in time for the October wedding. Because of a war scare, her train out of Vienna had been canceled, and she missed her sailing. Oliver might have guessed at other reasons; he felt too happy to look for them. Like a driver who has found a shortcut on his daily route, like a soldier who has won an objective without bloodshed, like a writer who has made his point thriftily, he drew happiness from his own efficacy. At the engagement party he realized that the money he had kept from Pauline's seven bad bets covered the expenses of his courtship down to the last dinner and drink. He indulged himself by confessing this deceit to her.

"You're a cad and a bounder," she said, "putting me through that torture for nothing."

"But we still have the money!"

"And what if I'd won, huh?"

"You're delightful and adorable, but when it comes to practical matters, leave them to me."

A note of seriousness in his words affected Pauline: "I want to leave everything to you! A propos—how about a date in your treehouse?"

Oliver took her in his arms and nibbled her eyebrows. "Why don't we wait? Let's make our wedding night a second first time."

"You're kidding—no? OK, if you say so." For a moment she felt stifled by the dog-day weight of his benevolence. She wanted to put her hand on his cock, in front of his parents, in front of their friends. She only asked, "No more treehouse? No more Mrs. Quilty?"

Oliver smilingly shook his head. He would never make the mistake of confusing Pauline with Elizabeth, or her demands with his own needs. She belonged to his life to come, the life that now stretched ahead of him like a succession of well-ordered, discreetly lighted rooms: the marble-flagged entrance where Pauline in long gold dress stood waiting by the door; the upstairs drawing room furnished in Louis XV, with a few cushioned couches and armchairs covered in softest gray and beige, their ease set off against the evening-dress formality of a grand piano; a dining room whose mahogany table, almost black in candlelight, was surrounded by tuxedoed cronies smoking cigars and drinking port; the ground-floor den with its chesterfield sofa and chair, its desk full of secrets, its private telephone, a refuge in which to explore the solitude that gave a man of the world his most substantial pleasure. She belonged to a perspective that he could enter without the slightest qualm or effort. If he could claim little originality for this perspective, he nonetheless took pride in it as in a personal creation, perhaps because he felt so entirely its possessor.

Oliver's self-esteem did not lessen when he learned, much later, the facts of Pauline's inheritance. He never overtly reproached her, and in truth the revelation left him almost grateful. After all, it confirmed that he had the right to manage things, the right to show condescension and pity, the right to control.

Owen and Phoebe: I

SUMMER 1961-SUMMER 1963

Y EARS LATER, ON THE VERY JULY FIRST THAT ALLAN LUD-
lam discovered Elizabeth, and in the same town, Owen Lewison
instructed his bank in the city to settle a large sum of money
on his daughter, Phoebe, then on the eve of her twenty-first
birthday.

This was not the first time Owen had decided to endow his
daughter: two years earlier, he had told her that he was estab-
lishing a trust fund to provide her with an income of her own.

He had spoken to her on a day in mid-August, while they
were sitting outdoors in a shade of maples. Beyond the blurred
distances of steamy fields and hills squatted blue-tinged Adiron-
dacks. Phoebe blushed through her damp tan.

"Poppa! What have I done—"

"Go on—you do everything wonderfully."

"You don't mean school? That doesn't even—"

"Oh, yes, it does. But this isn't a reward. I want you to learn
how to run your own life."

"Poppa, I plan to go to work—"

"Well, I *want* you to work."

"Then—"

"But with room to maneuver. So you can be choosy. So you won't be tempted straight off by some well-heeled john. Two hundred a month ought to help."

"That's fabulous, Poppa—"

"And with luck it'll grow."

"Poppa, what if—" She hesitated. "What if something special comes up—like buying a car? Not that I want to, but—"

"Ask me. It'll be a pleasure."

Owen explained that he would keep control of the capital: "That's what needs to do the growing. You do agree I can manage that best? You can see, too, that it would be a mistake to deplete it for something like a car."

Of course Phoebe agreed. She had already begun making a plan. Knowing that she would have money of her own was reviving a particular desire.

That spring she had attended an extracurricular lecture at her college. The students had invited as speaker the first long-haired young grown-up male she had ever seen. He wore boots and jeans with his suede jacket and string tie. He lived in the Rockies, and he spoke of their areas of unsullied wilderness. He spoke of the inroads being made in the wilderness by urban man. He spoke of the corruption in capitalist society, how it degraded whatever it touched, individuals included, out of its need to turn a profit. The wilderness, he said, encouraged individuals to remain simply themselves: it forced them to acquire a knowledge that proved incomparably useful for leading happy, self-sustaining lives. He had long held revolution as his political ideal, but he now saw that the time for revolution had not yet come. Until that time came, he recommended renouncing society. No one asked the speaker what, in the wilderness, people did with their evenings. Phoebe and her peers, usually so skeptical, accepted his precepts raptly.

Soon afterwards, in the city, she met a young man who
fleshed out the lecturer's vision. He was to spend the coming
year in New Mexico as a forest ranger. She had gasped her
admiration, which had led him to suggest: Come along. Although he loomed golden and vast, Phoebe could not then even
dream of such a prospect. Now she wrote to him: had he meant
it? He phoned back to say he had.

When Phoebe announced that she was leaving college to help
guard the timberlands of the southwest, Owen, who hadn't
smoked in a decade, compulsively clutched an empty breast
pocket. He considered himself swindled.

He knew enough to hide his feelings and dicker. He at first
expressed only surprise, commenting that it seemed a foolish
life for her to lead—she couldn't even do the work. Phoebe
claimed she could; she'd been a star on pack trips, better than
most men. (His own fault, he reflected—he'd raised her like a
boy. Her brother had been the indoor child.) Perhaps. But why
stop two years short of her B.A.? She replied that a diploma in
art from a progressive college didn't have much pull these
days—it could even be held against you. Owen asked: And the
art itself? For ten years she had wanted to become a professional painter. (Owen could accept that possibility. He didn't
expect his girl to go to law school, and everyone had pronounced her talent genuine. She should go on studying art.
Afterwards she might grow out of it, or she might succeed. He
imagined visits to her then, in the city. . . .) Art, said Phoebe,
what's so great about art? "I'll be doing something real."

"Even Marx knew better than that—remember 'productive
work'? Nothing very productive about staring at trees."

"Poppa, *you* said room to maneuver—"

"I meant, to get someplace in the world—the 'real' world.
Not run away from it."

"You're taking the money back?"

Owen wanted to know more. "These 'friends' in New Mexico—do they include a boyfriend?"

"What are you so afraid of? I'm not spending my life there. He's not a boy, he's a man," Phoebe couldn't help adding.

Owen was afraid—not of what Phoebe imagined, but of being excluded. He sincerely wanted Phoebe's freedom and saw himself as part of it.

"You'll be junking the benefits of nineteen years. You're too bright for the forest primeval—"

"But it's what I *haven't* learned—"

"—and if you want to go off with a 'man,' say so, for Christ's sake."

Of course there was a man—someone to provide the excuse for change. Phoebe got herself stuck defending this man she hardly knew. She embarrassed herself; she made herself angry; she grubbed for justifications.

"As soon as I want something, you welch."

"Phoebe, I'd be irresponsible—"

"Bullshit, you want to run my—"

"—what's best for you. Please watch your language when you're talking to me."

"The best is what *you* . . . That's what the money's for—to depend even more—"

"Forget about New Mexico."

"Goodbye, Poppa." She left before she started crying. (How could this clever man act so dumb?)

Phoebe went walking for two hours. Back home, she made some long-distance calls, packed two bags, and caught an evening bus to the city.

She left before her mother came home: Phoebe called Loꞏ ꞏsa the next day to explain her decision. Later, she kept in touch with her, so that both her parents would always know that "she was all right." Eight months passed before Owen saw her again.

Phoebe never left the city: the prospect of life in the wilderness with a golden youth had quickly lost its allure. She stayed for a while with the family of a college friend. She realized that her first task was to earn a living. Her old painting teacher helped her find jobs as an artist's model; daring to pose in the nude gave her confidence. She proposed herself to several photographers, some of whom did fashion work, one of whom shrewdly distinguished, among her many attractions, her slim feet and ankles. He specialized in shoes. Four months after leaving home, Phoebe became a professional model from the knees down. A few well-paid hours a week supplied her needs.

While Phoebe was learning how to support herself, her teacher introduced her to several artists. Phoebe went to their shows, visited their studios, met them after work. Their lives appealed to her. They had not yet been uprooted by a booming market; the Cedar Bar was still a flourishing club. Their work filled her with a passion of emulation, not of any one manner, but rather of the zany dedication the various manners expressed. She began coveting a style of her own.

She did not imagine she knew anything. She was preparing herself for art school, hoping Hofmann would accept her, when she saw a show by a painter called Trale, someone her teacher had often mentioned. This small retrospective, his first in many years, was hung in a gallery on East Tenth Street. Phoebe spent an hour there on her first visit and went back the day after, and the day after that, to make sure that in Walter Trale she had "met her master." She decided to make him exactly that.

Owen would have admired her efficiency. She persuaded friends of friends to introduce her to Walter, and later to recommend her. She let him often be reminded of her, strolling past him at the Cedar, for instance, on de Kooning's obliging arm. When at last she called on him, with six drawings, decorously smudged into a semblance of originality, he found himself on her side from the start. He looked at the drawings, and at her, and accepted her request to become his apprentice. She would do his chores, model for him occasionally, and work under his guidance.

Walter lived in a loft building on Broadway and the corner

of Ninth Street; he found Phoebe a kitchenette studio on the floor below him. She settled into a new life. Walter took his role seriously. Between what he made her do for him and what he made her do for herself, she scarcely had time to display her feet.

On a warm, drizzling mid-April morning, two months after Phoebe moved in, Owen paid her a visit. She had told him to meet her at Walter's, where the door was never locked and he could just barge in; which is what he did, a little early, having made the unfamiliar trip to the lower East Side in less time than expected. He did not see Phoebe at first. Near the far end of the vast room, Walter Trale was sketching a nude model, and the sight of her compelled Owen's attention. The model was not sitting still: she was slowly turning under the painter's gaze, as though performing a slithery dance, lying, crouching, kneeling in turn, shifting from one position to the next with a slow-motion regularity that struck Owen as both impersonal and hypnotic. The woman was young: her skin glowed, her nipples showed a uniform pink. He caught a glimpse of pink lips amid the slidings of her thighs before the long hair fell away from her face, which revealed itself as Phoebe's.

Owen told himself, it's a setup. Seeing him, Phoebe said, "Oh, shit!" Walter put down his stick of charcoal, wiped blackened fingers on a white cloth, and held out a hand to his dazed visitor.

"Oh—Mr. Lewison! I guess this isn't what either of us planned. Sorry—just trying to get in one last drawing." Owen watched Phoebe's bottom disappear into the bedroom. Walter said, "She's a great model. She knows how to move."

"Is that so?"

Walter forged on: "She *really* knows how to move. Not just lying there, like a still life. You know, the French call a still life a *nature morte*—who wants a model to be a cadaver? Like they're supposed to play dead, and we pretend they're 'problems in form.' Talk about treating a woman like a thing! I mean, why leave out the desire, the liveliness, if you're painting a nude, you *can't* leave it out, it's probably the most real thing there is—you remember Renoir, 'I paint with my penis'? So when Phoebe"—Owen's upturned eyes reminded Walter of Perugino's saints—"said, Let me try moving all the time, then I could keep seeing the life in her, I said, OK, and it works. You know, in a way it's not her I paint, it's her—"

"That's extremely interesting," Owen said as his daughter, dressed, came back into the studio.

"She's a remarkable girl, in more ways than one," Walter concluded. Owen took Phoebe out to lunch.

With her clothes on, Phoebe looked as radiant and unfamiliar to Owen as she had naked.

"Poppa," she told him when they were seated, "I want to say something right away." Owen thought: bad news. "Your giving me a hard time last summer was the best thing that ever happened to me. It made me learn what to do with my life."

"Hardly to my credit."

"Yes, it is. Taking the money back was great. I'm managing to pay my own way. When you came into Walter's studio (isn't he fab?) I realized that one good thing poppas can do is be mean, sometimes. I love you for it. I do love you, Poppa. I hope you approve of me a little."

"You're looking well." Owen made insinuations about her private life. Phoebe said she was too busy for men (she meant, one man).

"And your 'fab' friend?"

"He's *your* age, Poppa. Almost."

"Exactly."

A visit to Phoebe's studio nearly convinced him. The not-so-big room, bright even on a wet day, reflected a committed life: a thin couch, a chair, an armchair buried in laundry, in the kitchen a table strewn with the debris of breakfast assuredly for one. The walls were papered with drawings, gouaches, and unstretched oils; the floor, stacked along its edges with stretchers and rolled canvas and paper, was a labyrinth of paint cans open and shut. There were two easels, a large and a small, and by the window, with a swivel stool at either side, a ten-by-four expanse of thick plywood set on sawhorses, without a squinch free of professional clutter.

"Hey," Owen asked, wrinkling his nose at the turps, "you *live* here?"

Phoebe opened the window. Turning back, she found Owen examining the canvas on the larger easel. "Don't ask me, I'll tell you! It's been driving me bats. Ever since I got hooked on Walter, at that show in January, I've wanted to copy one of his paintings, except he wouldn't hear of it. I kept coming back at him, and one day he said, OK, you asked for it. What he's making me do isn't copying exactly. I have to get the same results the same *way* he did. He can tell—you know, if the stippling is done with a soft brush or a stiff brush, or the paint is laid down with a spoon handle instead of a spatula. Which direction his hand was going. What he drank the night before. . . . This was my favorite of all he'd ever done. An old thing—'A Portrait of Elizabeth.' "

"Elizabeth seems to have led a hard life."

"I've scraped it down four times already. I don't think I'll ever get it right. Each time I try, though, I get five hundred and fifty-three new ideas. If you see anything you like, Poppa, just ask for it."

From a pile on the table he picked a soft-pencil self-portrait. Phoebe's eyes looked bemusedly out of it into his, and, during the ensuing weeks, he looked back at them often, with a fascination made up of resentment, yearning, and uncertainty. He realized that he admired his daughter. The thought of seeing her again made him timid.

In those days Owen often came to the city without Louisa.

Calling Phoebe before one such visit, he offhandedly said, "I don't want to be bothering you. . . ." She answered, "You'd better had!" He offered to take her out for an evening. Where should he reserve a table? Would she like to see a play?

"Not much. Let's see how we feel. Whatever we do, I'll enjoy it. Come for a drink at my place. Maybe we'll just stay in and watch *Bonanza.* "

Owen had wanted to do as well by Phoebe as his own father had by him. His father, a hardworking small businessman, had had his career cut short by a fatal car accident during Owen's last year at Ann Arbor. Owen at twenty-one had found himself owner of a factory in Queens that supplied processed graphite to pencil manufacturers. Knowing little about the business, he agreed to run it: it was well organized, he knew he could learn quickly. A few months later a fire broke out in his stockroom, destroying the entire inventory and half the plant. Accountants urged him to collect the insurance and write off what was left of the factory. Doing so, he made a significant discovery.

Two companies of firemen had appeared during the fire. They had declined to do their job until Owen had the wit to offer them twenty-five dollars each (a week's wage at the time). A more experienced businessman might have known that this practice was common, but Owen was outraged; enough so to list this graft in his claims to the insurance company and thus symbolically denounce it. He expected no compensation. The claim was nevertheless paid.

From this windfall Owen drew a conclusion that eventually turned into a plan; this he submitted to an old friend about to graduate from Columbia Law School. The friend reacted favorably. Owen suggested they go into business together, using as their working capital the money he had collected from the fire.

Owen had realized that small businesses like his father's, low in reserves of capital and dependent on high productivity, were at the mercy of a single disaster. A delay in reimbursement by their insurers—his own had taken almost a year—could wipe them out. Such companies would hesitate to press ancillary claims that might postpone settlement. Owen proposed creating a service that would take over cases in which a natural disaster had crippled a business, reimbursing basic claims immediately, making its own profit by exploiting secondary liabilities covered by the insurance. The outcome of Owen's dealings with the fire department had suggested that such profits might be large.

Owen and his partner founded a company to supply such a service. They took great care in the choice of their first clients. They proved themselves industrious, clever, capable of rock-ribbed persistence, even lucky. Their venture was so successful that after five years their presence in a case often persuaded insurance companies to settle quickly rather than risk uncertain legal battles.

Owen prospered. His career brought him not only wealth but satisfaction: his initiative and ingenuity were constantly challenged; he felt that he was usefully serving small businesses and, later, businesses not so small. His success introduced him to the society of the traditionally well-to-do—bankers and professional men who set themselves higher than unassuming entrepreneurs like his father. Owen envied the confidence such people showed in their own distinction. Because he was both prosperous and amenable, they accepted him readily enough. Eventually he married a young lady who, although poorer than he, belonged to a venerable Philadelphia family.

Throughout their marriage Owen remained devoted to Louisa. She had soon given him what he most wanted of her: a child, and particularly a daughter. During her two pregnancies he looked forward so intensely to their outcome that by the time Phoebe was born she was already the focus of his desires.

Owen was relieved to have a girl. He could cultivate her happiness—his own happiness—without concern for the combative and methodical virtues required of males. He watched over her education in and out of school. He made sure she learned early how to swim and ride, and later how to ski and play tennis. He took her to the ballet to kindle wonder in her and then sent her to ballet school. At her first sign of interest, he exposed her to books, plays, and music; and to sustain her precocious artistic bent he kept her supplied with everything she might need, from clay and crayons at three to oils and acrylics at thirteen. He remained a consistently fond, demanding parent. Good-natured and smart, Phoebe thrived under his supervision. By the age of seventeen, the contentment she felt in herself shone out of her like whiteness out of snow. Owen rejoiced in his parental success. By then his work had lost much of its challenge—it had become a means less to achieve than to conserve. He began looking to Phoebe for surprising triumphs.

Ten months before, their quarrel and Phoebe's departure had bred furious disappointment in him. Now that they had made peace, he still did not understand her. She had thanked him with convincing sincerity for "being mean"—a strange conclusion to draw from his nineteen years' munificence.

He came to her studio at seven, a benign hour on this late June evening, when the hot, clear air was suffused with cinnamon incandescence. Phoebe had prepared chilled unshaken gimlets for him. What should they do? They drifted out into the never-ending dusk. She led him across town to a steak house off Greenwich Avenue, modish but not deafeningly so. From their table, Owen looked about warily. Here, at least, bohemia seemed ready to spare him.

A wine from the shores of Lake Trasimene, which he never had seen, nor would see, opened in his mind vistas of remembrance and expectancy. He had begun speaking to Phoebe about some incident in his past when a sturdy swaggering youth approached their table and cocked a hand in greeting: "Hi, Phoeb."

"My father, Owen. Harry."

"No shit!" Harry observed. "Listen, doll, Bob is blowin' at El Pueblo at ten. Thought you'd want to know." (Owen asked, "Blowing what?" Phoebe answered, "Horn.")

After dinner, with conscious benevolence, Owen said, "Why not?" They wandered around six corners to Sheridan Square. The near-dark sky flared with the refractions of fireworks upriver.

"It's a French horn," Owen disappointedly remarked, having savvily looked forward to trumpet or sax.

"That's life," Phoebe chuckled.

"Who's Bob?"

"Scott," Phoebe whispered. "And that's Woody Woodward on alto, Doc Irons on vibes, Poppa Jenks on drums"—three blacks and one white, all young, who at the stroke of ten filled the gloom of the Pueblo with a clangor so intricately sweet that Owen felt bewitched. A green smell spiced the air.

"They're very fine," he exclaimed.

Phoebe looked gratified. "They may join us after this set."

Owen felt a pang. He'd only conversed with Negroes who worked for him. How well did Phoebe know them?

She was explaining: "Walter's sort of their sponsor—at least, he got them this gig."

When, white-shirted and cool, the musicians sat down at their table, they paid no attention to Owen. A few customers, including Harry, came over to pay court. Otherwise they all sat together quietly and contentedly, as if after a long day they had settled on a veranda to watch the moon rise over cornfields, or Lake Trasimene.

At eleven-thirty Poppa Jenks drained his glass: "Owen!" Owen sat up like a schoolboy caught dozing. "Anything you'd like to hear?"

"Uh—'All the Things You Are'?" Owen hazarded.

"Right. Right?" he asked the others.

"What's that shift—"

"Down a major third. G to E flat, same as 'Long Ago.' " To Owen he added, "Mr. Kern was an attentive student of Schubert, and a thrifty one."

They returned to their instruments. A young man in tailored denims bent abruptly over Phoebe: "Fourteen West Eleventh. Domerich. *Vaut le détour.*" The musicians broke once more into their wry jubilation. The Kern ballad was disseminated in a bustle of counterpoint.

Afterwards, Owen again said, "Why not?" and they made their way eastward, in night now, deep but not dark: through ginkgo leaf, window-light stippled the sidewalks with pale orange. The air had scarcely cooled—only, by alleyways, mild gusts on face or nape suggested swipes of a celestial fan.

After half an hour at the party, Owen asked himself what, if anything, was happening. Something must be happening, because he wasn't bored. Phoebe had soon abandoned him—for his own sake, he knew: he would do better on his own. He stood near the bar and watched the other guests, many of whom were also watching. For a while a pickup combo—bass, piano, sax— played in a far room. What talk he heard sounded mostly small, a counterpart of the nudging and touching, friendly, not particularly sexual, that brought groups together and dispersed them. A California breeze was fluttering the Thai silk curtains. In this mildness a few isles of agitation survived: "Then he asked me, 'If I go to bed with you here, do I have to go to bed with you in New York?' and I told him, 'Sweetie pie, of course not!' " Owen failed to match a face to the melodious voice. He did not understand why he felt so much at ease among people whom he didn't know, who seemed no more concerned with one another than with him, who nevertheless acted neither hostile nor indifferent.

His impressions made more sense when the dancing started. The stereo came on like the summons to a Last Judgment where all would be saved. No one asked anybody to dance because nobody could hear. People danced or didn't. The notion of "couple" was dissipated in a free-for-all that spread across three rooms.

Owen loved dancing of every sort. Earlier that year, when the Twist had first appeared, he single-handedly imposed it on upstate gatherings still attuned to Xavier Cougat. Here the Twist had followed the Conga into oblivion; a new, less definable order reigned. Owen began reducing the apparently chaotic movements of those around him to a pattern he could imitate.

When he entered the arena, he found himself facing a woman, scarcely younger than he, who bore a compelling resemblance to Angela Lansbury and comported herself with stylish abandon. He tried to follow her lead and couldn't. She drew suddenly close to him—he thought she was going to kiss him—to shriekingly murmur in his ear, "Don't do *steps.*" He failed to grasp. . . . "No steps!" she insisted, leading him to the sidelines. "There aren't any rules. Just anchor one hip in space—make that your center, OK?—and let the rest go. Do what the music does—anything." She demonstrated. He tried. "*Any*thing!" she urged. "Shut your eyes and listen."

From time to time he stopped at an open window to cool off. He would then attempt, by smiles and gesticulations, to express to other bystanders his approval of the new culture. Once a young woman, as if to fortify his conversion, led him straight back into the action; once a young man. Owen's fear at the touch of that firm hand dissolved among the dancers.

He was progressing from exuberance towards fluency when Phoebe stopped him. In a quieter room she introduced him to Joey, a painter in his twenties with a problem she wanted Owen to consider: a fire in his studio, a landlord refusing to pay for repairs. Insurance? Not the right kind, according to the owner, who Joey thought was stalling in order to evict him. Owen told him to call his office the next morning and ask for Margy; he would phone her instructions. It occurred to him how easily he might extend his services to individuals so plainly in need of them.

The party was subsiding. Owen and Phoebe followed a gang of celebrants down the walnut banister, out onto Manahatta's stony pave. Arm in arm they headed west in search of a White Tower. Owen said, "Then I'll drop you home. I wish I felt sleepier."

"I see!" Phoebe turned them back towards Fifth Avenue. "You trust me?"

"With a vengeance."

She was hailing a cab. "Belmont, please. Service entrance."

"You want the hotel, lady, or the track?"

"The track. Take the bridge, please," she added. So they could see the dawn.

The not-quite dawn: the cab glided smoothly towards chalk dust cascading out of stars into eastern cloud-of-light. When they set down at the stables, Phoebe led the way to the cafeteria, which was half full and wide awake. They took coffee and Danish to a table at which five males were sitting, the youngest a diminutive adolescent black, the oldest a sixtyish Chicano. The group affably made room for Owen and Phoebe and went on with an earnest discussion of a horse called Capital Gain. ("By Venture Capital out of No Risk," Phoebe explained. "These people work for the McEwans.")

Walter Trale had kept friends from the days when he painted horses. He liked going to the track, and sometimes brought Phoebe along. She had met several owners, and because she knew horses, she had talked her way into the stable area and made friends there as well.

Pushing away his tray, one man said, "Let's try him out." All proceeded to the stables. Capital Gain was saddled and led forth. At the training track the young black was told, "Six furlongs, remember, and keep it tight. He may still hurt."

Dawn turned into day. When the horse pulled up at the end of the workout, the Chicano declared, "He's all right."

"He'll be up in six weeks," someone added. "Hey, Phoebe, want to walk a hot?"

The horse was huffing as it pranced sideways up to them. While a tall black held the bit, the exercise boy dismounted and handed Phoebe the reins. The horse turned a bulging eye on her, shaking his head like a wet-eared swimmer. Phoebe stood looking up at the head and spoke to it for a while before leading the animal towards the stables.

"Half an hour should do it," the man told her.

To Owen, his bare-legged and tight-skirted daughter looked alarmingly frail alongside the silver-gray stallion, three years old and foaming with power. Where had the others gone? He didn't say a word to her, he kept at a cautious distance; but when Capital Gain reappeared around a corner of the stable, Owen saw him jerk his head back without warning, pulling Phoebe off balance. As the reins went slack, the horse reared, wagging wicked forefeet above her head and whinnying huskily. Turning around, Phoebe held the bridle loose until the horse came down to earth and lowered his head. She stepped up to him and grabbed the reins closer to the bit, yanking them almost to the ground, holding them there with all her weight. The horse kicked and swerved and could not raise his head. A moment later, to Owen's horror, Phoebe with a stern cry of "You motherfucking" something-or-other began driving her small fist into the animal's neck. Soon after, she resumed her stroll, with the stallion again obediently in tow.

Near the end of Phoebe's stint, Capital Gain's owner arrived. Mr. McEwan had come to look at his horse. He was pleased to find him sound; pleased to see Phoebe, too. He invited her and Owen to the clubhouse for a second breakfast.

They ate a much bigger, better, and longer meal than their first: fruit, eggs, bacon, toast, buckwheat cakes, tall shining pots of coffee. They sat at their table for an hour and a half, in low eastern sunlight, in early-morning shade. At last Mr. McEwan left for work. He had behaved with perfunctoriness towards Owen, who realized that here he was no more and no less than his daughter's father, until Phoebe injected some helpful information into their talk. By the end of breakfast the men were chummily discussing business. Owen looked on Phoebe with freshened eyes.

The day had started hot and dry. The pair wandered across the track, where groundsmen readied the terrain for the afternoon and sparrows hopped about rare droppings. They bowed through a fence into the empty infield. They sat down on shaded grass. Fat robins policed the grounds; yarmulkaed chickadees pecked their way up thickset branches; beyond the linked pools, black cutouts of crows were pasted against yellow-green baize. A breeze carried vibrations of urban traffic and an occasional drone from the sky. Owen leaned his head on his knees.

Phoebe was poking him. "Poppa, stick around. It's nice out here." Owen grunted assent. His eyes would not stay open. "Don't forget Joey." He nodded, sighed, and sat up. Phoebe held out her hand: "Try some of this, Poppa."

"What is it?"

"Medical snuff. Poppa Jenks gave it to me—he endorses it one hundred per, and so does Freud."

"You're sure?"

"Just don't sneeze."

"Sort of like nasal Alka-Seltzer."

He sat in a phone booth with a diminishing column of dimes, chattering to his secretary like a telex as he transmitted, as fast as he could master it, the clear stream of ideas flowing through his consciousness. He solved the case of the thieving computer. He mitigated the death of the essential engineer. For Joey, he told Margy to check the insurance on the building, accuse

Joey's landlord of being criminally negligent, and point out that with Owen's help he could become an honest profiteer. "What do you mean, am I all right? On a day like this, who could *not* be all right?"

Phoebe had disappeared. He looked through the club rooms. On the terrace, Owen thought he might soon float away. The infield remained almost empty—one idle groundskeeper, another man standing immobile in the shadow of his Stetson.

"He should sell that hat to a developer." Phoebe was behind him, carrying a big paper bag.

In a clump of copper beeches by the stables, on a tablecloth spread on the ground, Phoebe set out lunch: two club sandwiches, four pears, a slab of rat cheese, a frosty thermos of martinis. They ate and drank.

From the stables came the bustle of nervous men and the stomping of hooves. The time for the first race was approaching. Owen felt pleasantly restless: "Let's go take a look."

"This is no time for camp followers," Phoebe told him. "We'd be in the way."

"Well, I feel like joining the party."

"They thought of that. You get to bet."

As they strolled back to the clubhouse, Phoebe said, "I'll go scout the field and meet you at the paddock." At her return she announced, "My Portrait in the sixth."

"My Portrait is a horse?"

"By Spitting Image out of My Business."

Preferring to "check the form," Owen bought a *Morning Telegraph* and through the afternoon studied it with the reverence of a Talmudic scholar. When they left, after six races, he had lost less than he might have. He had also paid Phoebe back for their lunch, and she had bet the money on My Portrait, who paid off at nine to two. She forced the winnings on him: "I did it for you. I never bet."

"You—Miss Spunk?"

Phoebe persuaded Owen to take the train back—the fastest way home, even if he dreaded an "awful crowd." Other early leavers entered their car. They seemed quiet—no beer-heads, no "youngsters." The last ones in had to stand, filling the aisle. The train started up with a jolt and a clang.

Owen soon regretted his forsaken taxi. He found himself hemmed in by bodies bulbous or emaciated, all clothed according to some perverse notion of unfunny clownishness, each swaying face stamped with metropolitan distrust. His gaze at last came to rest on a couple sitting across the car: neatly dressed, not bad looking, in their Latin way—he had caught a few words of Spanish. The man, who wore an open white shirt and beige slacks, had a slender body, dark, thin features, pepper-and-salt hair, and a black mustache. The woman, in a cotton print dress and white shoes, looked younger—pretty, a little coarse, perhaps, yet so amiable, her fine teeth flashingly set off by her black, brushed-out hair. The man's merry eyes caught Owen's at the moment Phoebe nudged him: "Just like us."

The man's eyes looked into his with cheerful indifference. Of course, a father and daughter. Like us: the man, therefore, "like me." Owen searched for feelings like his own in the alert face, whose nostrils flared ever so slightly as he stared. He thought: What signs do my feelings leave in my face?

He turned away to consider someone nearer: a man with florid swollen features, short strawy hair above a shaved pink nape, a heavy belly that bulged through a half-untucked Hawaiian shirt over low-belted pants of shiny plaid synthetic gabardine—And so on, thought Owen, ad nauseam. Why did he mind? His own body felt warm and stupefied. He noticed that the light outside the train windows had become detached from his perception of it; and he saw that a similar hallucinatory change was occurring in his neighbor. He was separating into disjunct entities—still a looming, monstrous straphanger, while his eyes belonged to another body, another space: through them shined light from afar. A disjunct light existed behind the appearance the man turned to the world. That slob body had become an empty vessel with autonomous light inside it—a Halloween pumpkin. The pumpkin grinned at him, as pumpkins should. Why? It was answering his own smile. All right. Owen extended his smile into a little nod, as if to say, Win some, lose some; or, Been quite a day. He lowered his gaze. The awful crowd—should he care? He shyly glanced at others near him: veterans of one summer afternoon, each encased in his rind, each accumulating incongruities, pains, shames, even signs of happiness, to conceal that uncanny light—their masks, their lives. Phoebe was snoozing on his shoulder.

From Penn Station she took Owen straight to Walter's. Walter was giving a dinner, to which she was inviting him: she was cook.

For a while they remained alone in his studio. Phoebe hustled in the kitchen. Owen stood in front of the northwest window, looking into a cherry-blossom sky festooned with jetliner trails. A molelike question was rummaging inside him: What is wrong with this? He ignored it and abandoned himself to the view of Jersey.

Walter arrived, then his guests—two women, two men. Each acted as lively and curious as a dog off its leash. Apparently they all led busy lives, in activities Owen could not recognize. What was, or were, sociolinguistics? Where was Essalen? Was a concrete poet a writer or a sculptor? Who was Theodore Huff? He was pleased to have discarded jacket and tie.

Phoebe made them all drinks (chilled gimlets for Owen). He did not know what to say to these people. They didn't mind. While he sensed that they were funny, the context of their wit and gossip escaped him. At last he mentally put his tie back on and asked them questions. They asked him questions in turn, and he told a little about himself. The others listened attentively. He succeeded in getting credit for helping Joey the painter.

Towards the end of the meal, after Walter had urged him to talk about his work, Owen revealed something Phoebe had never known:

". . . Neither of us had capital—just the insurance from the fire. But you're right: we needed more than that to expand. We might have raised enough money from the banks, but it would have been just enough—it would have meant being dependent on them for maybe ten or fifteen years. We talked about the problem for weeks, and gradually we agreed on a solution— actually, we backed into it, because it wasn't only risky, it was illegal. That was twenty-five years ago, and I haven't even *parked* illegally since then. This is what we did. There'd been an accident on the waterfront in New London. A tug banged up a wharf, pretty much wrecking it, and on top of that some gasoline drums spilled and set the whole thing on fire. The wharf belonged to a ferry company. It was a company with high operating costs and a low profit margin, so the owners were happy for us to take over their claims. We paid them right off what it was going to cost to rebuild the wharf. Normally we would have gone on and made our profit on secondary claims like losses due to interruption of service, damage to reputation, stuff like that. But we found out that the ferry people had taken out a policy for fire with one company and a policy for maritime damage with another company, and furthermore, even though the business was chartered in New London, because its services involved other places such as Long Island they'd used one insurance company in Connecticut and one in New York. So, since the wharf for all practical purposes had been wrecked twice over, once by the collision and once when it burned, what we did was press all the claims against *both* companies. I can tell you, we went through two very scary months. Once, inspectors from the two companies missed each other by minutes; and of course if they'd found us out, we'd have been through. But we got away with it. We cleared about a hundred thousand dollars—not enough to retire on, but that was still a lot of money in nineteen thirty-seven, and we felt a lot better set to take on the big boys. And that's what we did. We really buckled down. I don't know if I could work that hard anymore," Owen concluded. "Nowadays I do ninety percent of my business by phone."

A few seconds later he fell asleep. "Rack time, Poppa!" Phoebe shouted in his ear. Eventually she got him up and put him to bed in her studio. Their long day had ended.

When Owen woke up the next morning, he found a note from his daughter: she had "slept elsewhere"; he would find coffee, bread, butter, and eggs in the larder. She apologized for the evaporated milk: "I couldn't face shopping after the dishes." So she had gone back to Trale's place. Owen did not want breakfast. He missed his *Trib*.

Phoebe came in at ten. He warmed to her hug. She said to him, "Poppa, I've got to kick you out. This looks like a heavy day."

"A whole day without you? I don't think I can manage."

"It was fun, wasn't it? You keep right on playing without me."

"All right." He added morosely, "I really shot my mouth off last night."

Phoebe looked bewildered. "You were a smash."

"No kidding."

"Poppa, I just want to work. Why the soap opera?" Owen said nothing. "Want to meet for dinner?"

Owen said he'd see and put on his jacket. He felt hung over. Stepping out on peculiar lower Broadway, he looked forward to his office.

All day long, Owen talked to himself about Phoebe. She had downtown elegance, talent, and a passion for her work. She had friends low and high. She was attractive and smart. She had devoted herself to him without reserve. What more could a father want?

He wished she would demand the money he had promised her. Perhaps she could give him drawing lessons that he could pay her for. His irritation grew. He gave Joey's landlord a piece of his mind.

He imagined being old and widowed: Phoebe would take care of him. He would quietly watch her life out of the corner of his eye.

He wasn't old, he didn't need Phoebe looking after him. She had been cruel turning her back on him—you spend a hundred bucks, and next morning, see you later.

Remembering the bet on My Portrait, he silently begged her forgiveness. He called Phoebe to say he'd love to have dinner.

Phoebe that evening looked tired and worried. Some days, she told Owen, she felt she'd never make it. Her fingernails were caked, her hair bunchy, she wasn't wearing lipstick. Owen saw in these signs of trust a refusal to make an effort for his sake. She failed to suggest a next meeting.

He went on brooding about her. Something was wrong. Owen had become confused and didn't like it. Away from Phoebe, he thought wistfully of the night and day she'd given him. Why hadn't there been more? This first "why" soon led to others. Beyond all of them, "something must be wrong" lurked in a beckoning shade. If there was to be no more, why had Phoebe bothered with him? She had not merely been dutiful. Why had she led him on and then let him down? Allowing these questions to seem real planted a crystal of suspicion in Owen's mind, which crusted with cold like a pond in plunging frost.

He reviewed once again the time spent with Phoebe. He told himself that she had not chosen their activities accidentally. She had given him new experiences of new kinds of people: artists, jazzmen, stable hands, a "beautiful crowd." What did they all have in common? The answer came to Owen on a hot, windy afternoon at the corner of Madison Avenue and Forty-eighth Street. When the light turned green, he stepped back onto the curb to stare into a wickerwork-iron trash can. Phoebe had been making a fool of him.

She had been teaching him a lesson: these new people had nothing to do with him. Phoebe had lured him into enjoying activities and attitudes that belonged to her, not to him. She was telling him, If you like my life so much, what can yours be worth? The year before he had opposed her; she was taking her revenge. She was showing him who had been right and was still right.

Owen had found something clear and nasty to batten on. He disregarded the noticeable thrill of suspecting that his daughter had betrayed him; he only relished his relief at having an explanation. He enjoyed his discovery so much that his sentiments towards Phoebe brightened perceptibly.

Owen saw Phoebe twice in August and once in September. He tried to make their meetings altogether casual. To Phoebe he seemed determined to undo what they had shared, pointedly refusing a stroll down Third Avenue one hot night because of "all the people," not going to a party because dancing was "no fun anymore." Owen would have denied such intentions. He had so thoroughly become the mistreated father that he forgot all his once-happiest expectations. He was defending this identity "innocently."

Phoebe occasionally prodded him. When Owen declined having drinks at Walter's, saying, "Walter's OK, but you know I can't stand his friends," Phoebe asked, "Like Jack McEwan?" With whom Owen had recently dined.

Usually she accepted his comments docilely. Owen was therefore surprised to notice, after a time, an undisguised aloofness on her part. He had sometimes spoken frankly to her, he knew; didn't she pride herself on her broad-mindedness? Her coolness did not discourage him, but rather confirmed him in his role of responsible, misunderstood parent.

Something more preoccupying had strengthened his commitment to that role. In the course of the summer Phoebe gradually succumbed to what was first considered a mood, then a psychological state, and at last—much later—a disease. The condition revealed itself, slowly and relentlessly, in symptoms of fatigue, morbid emotionalism, and depression. During the following autumn and winter, two good doctors assured Owen that Phoebe was suffering from a type of neurasthenia. Influenced by his own passionate conviction, they attributed the source of her trouble to the irregular life she had been leading.

Whatever a child's age, her health remains a parent's prime concern. Owen found Phoebe the best doctors he could trust. Otherwise he kept to the background, reserving for himself the right to protect his daughter from the prime cause of her disorder—her wayward life. Wary of Phoebe's stubborn independence, he waited for an opportunity to intervene. One came late in December. Chronic insomnia had left Phoebe exhausted. Her resistance to infection had been sapped. When she caught the flu it turned into bronchitis, then pleurisy. She had to stop modeling; her money ran out. Having learned as much from her psychiatrist, Owen called up Phoebe and went to see her.

Her studio looked a mess; so did she—a frail, livid derelict. Owen made her some tea, chatted a while, then offered to resume the payments from the trust fund he had set up the previous year. It "was still there, waiting for her."

Phoebe began to cry. She cried like a six-year-old, with long, violent sobs. "I *am* tapped out. I thought you'd given up on me."

"That's nonsense."

"You've been very hard. I felt so close to you last spring, last June—it seems ages."

"I've been worried about you, that's all."

"I feel so awful. Sometimes I feel like I'm dying."

"You don't take care of yourself."

"I do. I go to the doctors and take all the pills, and it doesn't ever help, not for long."

"Tell me one thing. Are you still taking drugs?" Phoebe looked at him incredulously. "Can you honestly promise me you'll stop taking drugs?"

"You should ask Dr. Straub. He tries out a new one on me every week."

"Not that kind of drug—marijuana, amphetamines, cocaine . . ."

"Do you think I'm crazy? I mean I'd *have* to be nuts to, the way I feel."

"It's not you—it's your friends I worry about. Can't you just promise?"

"No sweat."

"Good. With your money you could take a good long rest and get really well again. How would you like a week in the Bahamas? Be my guest. If it's good enough for Jack and Mac, why not us? One other thing—" Owen neither paused nor altered his tone of voice, warm and urgent. Why should he hesitate? The sight of Phoebe had not only appalled him, it had mightily reinforced his disposition: he knew what was holding her here, what had to be given up. "I want you to go to a real art school. You haven't been making the kind of progress you should. I know Walter's a nice man, and I know how fond of him you are—I'm fond of him too. But he's not a good teacher." Owen thought that through her sunken cheeks he could see Phoebe's teeth. She said nothing. He concluded: "That's something I consider essential to your well-being. That's the first thing you have to do before we get you organized."

Phoebe glanced around the studio, its walls crowded with

work that Owen had ignored. Copious tears again flowed over her face and dripped off her chin. In a voice steady enough, only a little hoarse, she told him to get out.

"I know it's difficult," he replied, "and I know you're upset—"

"You are a bleeding asshole."

"—but sooner or later you've got to face the fact that you're unwell *and* unhappy. Think it over. Ask yourself why."

As he left, Owen thought: She's a very sick girl. He had done what he could. He was glad she was in good hands. Calling on her had depressed and somehow elated him. Phoebe's insults had provoked a warm rush of what he did not dare recognize as relief.

He phoned Dr. Straub to say how concerned he was. He would appreciate being kept informed.

During the ensuing months, Phoebe kept getting worse: depression, insomnia, feverishness. In late spring she was taken to a hospital with pneumonia. Her doctors refused to release her unless she allowed them to perform certain tests. These enabled her disorder to be identified as acute hyperthyroidism, also known as Graves's disease. Phoebe began a treatment with a drug called methyl thiouracil. Its initial effect proved slight. At the beginning of June she agreed to return to her family's house upstate, not because she wanted to, but because her mother's insistence and her own helplessness left her no choice. Ten weeks afterwards, her treatment, no doubt begun too late, was abandoned, and she consented to undergo a subtotal thyroidectomy at a nearby hospital, which she entered on the fifteenth of August.

At the time of Phoebe's earlier hospitalization, Owen's attitude towards her changed. He had plainly done her an injustice, and he knew better than to claim good intentions as an excuse. He had blamed Phoebe's condition on her behavior—a judgment that, as well as wronging her, encouraged the doctors he had chosen to persevere in their mistaken diagnosis. He told himself that she could never be expected to forgive or understand him. He must simply make what amends he could and pray that she would find a way to leave him in peace.

When she came home, he committed himself to a program of discreet and fervent atonement. He did whatever Phoebe asked of him without the least complaint. Owen's contrition was matched by Phoebe's contempt. As a condition of her return, she insisted that he move to the guest annex at the far end of the house. When she heard his voice, she often asked her mother to shut him up. Sometimes she summoned him to her bedside to supply new fuel for her scorn. ("What rich creeps did you insure this week?") Or she would demand things of him (such as reading *Two Serious Ladies* out loud to her; she wept at its beauties and raged at his boredom) as if he were a lackey whose career of swindle and rape had just been disclosed. Whenever he appeared she stared at him out of bulging, hateful eyes. When Owen came into possession of Walter's portrait of Elizabeth, he let her ridicule his motives for acquiring it and did not try to explain them. She was so outraged that the picture belonged to him that he had it sent up from the city to be hung in her room.

Phoebe's treatment of him comforted Owen. It allowed him to go on playing the dutiful, now penitent father. The role, hard and forthright, continued to reassure him. Owen dreaded above all the agitating uncertainty into which Phoebe had twice led him. Of course she still loomed dangerously in his future. How would she behave once she was cured? Most likely she would want to be reconciled with him. Her harshness towards him could become the pretext for excusing his own unfair behavior. Owen abhorred this possibility and preferred being punished. He longed for Phoebe to live her life and leave him out of it.

On July first, Owen settled a large amount of money on his daughter. Unlike the trust fund, this arrangement made Phoebe

truly independent. She would have no further need of him. To
outsiders, his gesture seemed generous; intimates saw in it an
expression of remorse and hope. Owen claimed he was fulfilling
a father's obligations. He could scarcely acknowledge his eagerness to escape from fatherhood altogether.

In late August, after her operation, Phoebe asked Owen to
visit her in the hospital. He went to her late in the afternoon.
In her room, the dark glow from the lowered blinds and drawn
purple curtains revealed an emaciated shape.

Owen had not seen her awake since the operation. Phoebe's
hair, cut short and flattened with sweat, looked like a skullcap
on a skull. Her skin lay waxily over the bones of her face. Owen
experienced fright, revulsion, a spasm of pity.

At first she said nothing as she gazed at him out of huge
inexpressive eyes. She held out her hand. The thin hot hand
gripped him hard. He didn't know what to do or say; he began
sweating himself. She finally spoke, in high, almost whimpering
tones: "You're my father. I feel awful. I don't know what's
happening to me. I feel so awful I don't feel anything else. I
can't talk much. You mustn't stay long. I do want you to
know"—from a box at her side Phoebe pulled a Kleenex and
spat into it—"I wanted you to know . . . something. It was when
my feelings got wiped out I understood, I understood something about you and me. We've been playing a dumb game, both
of us. We've been turning you into a shit. You can keep playing,
that's all right, but not me. I plan to love you whatever you do."

Owen felt himself being gathered up into a wet, smothering
shroud. He longed to scramble away from that room and his
bony daughter. Her grip tightened. He cleared his throat:
"Phoebe, you have to believe me, I've done everything I could
to you."

He did not realize what he had said until she grinned:
"Maybe, but I gave you a lot of help." She let his hand go. She
shut her eyes, spreading wrinkles across her face. She looked

like a crone. "I love you—ring that buzzer, will you? Please do it fast. Bye bye. Come back soon."

Owen hurried through the cooled corridors and lobby, out into the dank brightness that smelled of wet grass and decay. Tears simmered in his eyes. He had behaved so cruelly to Phoebe, so many times: how dare she love him? She had trapped him. She had had the last word.

Owen would have liked to cough up his feelings, as though he had breathed a beetle into his lungs. He could not identify his feelings. He got drunk. He woke up at three in the morning and wove fantasies of living under another name in a country he had never seen. He thought that he, or at least his life, had gone insane. He wished that Phoebe had never been born.

The Labor Day weekend passed. One afternoon Owen went into Phoebe's empty bedroom, where the portrait of Elizabeth, brought back from the hospital, had been set against a wall. Owen stared at it malevolently. He knew the woman in the painting all too well. Her masklike abstractness had made of her an unrelenting, unresponsive witness of his past mistakes and present helplessness.

He said aloud, "Up yours." He wished he had the nerve to piss on her. He spat on her instead and with his fingertips rubbed the spittle over her face. The paint felt slick and tough. Owen became deliciously aware of being alone in the house, as if the house belonged to someone else and he'd sneaked into it like a marauding boy.

By the window stood a table littered with Phoebe's makeup. Owen took an eyeliner pencil and with a grunt of satisfaction drew blue whiskers across Elizabeth's ivory-gold cheeks. Under the soft point the surface held firm. Encouraged, he picked up tubes of scarlet, purple, and orange-red lipstick. He bedizened the mouth and eyes with spots, stripes, and flourishes. Holding the three tubes in a cluster, he enclosed the entire head in a whorl of grease.

He felt better. He even laughed at himself. Through the window he looked across his lawn and the lawns of his neighbors into the dark woods nearby, warped here and there by clear vapor rising in hot, late-summer sun. He found a box of Kleenex and began erasing the mess he had made. Tissue after tissue fell to the floor blotted with the colors of Phoebe's mouth. He used a soapy washrag to remove the remaining traces.

Soap and water proved less than sufficient. The paler areas were still misted with purple or pink. To complete the task, he fetched a can of turpentine from the cellar, tore a clean shirt into rags, and began lightly rubbing away the last stains. He had finished cleaning one cheek and was proceeding to the eye above it when his rag caught on a crust of paint running along the rim of the eyeball. Burnt sienna surged into the eye's light ocher. He wiped it off as gently as he could; the ocher in turn spread into the nose. Owen swore. He went into the bathroom and came back with a toothbrush. Having dipped it in turpentine, he shook it out and rubbed it half dry on his sleeve. Leaning his elbow against the canvas, he started to slowly and scrupulously brush away the misplaced paint. His diligence was succeeding when a brown speck sprang from the elastic bristles and slid down the upright surface. Instinctively Owen jabbed at it with the cloth in his left hand, spreading a fresh blotch of softened paint beneath the injured eye.

Stepping back, Owen saw that he had inflicted serious damage. He wondered how to repair it. Half irritably, half jokingly, he told himself: I own the goddamn thing, I might as well enjoy it. With a turps-soaked rag in either hand, he vengefully attacked the painting. Soaking the pigments of the right eye, he smeared its colors across the fiery hair into the pale landscape above Elizabeth's head. The smear looked like a horn. Who ever saw a cow with one horn? He drew a second streak from the other eye. He drenched the mouth and blurred it into a haze of mauve. The rest of the face he obliterated with the orange of her hair.

Owen carried the painting, toothbrush, and turpentine down to the cellar. He used a chisel to loosen the tacks on the back of the stretcher before stripping away the canvas. He pulled the stretcher apart and sheared the canvas into ribbons, packing them into a burlap sack along with the rags and toothbrush. Outside the back door, he stuffed the sack into a garbage can underneath other refuse. He took the disassembled stretcher to the garage and with a hatchet split and chopped the wood into insignificant slivers, which he dumped on a pile of unstacked kindling behind the neighboring shed. He then retreated to his room to wash his face and hands.

Owen and Phoebe: II

1962-1963

W HEN OWEN TURNED AWAY FROM HER THE SUMMER BE-
fore, Phoebe could see what was happening; not why. Owen had
begun treating her as an enemy. What had she done to antago-
nize someone she so loved? She kept her patience, hoping that
if he did not end his hostility he would at least explain it. Later,
she turned cautious and, sometimes, hostile herself. Owen then
stared at her without surprise, as though looking at a curious
old photograph.

Phoebe had begun suffering from two misfortunes. First, for
several months she lost Louisa and Walter, either of whom
might have helped her. Second, her insidious disease con-
taminated both her life and her perception of it.

When the thyroid gland misfunctions, the effects are not felt
as symptoms. Depression and excitement, even indigestion, are
interpreted as private, "natural" experiences. Not until September did Phoebe consult a doctor—a general practitioner who

74

identified her trouble at once. She should, he said, be given the customary basal metabolism test; for that, he advised her to see a specialist in endocrine pathology. Owen recommended someone; she made an appointment; and her misfortune was then compounded by misdiagnosis.

Dr. Sevareid had an expert's insight: he had treated thousands of glandular disorders and could spot them at first glance. As soon as Phoebe walked into his office, he saw that she did not have thyroid disease. He told her so. Of course she should take the basal metabolism test—it could only prove him right. He forthwith introduced her to the nurse who administered it.

The test measured metabolic activity by recording the units of oxygen a patient consumed in a given time. In an adjoining room the nurse blocked Phoebe's ears and nose with rubber plugs and fitted a mask over her mouth. Through the mask she would breathe oxygen from a nearby cylinder; the plugs would restrict her oxygen intake to what the cylinder supplied.

After Phoebe had started breathing through the mask, the nurse went out of the room for about a minute and a half. When she returned, she checked the results on the monitor and was dismayed to find them abnormal—dismayed because she believed in her employer's flair as much as he did. During her absence, she said, one of the plugs must have worked loose and let in air. Since she could be fired for such negligence, she begged Phoebe not to tell the doctor she had left her alone.

She had no need to worry. Dr. Sevareid glanced at the results and remarked, "A little high, but nothing to write home about. You must have leaky ears."

Phoebe was pleased not to have to lie about the nurse and pleased not to have thyroid trouble. She was surprised to learn that she suffered from cardiac neurosis.

"Don't worry, your heart's OK—it's only a minor disorder of the nervous system."

Dr. Sevareid gave Phoebe what she craved: an authoritative

explanation of her unusual feelings. She never doubted his judgment. He could describe symptoms she had never even mentioned—her breathlessness, her blushes. When he asked her to hold out her hands, they trembled helplessly.

"You can see the condition is physically real, even if it has a psychogenic origin. It's what people used to call 'nerves.'" Phoebe blushed on cue. "You've probably been upset for a while about something or other, natural enough at your age— or *any* age." He smiled warmly and prescribed Miltown in moderate doses. If she didn't feel better within a month, she could always try psychotherapy.

The tranquilizer took the edge off Phoebe's anguish. But her spells of depression grew worse, with each passing day and night her angry heart beat faster, and she spent nights no less wakeful than before. She was perhaps most discouraged by the voice in her head. Originally no more than a murmur, it now grew into a merciless yammer, berating her with things she could hardly bear hearing—her own voice turned mean.

Phoebe named this voice her squawk box. She blamed it for making her heart pound, for keeping her awake at three in the morning, for rousing her every two hours when she slept. When, one day, she realized that she had begun talking back to the voice, she asked Dr. Sevareid for the name of a therapist. He advised her to speak to Owen. To Owen he confidentially recommended his colleague Dr. Straub.

Like Dr. Sevareid, Dr. Straub was experienced and honest. Phoebe could not know that to both doctors Owen had described her at length and in terms confirming his own prejudices. To Owen, that Phoebe was neurotic proved her way of life wrong and justified his mistrust of her. She had been mistaken from the start. He should have forced her to listen to him, forced her to stay home. Owen wanted her doctors to support these views, and he drew them a portrait of Phoebe that approached caricature: her life had lost all regularity, her friends belonged to the fringes of society, she took drugs, she indulged in sexual promiscuity.

Phoebe knew what Owen thought of her. Whenever she discussed her life with him, he remained earnestly uncomprehending. When she told him she had a hard time getting to sleep, he suggested she stop staying up so late. She disliked being given advice fit for children and detested his conviction that he understood her. She decided to keep silent in his presence. She said to her squawk box that explaining things to him was like trying to change a political party by joining it. Her squawk box scolded, *Baby, is that how you talk to the doctor? He'll tell you who wears the nuts in the family.* Phoebe: "You're so *cheap.*"

Phoebe inspired kindness in Dr. Straub, and she welcomed this kindness. She could not guess how pathetic Owen's description had made her appear. Dr. Straub had readily accepted the description because she came to him tagged with Dr. Sevareid's unimpeachable opinion, and he needed evidence that her neurosis had substance.

Phoebe herself supplied further evidence. Her feverish excitement provoked a sexual itch, and she masturbated frequently. She had no male friends that especially attracted her, and she was misguided in her choice of strangers, even at social gatherings (the only occasions where she dared approach them). She had three one-night stands that left her feeling degraded. When Dr. Straub learned of them, Owen's account of her seemed even more plausible.

Unaware of her disease, beset with disagreeable sensations, Phoebe concluded that she must simply be strange—perhaps truly neurotic. A sense of solitude invaded her, whether she was alone or not. She decided that the world was leaving her to herself; and because she did not make the easiest company, she wondered what else might comfort her. Since even the most ordinary experiences now took on unusual intensity, she began speculating that the world around her represented more than what she had heretofore seen in it; that life, and her life in particular, depended on a less visible, more abstract, more significant reality. Looking for manifestations of this idea, she found them in abundance: in the unwittingly expressive gestures of others, in the penetrating glances they gave her, in words that leapt at her from the humdrum contexts of what she heard and read.

Louisa, who saw Phoebe several times in November, was disheartened by her appearance, and even more by her obscure new way of speaking. Once, discussing Owen over the phone, Phoebe breathily said to her, "Darling Momma, how is it he can't understand? The bads, OK, but even when I'm ecstatic? I know that it's always just Nature working on my mind. So I feel it working on my mind—"

"Everyone has their ups and downs—"

"No. It's why can't *I* be a little voice in the big chorus? I'd settle for being a pocket thermometer."

"A thermometer?"

"You know, when the sun moved to the heart of the earth (it's still there, actually), anyone could feel it—even the Presidential Mediators."

"The who?"

"There's only one planet, Momma, whatever the astronomers say. You know what I call it?"

"No."

"An apple of love divine! By 'divine' I just mean a coherence of *apparently* contradictory vectors. That's what gives us a glimpse of the holy spirit. You know, the spirit of the hole? That's where the thermometer goes in. A joke, Momma."

"Oh—I see."

"Anyway, it's all the same, and it's *me.*"

Louisa apologized for not understanding her and asked for time to think about it. Soon, however, all Louisa's time would be devoted to her son, Lewis, and she would leave Phoebe to Owen—he had always "adored" her and had her best interests at heart.

The words *hole* and *Presidential Mediators* had drifted into Phoebe's speech from conversations with her squawk box. She had told it, "I'm just a worm in the Big Apple. . . ." *So, what did you see, huh?* "Cuter girls than me, I can tell you." *Cute boys, by the Lord. I know you—every boy's a cute one.* "No, they make me sad. They find a girl and lead her straight to the icehouse, to see what she'll be like when she's old. It's crazy." *You walk down the street and all you think about is love. You better keep your girlie hands to yourself, you little bitch.* "I do that all the time." *I don't mean that. It's the far slope I'm talking about.* "You mean the hill, with the convent of the Sacred Heart?" *Oh, you're the heart—the artichoke heart! Not the holy heart, because that wouldn't be a hill but a hole. . . .* Phoebe was stuck with this pun on *holy.* She pierced, she was pierced with the holes of her body. Through them she thought she might penetrate to the exalting light coursing through her.

In October, at the climax of the missiles crisis, the general fear affected Phoebe violently. With the danger gone, the abstract meaning she looked for in the world was briefly embodied in a heroic image of the President. She wrote him a letter:

If we admit that Nature works upon the mind, war is then a question of mind. I know that you know this. While the sun was floating up over Brooklyn this morning, I saw that you had mastered the coherence of contradictory vectors that alone gives us a glimpse of light, which some call love divine, since it harmoniously fuses races, nations, and religions in a peace that passes understanding. Because you have mastered this conflict, I feel as if stunned with love, like a bell in a wedding of angels. You have (not on purpose) decked out each corner of my heart with exquisite fiercely scented flowers. Nor, walking beside you,

would I forget her, still and ever an adorable feminine apparition pursuing me and encouraging me like the spring breeze in
her smile. That's how I've been cured of my regrets, in fact.

Squawk box said: *Don't bother him when he's so busy.* "OK, I'll
send it to the Presidential Mediators. They'll know what's
best."

Phoebe showed Walter her letter; he suggested she sleep on
it. If she liked writing, he asked her, why not keep a working
journal? A great idea, Phoebe replied. The letter read like
gibberish when she next looked at it, and she put it away
in a drawer, while her squawk box sniggered, *You still adore
Him.* . . .

Phoebe saw Walter less and less. Priscilla had come into his
life, looking after him, taking up his time. Phoebe inwardly
relied on Owen, because she still loved him and because he
dominated her visions when, for instance, she woke up to challenge another long day in late-night blackness, alone, in a sweat,
with her heart clobbering her from within. Owen did not call
often.

At the end of November her brother, Lewis, was arrested in
scandalous circumstances. Phoebe refused to believe what was
publicly said about him. Dr. Straub saw in this sympathy a
confirmation of her tendency to dissoluteness. He became more
confidently paternal than ever.

Phoebe began her journal:

In art we must start by eliminating all historical classifica-
tions, which only produce stifled characters. We want beauty
novelty style for all ages and lands. It's Christmas, isn't it—"No
Hell"? . . .

As if to acknowledge the season, her squawk box softened
its tone, doubling her own voice in dreamier obsessions:

"Gounod's 'Ave Maria' . . ." *Vacation's starting—but not for Mary Stuart. Ave Maria Stuart! It's like Christmas in wartime. Oh, you remember! The dead on a picket fence at Gettysburg, and: 'Hordes across the Yalu.'* "Fronds and spines on those corteges. Wouldn't it be kindly to be reborn into happy

> Old nights of Holy Mystery
> Hearing Noel sung in Your honor
> To the ends of the earth."

You've lost your French, Maria Stuart says. "I remember beautiful Christmases. Reproductions in gifted books—Christmas was a Prussian-blue sky with Wise Men and star. Also organ and bells. Sometimes they boom death Mass—fears and pains." *We do have peace, sort of.* "Only divine hands can stanch tears. Away on country hillsides steeples are counting out solemn carols. In small-town streets they sing in a smell of snow and ozone. Here shadows are all over the snow, with shouts not hymns." *You don't dare step into a church. You'd want to kiss people, and they'd only let you sing and cry.* "Fervent wishes in the wind! Deliver our hearts and eyes from irritation. Let's raise one Christmas tree in the Morosco Theater, and another in the Beekman meat market."

She spent most of Christmastime in bed, feverish, besnotted with her entrenched bronchitis. The infection aggravated her usual symptoms. She got up for Owen, who came with an offer of help in exchange for her giving up Walter. Breaking with him left her in a morbid state, even though he sent her money afterwards. She celebrated Christmas day in bed alone.

Walter went away for a few days with Priscilla. Phoebe agreed to look after a friend's cat. She soon began thinking that it was all the society she would ever have. And nobody's fault but her own. She didn't blame anyone for neglecting her, not even Owen. Not even Louisa, who was hiding behind him.

"Look at me, twenty years old, with breasts as wrinkly as the skin on hot milk."

Phoebe gave up all thought of modeling. She painted less and less. (Her hand shook, exhaustion led to distraction and excused it.) One morning her jeans fell down, slipping off her unfleshed hips. She hugged the mess of her body. She hurt. Sometimes the ache of her thrumming heart soared into a dazzling pain that sent her back to bed curled up and enduring. Because her sensations, feelings, and thoughts never abated, she came to the conclusion that she didn't stand a chance against them. What was she proving by lasting as long as she could? Survival meant only unremitting punishment. She didn't deserve it; she didn't deserve herself.

One evening in early February, she got out of bed and on the way to the bathroom picked up an X-Acto knife from her worktable. She ran a warm bath and sat in the tub with the knife in her right hand. After a few minutes she traced a tentative incision across her left wrist, perpendicular to the veins that ran blue and swollen underneath the transparent skin. A rosary of red droplets sprang up under the point. Her friend's cat had followed her into the bathroom and was sitting on the toilet, perched on its hindquarters, staring at her. Its gaze, one of perfect attention and indifference, was suddenly interrupted by a pink-and-white yawn, during which the cat's head disappeared behind its mouth. The animal then settled on its belly, crossing its forepaws. Phoebe shifted the knife to her left hand. Leaning her neck on the rim of the tub, she began masturbating underwater. Her pleasure—faint, short, unsettling—kept her alive.

Phoebe flipped the drain open and stepped out of the tub. She put on a can of consommé to heat while she dressed. She took a long time dressing. Later she went outside and started walking, working her way east, through the clear and windless night, cold but not frozen. She felt both numb and alert crossing the city, numb to cold and filth, alert to a thrashing rhythm within her. As she passed from one streaming avenue to the next, each dark block between became a bridge that lifted her into another half-abandoned hive where beings from uncreated dreams slept and drifted, giddy from the shock of their birth. They did not sadden her, she felt no sorrow for them, and a glance from any one of them could only mean that someone wished her well; she went on. A half hour later she crossed under an elevated highway and found herself at the "river." She wiped her eyes stung wet by cold and airy dirt. Above the city glow, scattered stars glistened in a moonless sky, drooping close, teetering not unkindly over the convulsions of her thought.

She had grown cold. She hurried up to Fourteenth Street and found a coffee shop. She was wearing Russian boots, men's corduroy trousers, a Navy pea jacket with two sweaters underneath, ski mittens, and a plaid wool cap with its earflaps down. After ordering her tea, she took off the cap, the mittens, the pea jacket, and one of her sweaters. The other customers relaxed. Someone from space had become a nice girl with rather large eyes. Three young men at the counter began teasing her, betting how long it took her to get into all those clothes. And how about getting *out* of them? Phoebe hardly minded. She had attracted no attention in a week, or since wanting to die. One of the men said it was a crime to bundle herself out of sight like that—a pretty girl was what life was all about. His words gave the world back to Phoebe. She wanted to cry. When he asked if he could take her home, she said yes.

Back in her studio, he treated her gently and a little impatiently. Because of her skinniness she turned out the lights and got under the covers first. He started rubbing his hands over her. She cried out. He took this for a sign of pleasure; she meant something else. She was experiencing a visitation, or at least an unusual visit. It had begun snowing inside her room. Out of the fathomless dark ceiling, snow was falling and soundlessly pelting her. The flakes felt light and warm as they cascaded onto her and through her. "Wait," she pleaded, "it's beautiful—" The boy grunted knowingly. She let him be, surrendering to the soft tumult. She rose to meet and savor it, gliding through rings of splintery light, up, up. Where was she going? Higher, she found or mentally assembled webs of incandescence out of which the flakes came sprinkling. She guessed, she *knew* what they were: stars. The teetering stars had spilled into the gloom of her mind. She had no strength to resist that shower or the spidery filaments above it that sucked her in. She recognized where she had come: into the abstraction called love. She was being pelted with love and sucked into it—and this poor boy was still bumping against her. Sure he was. Love had been broken into bits among us, the way light was pieced out around the sky: here and there, the same thing. A showering, never fixed, except in a fixity of change, in the motion of its fragments. Each star moved in its ring, each man in his life each woman in her life, longing to touch and never able to, and still one life, one us. That's why I love cloudless nights, Phoebe thought. Truth was shining around her. She drifted into the welter of light. She laughed incredulously, "It's us!" Her body shook with glee as he lost himself inside her. For a few days she had a hard time keeping him away.

Phoebe had to talk to someone about this joy. She approached Walter as soon as he came back. When she confessed that a stranger had restored her faith in life by telling her she was pretty, Walter scolded her. She was peddling herself to bums. They didn't care a damn about love and truth: "Their guiding light is getting into your pants."

She was disgusted with herself when she left him; and the disgust permanently cured her of suicide. Her piddling life did not deserve dramatic remedies. No sooner had she thought, When I got to the river I should have jumped right in, than her squawk box barked sympathetically, *The East River? Honey,*

you wouldn't have drowned, you'd have choked to death. Phoebe
wrote in her journal:

> A leap into the unknown is a leap back into childishness—
> another dream that doesn't work, and pretentious, too.

She resigned herself to living as a sick, childish adult, as a
succession of hopeful and shameful incarnations. She remembered her father, with whom she had shared years of love and
to whom she had spoken viciously. She wanted to speak to him
again, in some other manner.

Phoebe had not seen Dr. Straub for a month. At her next
visit, in mid-February, he remarked that she had behaved irre-
sponsibly by not keeping her appointments. Not only had she
harmed herself, she had prevented him from reporting on her
condition to Owen, who was greatly upset. Phoebe thus learned
of the therapist's complicity with her father. She saw an opportunity to wipe the slate clean, since both she and Owen had now
put themselves in the wrong: she had yelled at him, he had
acted behind her back. She wrote him a letter:

> . . . I was painfully surprised that you could talk about me
> to someone, even a doctor, so confidentially. It's too bad you
> haven't observed the results. At least I now understand why he
> stares at me so hard without ever seeing me. (It's true I always
> wear the magic ring you once gave me!) Since I can appreciate
> your desire to talk to someone about me, perhaps you can
> appreciate that to me it seems fairly disgusting? I know you
> meant well—that's the way "your kind" behaves, you're all so
> *good* at that: summing up a life in a few words. Has anyone ever
> looked right through you and out the other side? . . .

Owen did not respond. Phoebe was afraid of saying what
she didn't mean if she used the telephone; so she wrote an-

other letter, this time to Louisa. Discussing Owen, she asked for help:

> . . . A question becomes evident: is it possible to communicate with a human being? To communicate what my life is—
>
> Life goes on and keeps becoming what it already was. There are differences of form, that's all. Or I may feel that I'm still a lot of different people, but it's still one person struggling like mad—madly degrading myself—. . . .
>
> There were moments when you smiled—you were irresistibly yourself, even if you checked the smile a second after it showed. I know all about that. . . .
>
> I'm getting weaker and weaker, I let things happen abjectly. My room is a dream. So are the things in it, including my feet. Sometimes I scream dream screams. What I've lost is my confidence—my "insolence." I need tenderness, too—the infinite tenderness that goes with beginnings. So I scream like a little child who's been left out. Not just left out by people, by *things*. However, this does not make me feel inhuman, I feel *very* human. . . .

Louisa, when she came to see her, found Phoebe more than she could face. She did not know where to begin. She encouraged Phoebe to trust the medical help she was getting and withdrew—into Owen's shadow, as Phoebe saw it. Phoebe still refused to condemn Owen, reminding herself that he was paying for her doctors and sending her money. She reduced him for the time being to someone who wrote necessary checks.

With no one else to rely on, she clung earnestly to herself. That self had become more and more fugitive: she kept losing hold of her pain, her tremors, and her explosive feelings. One afternoon she went to a movie, *The Diary of a Country Priest.* In one scene, an older clergyman tells the young protagonist that anyone called to holy orders will find in the history of Christianity a precedent for his vocation. Walking home between ridges of grizzled snow, Phoebe asked herself if hers might not be Saint Lawrence on his griddle. At home she wrote in her journal:

> If the old ways had not been hidden, we could deliver ourselves from death by death. The divine directive points toward voluntary consumption—best by fire, "to cleanse the errant soul."

Reflections such as this reconciled Phoebe to the "fire" cauterizing her from within.

Occasionally she would return to places and people she had enjoyed. Her volatile temperament prevented these outings from soothing her as she hoped they might. In the Cedar one February evening, a writer told a group at the bar a supposedly true story that amused everyone except her. The previous summer, two of his friends had traveled through New England by car. Late one afternoon, on a back road in the White Mountains, they had overtaken a line of forty-odd girls returning to camp at the end of a hike. The girls, who were ten to thirteen years old, looked tired out. The procession was led by a group of four counselors, young women in their late teens. The writer's friends pulled up near the end of the straggling group. They asked how far the girls still had to go. About three miles, they answered. Any of them like a lift? You bet! Four of them got into the back seat. The men explained that in exchange they would have to "give head." The girls didn't know what that meant; as soon as they were told, they scrambled out of the car. The men stopped to renew their invitation farther up the line. Other girls climbed into the car and climbed out. At last the men, drawing level with the counselors, asked, "A lift, anybody?" "OK." "Hop in." Two of the counselors settled in the back seat, nothing else was said, and the car drove off under the gaze of forty-six freshly enlightened little girls.

Phoebe at first missed the point of the story. When she understood the trick the men had played, she began to cry. Her friends looked at her incredulously. She smashed her beer on the floor and ran outside.

She felt angry less at her friends than at humanity at large. Men and women looked at one another and saw only the stuff of contemptuous jokes. Tag thy neighbor, and any tag would do—Pole, Jew, cocksucker. She shuddered remembering the women who had been stuck with this ingenious disgrace. In spite of herself she laughed at the ingenuity and thought of the disgrace as something less than disastrous, an impulse that made her break out in fresh tears. She was no different. Even she could forget "love divine." She told herself after a moment, "Of course I'm no different. And *that's* part of love." Nevertheless she had begun excluding herself from the world that her love embraced.

A few nights later Phoebe had a dream. She called it her "dream of dissolution." She is attending a group event in a sort of sunken theater inside a big, old-fashioned hotel in the city. A froglike man is directing the group. Again and again he tells them, "Accept things as they happen." Long sessions of explanation and mental exercise are separated by five-minute breaks. After the first break, she notices that the cat sitting near her is missing. After the second, the woman on her left disappears. No one can leave the theater unobserved.

Phoebe now realizes what she has been warned to accept: creatures are disintegrating. They are vanishing definitively, without cause, without justification. Phoebe feels a fresh confidence. Although she knows that sadness awaits her, she no longer worries about what will happen. During another break, chatting with a short, lively woman in her sixties, she senses that this woman will go next.

When only five participants are left, Phoebe is possessed with a desire for a "saving egg." She does not understand what this means. During the next break, in a hotel shop full of exotic bric-a-brac, she finds a cream-colored porcelain egg and buys it. Rolling it in one hand, she experiences an elation both austere and sensual. Nearby, the froglike leader is talking to a dark intellectual boy whom Phoebe had known at college. The three go back together and sit on the floor of the pit. Phoebe squeezes the egg, filling up with power. The frog man, who has begun a long speech, turns to her and softly tells her, "All right, lay off. I get it. You have the power."

A consoling warmth was stealing over Phoebe. She looked forward to waking up. She could not wake up because she had not fallen asleep. The dream, vivid as a movie, had come to her as she sat on the edge of her bed—the first of many such hallucinations. She clenched her left hand around the absent egg and hummed an old refrain:

> Earth is mother to all kinds,
> Crazy men and women.
> Earth is mother to all kinds,
> Crazy women and men.

Phoebe became chronically frightened. Her tenacious depression had convinced her that "she had failed." What had she failed at? Who was the "she" that had done the failing? She was frightened by the loss of anything she might call herself. Whatever she now was eluded her; "she" had dissolved into pure confusion. When she told Walter this, he replied, "Why the hell do you think I paint?" She noted:

So there you are with two fingers up your nose. Remove them. No problem.

She made herself go back to work. She decided literally to see who she was: she would paint nothing else.

. . . First, drawings of myself, in the old manner. Divide the surface into squares. Draw fainter lines through the center of the squares to form a secondary griddle. Insert my parts one by one:

P. Lewison, of medium height from head to toe. The length of her head equals the distance between her chin and her nipples, the distance between her chin and nipples equals that between nipples and bellybutton, the distance between nipples and bellybutton equals that between bellybutton and crotch. Shoulders are two head-heights broad. Bones: through the skin you can identify ribs, also knobs of femurs, humerus, radius. Elsewhere: frontal bone, parietal bone, temples, brows. Features: eyeballs, hair, thin nose, middling mouth, rounded chin, scarlet cheekbones. Legend: draw two horizontal lines, letters between them in large and small caps: PH. LEWISON. Inscribed above: ST. LAWRENCE IN DRAG. Or BLEEDING HEART OF JESUS. Or SACRED CUNT OF JESUS.

Phoebe gave one such sketch to Dr. Straub, the person she most talked to, someone she wanted to thank. At their next meeting he analyzed the drawing for her. In it, he pointed out, he noticed blank eyes, hands hidden behind the back, genitals more detailed than the face. His comments made her cry. Because she rarely cried in his presence, he imagined that she had come to the verge of a useful discovery. She was crying for him. That night she wrote him a farewell letter:

. . . O my psychiatrist! The human being has turned into a farm animal. The hands that handle her take all they find and give nothing back to what *must* be the source of life. You yourself pay taxes to the animal farm—you know we all end up in the stewpot. People love to eat out of it, and orders have been issued to the young to multiply and then suck each other's juices right down to the marrow. First we're pigs and donkeys, then animal suckers. . . .

This letter at last elicited a phone call from Owen: "You can't do this to yourself. You're in bad enough shape as it is, and now what's to keep you from going to pieces completely?"

Her squawk box had already been telling her this, in these words. Phoebe wondered in terror if she had not already gone to pieces. No—she still had her feelings. They rampaged through her every hour of the day. Whatever being endured them could lay claim to a real existence. Only her body, the ground of that existence, kept letting her down. Each day she tried to will it back into wholeness if not wholesomeness: "Two feet, like everybody else. Left big toe, right big toe, left ankle, right ankle. . . . Stomach with diaphragm attached, ribs enclosing me like two hands. Lungs . . ." Her lungs remained sopped; when she ate, her stomach burned; a skinned rabbit's head stared back from her mirror.

Asking the head in the mirror if she was insane comforted her, because as long as she accepted insanity as a possibility, she knew she had some sanity left. "How can the possibility of insanity be cured?" she wrote. "By food, work, and faith."

She forced soup through her teeth. No matter how exhausted, she stuck to a daily schedule of sketching, writing, and reading. Faith proved harder. A relentless awareness of loss stuffed her thin chest with dated movies of lovers, parents, and friends.

Consolation began in a book. She had become the kind of reader authors dream of, for whom each sentence revises the universe. She could have sworn Sir Thomas Browne knew her plight when he wrote that

Thy soul is eclipsed for a time, I yield, as the sun is shadowed by a cloud; no doubt but there gracious beams of God's mercy will shine upon thee again. . . . We must live by faith, not by feeling; 'tis like the beginning of grace to wish for grace; we must expect and tarry.

A passing cloud had come over her. This did not mean that her sun was dead.

Life is a pure flame, and we must live by our invisible sun within us.

She remembered her autumn ecstasies—"light and love divine." Others had looked at her strangely. In Sir Thomas's company she felt less strange, less alone: I don't know what it is, but I know I'm something, and it's all I've got.

The sudden spring fostered her confidence. After five months she at last stopped coughing. She imagined that soon her hands might no longer tremble. Lewis and his friend Morris took her into the Hudson River valley for a weekend, among reservoirs and rolling orchards. Sunday night she wrote:

Grapevines budding. I'm still only twenty. Yesterday apple trees opened petals of primal cream and pink. In a few months, Rubens's wreaths of fruit—vines ripening, apples on boughs. Tonight, light dripping with shadow, hill moon rising, sun withdrawing, forest shivering in the breath of summer to be. Someone told the hawthorn, Blossom!—Ph. unfolded. Someone told the whippoorwill, Sing!—Ph. sang. Brother and friend spoke hymns of farewell to this natural day. A beloved woman must speak with the breath of corollas brushed by a shuttling bird.

She went back to work in a loving frenzy. She started calling her friends again and went out to meet them. She wanted to wrap them all into her billowing cloak of love. They were busy, they were worried, they had to leave. Her work happened in visionary outbursts. Walter came to see it. He told her, "You're crapping all over the canvas. You *know* better." Even though she had met her only ten minutes earlier, Phoebe implored Elizabeth, who heard this judgment, to wait in her studio after Walter left. While Elizabeth watched, Phoebe destroyed her new work.

She then planned another self-portrait in the manner of the old masters. But she didn't have the patience for such things. Her hand lusted after scrawls and tangles, "dirty combinations," dull orange smeared with dull green. Her brush scampered away from her.

In mid-May she gave up. She stopped seeing her friends. She stopped painting, although she still wrote a little. Increasingly she spent her days and mostly sleepless nights trying to guess the cause of her disintegration. What had she or anybody done that must be so painfully atoned for? Something—something obvious and stupidly hidden from her: "a secret lesson any old ocarina can repeat." She was condemned to learn this lesson the hard way.

In late May, her brother, Lewis, again became the object of public scandal. Louisa, who had spent months watching over her son, collapsed and was committed to a hospital. Phoebe went to see her. In Louisa's hospital room, mother and daughter broke each other's heart.

Phoebe stopped at a bar on her way home. She stepped from the sweltering day into air-conditioned chill. She sneezed into her whiskey sour. Her nose started to dribble. By evening she was coughing violently; before morning she was burning with fever. She phoned Walter, who took her straight to Saint Vincent's, where she was admitted with double pneumonia.

The two doctors in charge of Phoebe were appalled by her condition. They disregarded her psychosomatic explanation and quickly guessed at the truth. Phoebe did her best to frustrate them. She regarded them as mortal enemies. Whenever they approached her, her eyes glittered with wary loathing, and her squawk box, in a harsh mood, speaking on her behalf, pestered them with resentful insults.

As Phoebe saw it, two strangers had decided to meddle with her secret life. Under the pretence of caring for her, they were hunting down the scurrying, tiny identity to which she was now reduced. Her mistrust of them survived their successful treatment of her pneumonia and the prodigies of tact the doctors exercised in discussing her chronic disorder. Their suggestion that this disorder might have a physiological origin infuriated her. The ecstatic pain that had grown in her over the past year had by now become the center of her reality. She could not bear having it made medically predictable. She refused to be helped. Only when Louisa arrived, four days after Phoebe's admission, was she lured out of her corner.

Louisa promised Phoebe that she would never abandon her again; she promised never to let Owen, or anyone else, interfere with her. Phoebe let herself be convinced, after exacting one more promise: she must never be left alone with her doctors. She then agreed to do what was asked of her, giving up responsibility for her nightmare illness with a relief that surprised her. For the first time since December, she menstruated.

Phoebe was given a second basal metabolism test, this time correctly administered. It recorded her metabolic rate at an abnormal +35. Methyl thiouracil was prescribed for her, one hundred milligrams to be taken daily. Louisa was told that Phoebe could leave the hospital as soon as she recovered from her pneumonia, probably in three or four days. She would need several weeks to become healthy again. During that time she should lead a restful life, she should be taken care of—in other words, she should go home.

After her first wild resentment, Phoebe endured her stay in the hospital with petulant resignation. Her fever came down, her lungs cleared; nothing else changed. Her heart still banged, she trembled and sweated, and the best pills brought her only brief sleep. When Louisa said she was taking her to their home upstate, Phoebe did not protest. She nonetheless took the decision as a defeat—the two years she had lived on her own were being written off. Her squawk box, meshed for a while with her own passionate voice, reasserted itself to denounce her surrender. It suggested that Owen had instigated what was happening. Louisa was doing the dirty work while he rubbed his hands in the wings.

Phoebe's own voice fell to a whisper. It whispered more sound than sense, as though the squawk box had requisitioned the attributes of reason. One day it started saying, over and over, without apparent cause, "I quest, request, bequest . . ." (By now she could control her own voice no better than the box's.) At another time it repeated an inexplicable succession of letters inside her docile ears: b.s.t.q.l.d.s.t., b.s.t.q.l.d.s.t. . . . Phoebe could not decipher the series. After making it yield "Beasts stalk the question lest demons sever trust" and "But soon the quest lured drab saints thither," she rejected the possibility that the letters were initials. She found it even harder to make words out of them, especially without a *u* for the *q*. No matter what she did, they refused to be dispelled. No matter what she did. Without meaning, unthreatening, merely insistent, the letters turned into a regular refrain inside her head. Phoebe had to insert her voice's other whisperings between them: "I b.s.t.q.l.d. quest s.t. I b.s.t.q.l. request d.s.t., I b.s.t.q. bequest l.d.s.t. . . ."

Phoebe quickly lost interest in the new diagnosis of her condition, which might have pleased anyone—anyone else.

Before she left, Louisa repeated to her again and again that she would take care of her until she was completely cured. She would not be sent to a "clinic." She would be protected from Owen as long as she wanted. For the eighteenth time Phoebe consented to go home. She set a condition, however: she would go alone, and by train—the way they had always come back from the city when she first traveled with her parents as a little girl. Phoebe's doctors urged Louisa to indulge her.

During her trip, Phoebe learned something about the series of letters. B.s.t.q.l.d.s.t. signified an old train careening down an old track. At slower speeds the train said,

> Cigarettes, tch tch
> Cigarettes, tch tch.

She found nothing to eat or drink during the four-hour ride. The carriage shook so hard she could not read. Before Poughkeepsie, under a three-o'clock sun, the air-conditioning broke down. People sitting near her kept moving away. When she saw Louisa, the pang of joy made Phoebe yell. Afterwards, in her unaltered room, she yanked off her clothes to slide between the sheets of her blond-pine bed. She slept.

Owen arrived the next Friday. When she saw him, pain came back—an unfamiliar pain, which Phoebe lived with for several days before she could name it.

At two in the morning, awake in her room, Phoebe sat by her window, staring out through hot moonlight at the trees, lawn, and houses that beleaguered her. She listened to the voices inside her. With obscure insistence her box kept reminding her of a photograph in her father's room. Thanks to her, that room was now unoccupied. Phoebe got up and found the photograph, a sepia portrait framed in engraved silver of her paternal grandmother, who had died of a stroke when Phoebe was two. She was dressed in black, with a wide-brimmed hat pinned to the back of her head, a jacket with enormous lapels, a tapering ankle-length skirt, and long silk gloves held loosely in her hands. Her features expressed gravity and alertness. Averted from the camera, her gaze seemed fixed on some disaster that confirmed all she had ever suspected. Phoebe put the photograph on her bedside table.

The novelty of Phoebe's pain lay less in its symptoms—the familiar ones of her disease—than in its source, which she imagined as outside herself. She could not at first identify that source, and only did so after Louisa revealed to her the settlement Owen had made on her behalf on the occasion of her twenty-first birthday.

What she then discovered would not have surprised anyone who had observed her in Owen's presence. Her every gesture and word expressed resentment and disgust. Whenever he appeared, she would draw up her knees and grit her teeth, reminding herself of demands to be made, reconnoitering opportunities for attack. Unable to see herself, Phoebe remained unaware of the obsessiveness of her feelings. She almost realized the "truth" while Owen was reading to her late one afternoon:

> Mr. Copperfield chuckled. "You're so crazy," he said to her with indulgence. He was delighted to be in the tropics at last and he was more than pleased with himself that he had managed to dissuade his wife from stopping at a ridiculously expensive hotel where they would have been surrounded by tourists. He realized that this hotel was sinister, but that was what he loved.

Phoebe would have shouted "Just like you!" if at this moment her father had not dozed off. Her rage diverted, she only growled him awake.

A few days before Phoebe's birthday, Owen deposited several hundred shares of high-priced securities in a custody account opened in her name, and ordered the monthly transfer of five hundred dollars from his checking account into hers. The news of these arrangements brought Phoebe's emotions into perfect order.

"He hates you," a woman said. In astonishment Phoebe looked at the photograph by her bed. Two ravens rose out of a summery field and winged their slow way out of sight above the house. "He'll do anything to stop you."

"Why, you fifty-pint-old drunkess," Phoebe replied.

"I know him better'n anybody," the woman cawed. "Remember the first time he stuck you with money? He'll never change."

Owen congealed for Phoebe into a repellent image of selfishness. She saw that he had pretended to encourage her freedom only to attack it better. He no longer even pretended an interest in her painting. Of course he must hate her. Perhaps he had always hated her, and he had lavished care on her as a child only to control her, to make sure she complied with his desires. To think how she'd loved him!

"Don't expect me to thank you," Phoebe told him after learning of his extraordinary gift.

"I don't," Owen answered, with a meekness that made her yearn to draw blood.

"I'm only accepting to make you pay something." Her grandmother coaxed her, "Tell him he's a fox and a pig!" Phoebe's throat choked with sobs of fury.

She sometimes spied on her parents, hiding inside the door of the terrace where they had drinks before dinner. One evening she heard Owen suggest to Louisa that Phoebe have a thyroidectomy. She thus made a second discovery. Her father would not content himself with dominating her life; he wanted that life itself. She thought of the ways he had intervened since last September: choosing her thyroid specialist, choosing her psychotherapist, insisting that her troubles were psychological, belittling her flagrant symptoms. He had pushed her to the limit of her disease; now he wanted to finish her off.

Mrs. Lewison Senior's black silks flapped around her fussily: "He may think he doesn't know what he's doing, but he sure is doing it." Phoebe, who had wet her pants downstairs, was sitting on the toilet in her bathroom. She had become fiercely determined. She would survive and win. Her father would die first. Or she would teach him pain. That would be even better.

Louisa never failed her. When Phoebe called, she came.

Phoebe called her more and more often. Louisa had become company, and also childhood love, belated and never too late. Phoebe wished she did not hang on to her mother so greedily. For Louisa, apparently inexhaustible, this dependence was in itself sufficient reward. That Louisa never mentioned the operation did not disturb Phoebe: it meant that her mother had turned Owen's proposition down. After all, she herself did not speak about certain matters, such as her grandmother's eerie voice.

That voice was raised urgently when, on August first, Phoebe learned that Owen had acquired the "Portrait of Elizabeth": "He's at it again. Why, he never cared about painting. And you know how he feels about Walter." (Lewis had told her that Owen referred to Walter as "the man who ruined my daughter.") "But then, maybe he's speculating. To people like him, you know, art's just a commodity. No, that's not it. He knows how you feel about that picture, doesn't he? Take it from me, *you're* why he bought it. He doesn't want to leave you one single thing. He wants you to see he's running the whole show. . . ."

Phoebe rasped, "Shut up, you old bitch!" She'd been stung. Although she was willing to see vengefulness in anything Owen did, his simply owning the portrait hurt her most. When could he have bought it? Suspicious, she telephoned Walter's gallery. The painting had been sold—to Maud Ludlam. They were sure: it had been shipped to her in late June.

"What did I tell you?" the old woman sighed. "He's a dark one—dark as the ground owl of childhood fame."

Phoebe confronted Owen with what she'd learned. Since he now approached her like a sinner at confession, she could not tell whether her words truly upset him.

"Of course," he said. "I bought it from the Ludlams."

"Maud got rid of it after a month?"

"Why not? What difference does it make?"

"What the hell are you doing with that painting?"

"If you really want to know, I got it for you."

Phoebe sensed he was lying. She would pin him to the floor. "So why haven't you given it to me?"

"It'll be arriving any day."

"Is it mine or isn't it?"

Owen hesitated. He *had* thought of reselling the painting. "Would that make you happy?"

"Nothing you do could make me happy. Your owning that painting makes me puke."

"It's yours."

"I want papers to prove it."

"There's no need for that, darling."

"Yes, there is, *darling*. I want to make sure it's out of your fucking hands."

"When I promise you something—"

"Uh-uh. I want a legal document of ownership. Otherwise the world is going to learn about your hanky-panky with that wharf in New London. Remember, when you got two companies to pay off one claim?"

Owen laughed. "Phoebe, stop it. That's ancient history. Nobody gives a damn. I even told complete strangers about it—you were there."

"Not Louisa."

Watching him, Phoebe could not stifle a grin. She had guessed right. He walked out of her room. She would have her way.

Louisa took advantage of Phoebe's good spirits to broach unpleasant business. She told her that her treatment had conspicuously failed and that she should consider a thyroidectomy—the sooner the better. "You haven't gained five pounds since you came up here, and you're jumpy as ever. In your shoes I'd go crazy in a week."

"I went crazy months ago. If I could know—if I could be

sure I'd get better someday, I wouldn't mind waiting. I suppose
Owen thinks I should get my throat cut."

"He's got nothing to do with it. *You* think about it, and *you*
decide. I don't want to keep secrets from you. I did find out
there's a good surgeon at Albany. He does four or five thyroids
a week, there and in Boston. I told him about you, and he's
available."

Phoebe said nothing. After a while Louisa again spoke: "I've
told you *my* secret."

"I'm scared. It's mainly the anesthetic. I don't want to face
that. It's like death."

"Not anymore, not with Pentothal. It's not like going under.
You just disappear in a second, and then you're back. No
anxiety, no memories—"

"I believe you, but that's *not* my secret."

"I don't follow."

"Momma, if I'm going to live, I have to agree to die first. Can
I be alone for a while?"

Phoebe wrote her brother, Lewis:

> . . . Louisa is all kindness—real kindness—but I feel I'm
> losing her too. The sympathetic string of motherhood vibrates
> with hypocrisy. It has to—she has to disconnect from me if she's
> going to help. Is life always going to be like this? Yes, at least
> until death. That will do for an answer.
>
> Can you understand? I need someone to understand, and you
> can—you've survived worse than I. Will you come here to be
> with me? With you at my side, I might let them cut my throat.

Phoebe's grandmother attended her constantly—a presence
not disturbing, not reassuring. She had been permanently transformed into a bird. Although large and black, the bird brought
to Phoebe's room a sense not of ominousness but of placid,
continuous movement, like the sound of planes regularly land-

ing and taking off at a distant airport. The bird spoke less and less.

The portrait of Elizabeth arrived. Lewis brought it to her room as soon as it had been uncrated. When she saw it, Phoebe was overcome by giggles. "It was mine all along! Hang it on the wall, over there. Lewis, please let me love you."

Her twenty-first birthday passed discreetly, marked only by a cake for three. The day before, Louisa had driven Phoebe to the Medical Center in Albany, where a surgeon examined her. Phoebe had taken to him at once, something that so astonished Louisa, after her lengthy precautions, that it made her almost cross. During the days that followed Phoebe thought only of her next encounter with the doctor, ruddy, plump, irresistibly confident. When she first looked into his eyes, calm as a cow's, life became manageable. Later, she experienced fright, and a familiar hatred of created things, especially herself. In her bedroom she rediscovered an owlish raven circling the ceiling, and Elizabeth in paints, whom she did not hate.

Following Phoebe's instructions, Owen brought the portrait to the hospital during the operation and hung it in her room opposite her bed. On the bedside table Lewis installed a record player that she could reach lying down.

Louisa and Lewis were waiting for her on her return from the recovery room. Whenever Phoebe opened her eyes—for a long while they merely rolled absently under half-closed lids— her mother said to her that she was doing fine, and Lewis grimly echoed her. They were not saying what they thought, only what they had been told. Phoebe's face looked bloodless and shrunken above her bandaged neck, to which two drains were taped.

Phoebe at first did not hear them and later did not believe them. She was emerging into a welter of drowsiness and terror. In spite of the tranquilizers she had been given, she had never felt sicker. The consequences of surgery did not frighten her: she simply knew that her symptoms had grown worse.

Her heart bedeviled her ribs like a spike; sweat filmed on her arms and legs; her body had disintegrated into pockets of anguish.

The operation had succeeded, and Phoebe's reaction corresponded to a new condition. Four-fifths of her thyroid gland had been removed. Left unchecked, the gland could only respond to the body's demand for the excess thyroxine, to which it had grown accustomed, by starting to grow back. To prevent this, Phoebe was given thyroxine in amounts greater than any she had secreted during her disease. In the course of her operation her pulse had not gone below 160; it now rose to 180. No one could have persuaded her that she was being cured.

For seven days she endured in virtual immobility because of the drains in her neck and the intravenous drip in each arm. She again lost all control of her thoughts and feelings.

The feeling of fear never left her, oppressive with someone at her side, unbearable whenever she found herself alone. Without either Lewis or Louisa, Phoebe would ring for a nurse every two minutes, although she soon learned that others provided only an illusory relief. Others could distract her, not calm what she most dreaded: that the next moment would prove as intolerable as the last, as it always did.

Lewis sometimes read out loud to her. Phoebe did her best to listen; in less than a minute her attention would unravel. Music worked better. She had brought her favorite records, among them some Haydn quartets. Halfway through one of them, at the end of the "Emperor" theme and variations, Phoebe grabbed Lewis's wrist: "Leave that." She played the movement over and over, at least four hundred times. She said afterwards that without it she would have tried to kill herself. Often her head filled with words that Haydn's familiar tune trailed after it, words she thought she had forgotten, a hymn from school days: "Glorious things of thee are spoken, Sion . . ."

Her bird still attended her, voiceless and mechanical, speeding incessantly from one corner of her ceiling to the next as if hung on an elliptical track. It made a whirring, whispering noise: *essesso, essesso* . . .

These things constituted her days and nights: the whispered *essesso* of the bird, the fourth variation coming to an end, grappling with the pillow to find the bell, reaching for Lewis's or Louisa's hand.

Before she left home, the portrait of Elizabeth had entertained if not consoled her; here it gave no comfort. Phoebe had her room kept dark. In the meager daylight from the blinded windows or by the light of the night lamp, the painting was blurred and distorted. The yellow blank eyes floated above the head; the folded hands, whose nails suggested a silver smile, shrank to dull stumps; the fiery red of the hair streamed down the canvas in muddy pulsations. Phoebe would look at Elizabeth, shut her eyes, and sing in time with the record,

> See the streams of living water
> Springing from eternal love

wishing for one thing: make it end.

She never cried. She never had time to collect her tears: too busy getting the Haydn restarted, clutching the bell, watching the door for the tortoise-footed nurse, waiting for the next moment to be less painful, and the one after that. If she had been able to cry, she would have cried for her poor body, regularly devoured by an insatiable, rubber-toothed monster.

After a week, her dose of thyroxine was reduced. Although Phoebe did not know she felt better, her sensations gradually came off the boil, and the terror that had swamped her subsided into a calmer sadness. The sadness filled her whole body, as the terror had, coldly now. The whir of the bird, the inexhaustible sweetness of the quartet, the portrait of Elizabeth assumed new functions as emblems of this sadness to which, without realizing it, Phoebe turned as to the purest hope. She had nothing to look forward to; she had simply rediscovered something that she could call "herself." For the first time, she accepted her disease as a reality, as her reality. If her sickness meant sadness, she would become that sadness, keeping it all for herself, in the remnants of her body. "My body lies over the ocean," she sang. She also sang,

> 'Tis His love His people raises
> Over self to reign as kings.

She smiled at the thought of loving her sadness—surely better than not loving at all, than not loving herself at all? Self-pity provided a first step towards sanity. Only a step—what next? Elizabeth's ivory cheeks and smiling hands had fallen into place. Phoebe sighed wistfully, "My Elizabeth, I'd like to set lighted candles at your feet. I'm better now." *Essesso,* went the bird.

Louisa and Lewis knew Phoebe was recovering when she made a small joke in a mode of that time: "If Stella Dallas married Roger Maris, she'd be known as Stella Maris." In their perpetual shadow, Elizabeth's unpupilled eyes became her stars.

Phoebe's convalescence remained slow. In the course of a year her disorder had disrupted the normal functioning of her lungs, her heart, and her digestive system. She had no physical reserves to draw on. Her doctors spoke about her condition with optimism and advised that she spend another week in the hospital.

Hallucinations still afflicted her. Voices neither hers nor the bird's rumbled through her darkened room: ". . . Who is she who on earth brings forth the sea? Who is he who on earth brings forth the sea? Who is she who lights up great days?" *Essesso, essesso.* "Who is he who devours? Where is the shoe-

maker the blue one?" *Essesso.* "Where is the red-white-and-
blue shoemaker? . . ." Phoebe did not take these voices seriously. Even the bird could now have left without being
missed, although she thanked it frequently for its attentiveness.

Phoebe reminded herself never to use her sadness as a pretext
for not acting. Acting meant getting what she wanted, and she
knew what she wanted: happiness. Happiness required a world
with no monsters in it. She had said to Lewis, "Something's out
there in the dark prowling around. You can't see it, but you
keep getting these horrible reports," and even as she spoke she
knew that she was only telling a convenient story—an excuse
for giving up. She had nobody to blame. She asked Owen to visit
her. She would not let him prowl outside in the dark any longer.
When he had left, she thought, "So that's what heaven is: the
living around us, no one left out." This recognition brought her
only a distant joy, because she had become feverish again. In
dog-day heat, she had managed to catch cold.

Several nights later she had another visitor. Her fever had
gone and returned. She was lying in the dark, licking her dry
mouth and smiling at the viola's turn:

> Who can faint when such a river
> Ever will their thirst assuage?

She became aware of a glow to one side and a sound like a
voice speaking. She turned off the record player. The glow
was emanating from the only blank wall of her room, to her
left, beyond the window. At its center a circle of crystal had
formed. Superposed rings of crystalline rock began appearing
within the circle, tinged with blue light from behind. These
blue rings opened inwards, brightening as they receded
through a self-creating distance that narrowed into a radiance
deep within the rock—an endpoint that Phoebe perceived as

pure white, dazzling and warm. As she lay there smiling into that charming light, her bird flew noiselessly out of the hole. "Is my bird going to speak to me again?" The owlish raven had itself turned white. It vanished among the shadows of the room, only to reappear inside the blue-white tunnel, once more flying towards her. Phoebe again heard the voice. It was calling her by name.

"Who is it?" she asked.

"It's your old pal," the voice answered. "You know who."

"Walter?" Staring into the shining circles of stone, she glimpsed what looked like a man in profile. She could not recognize him, although he reminded her of a stranger on the train home from Belmont. "I can't see you."

"No need," came the answer. "I'm waiting for you."

"Thank you, but I'm picky about my friends."

"Come on, Phoebe. It's great in here." The hovering bird turned back into the tunnel, showing her the way. Phoebe's body tingled with sprightliness.

"Thanks. It's not bad out here, either."

The apparition slowly dimmed. A minute later no light showed in her room except for the glint of her water glass, the faint blue aura of the night lamp, the red dot on the panel of her record player. Phoebe lay in bed wishing for someone to laugh with.

She felt buoyant when she woke up. The tunnel's glow still warmed her, and she remembered the profiled man with intense affection. He's my mentor, she decided. He's the man I'll go looking for as soon as I leave this dump.

Her unusual cheerfulness made doctors and nurses beam. She promised herself to pay no more attention to her discomforts. Later in the day, as her temperature exhaustingly rose and fell, she realized that her body was once again in crisis. Like the medication given for it, its disorder now belonged to the world outside her. She hoped, as night approached, that her anonymous mentor would appear in his tunnel. Even though he did not, his memory continued to enchant her; and early the next morning, before dawn, she was granted some solace. Her bird, which she had not seen the day before, came back to her room, its first blackness restored, describing once again its customary ellipse. Its wings, however, made no sound. It rapidly gathered speed and soon was flying so fast that Phoebe could not follow it. She did not mind, she was elated. Out loud she said, "Look at that birdie go! Granny, you're wearing me out. I thought you were on my side."

The bird spun like the knot of a twirled lasso. Phoebe's heart raced as she watched.

"I wouldn't mind if you could just unlock the kettledrum in my chest of drawers and slow it down a notch. Granny, talk to me at least."

Phoebe sat up.

"Where is my chevalier, pray tell? Catalepsy got your tongue? OK, but someday I want to go riding again. Think of it, I can buy myself a chestnut now. Horseflesh will be mine. I'll go out riding in pursuit of my faithful bird's-eye, hear that? Meanwhile, the birthday girl is full of thirst."

She cleared her throat and coughed.

"My throat is full of thistledown. There are so many thirsts I want to do. First it will soon be time for love. I haven't had an orgy in thirteen weekends. It's a boycott, no less. And that's exactly who I want to start with—boysenberries and their big banjos."

Phoebe no longer cared if the bird was listening.

"Then a nice older piece of lettuce for salad days, full of suggestions and spinal trappings. And finally I want the man of my dreamy legs from somewhere in betweentimes. When I love that personality he'd better watch his outlooks! As former corpus delicti (almost) one will have knucklebones and depravities comparable to those of the avidest Elizabethan desperadoes, and you know how swank and murderous they can be! . . . Oh . . . Elizabeth—"

She tried to make out the portrait in the gloom.

"I haven't forgotten you, not for one secret. And what if you were the one? I can see us in our warm and lovable drawing room, two wombs as one, wife to wife. I could fancy that. Witnesses of each other's dreams. . . . But then who could I be butterfly to (and housefly to, too)? Who could I waffle, who could I babushka? I need real babes to sillytalk, and I can't help thinking of all those malcontents with their malarkey and solo prongs strewn around like landmarks, like pieces of forgotten furniture."

Phoebe started laughing.

"Now there's a dimpled prognostic for a life! A dimity landlady turning sprung floperoo easterners into pidgin pies and daffodils of her cosmology! Because for me myself and I, what will they add? Noteworthy nothingness. I'm my own cosmonaut, thanks just the same, and my private universe spreads from world-eaten rosaries to the swivels of skyrider Galahads— and whatever that may mean," she added, "I swear it's true." She looked around her. "My birds are spreading—hi there, Granny!—or maybe it's my bod."

A shower of sparks burst along the path of the bird.

"I haven't forgotten you, either. You ever were and shall be my ethereal booms. Zowie! You came out of my cecum, the heaven-mapped loins, you and your flaky rinds, and it was then I knew. What else can I ever know? East River to Long Island Sound and out to sea, over which you so cunningly twinkle. Winter, summer, winter again, going places we never left, and all we have to do is sit through the movie and we're there! Christmas! Why isn't it motherland? Granny, tell me you're a nighthawk. I want to go outside and look, all that fun and nonsense I'm missing—rockets zooming through bones. Granny, where's my skylight? What's wrong?" Phoebe loudly asked this of the circling bird, which was wearying, and she could sympathize with that, since her enthusiasm had left her breathless. She watched the bird slow down as it descended, blindingly white now, settling gradually until it came to rest on the floor next to her bed—except that, to Phoebe's surprise, that part of the room had no floor: the bird plummeted abruptly out of sight and hearing.

Allan and Owen

JUNE-JULY 1963

A S A RULE, THOSE WHO DIE YOUNG LEAVE THEIR PERSONAL affairs in a mess. Perhaps because chronic illness had long made his life seem precarious, the rule did not apply to Lewis Lewison's friend Morris Romsen. Long before he died at the end of his thirtieth year, he had drawn up a satisfactory will; and he had recently supplemented it with a generous life-insurance policy whose beneficiary was his associate, Priscilla Ludlam.

The provision for Priscilla came as a surprise to Lewis, and even more to Morris's sister, Irene Kramer. Particularly devoted to Morris, Irene was startled to learn that Priscilla had known her brother so intimately, amazed that Morris had never mentioned making her his beneficiary; and her amazement turned to mild suspicion when she found out that the policy had been written shortly before Morris's death by Allan Ludlam, Priscilla's father. While realizing that coincidence, or friendship itself, might explain the fact, Irene still wondered if some

III

professional ethic did not forbid a father's writing such a policy
on his daughter's behalf. She decided to consult Owen Lewison,
since he had every aspect of the insurance business at his fingertips and she knew him well enough to trust his discretion.

Owen told her, "I'll be happy to check things for you." He
had time on his hands, and worries to forget: Phoebe, about to
emerge from Saint Vincent's, had refused to let him see her.
"I'm sure Ludlam's clean, though. I've worked with his office
a lot, I even know him slightly. There's no chance he'd try any
monkey business."

"I know him too, and I know how well off they are, or Maud
is. It just seems strange."

From an old acquaintance in Allan's company, Owen discovered that Allan had been recommended to Morris by none other
than Phoebe; that on learning that Priscilla would be named
beneficiary, he had at first declined to write the policy; that he
had later agreed to do so only after Morris assured him that
Priscilla knew nothing about it.

Irene ran the Kramer Gallery, which had opened on the
West Side several years earlier and recently moved uptown.
During a subsequent meeting with the Ludlams at her gallery,
Irene confessed to Allan her "curiosity" about Morris's life
insurance: "I didn't know it could be so all-in-the-family."

Allan blushed. "It usually isn't. It bothered me too, you
know—"

"I do know. You're scrupulousness itself."

At his office the next day, Allan asked if Morris's policy had
raised any problems. He learned of Owen's inquiry. He called
Irene: had Owen acted at her request?

"Yes, he did. It was dumb of me, but Morris had just died,
and, for reasons I still don't understand, he'd never spoken
about Priscilla to me. Mr. Lewison said your conduct was
exemplary."

"Irene, it was standard procedure."

Allan was relieved by Irene's reassurances. If Morris's policy gave him no cause for worry, he dreaded the possibility of having other cases come accidentally to Owen's attention—cases that might reveal his secret career of repeated fraud. This career had always exposed him to high risks; to have an expert like Owen investigating him entailed a risk he couldn't afford to run.

Owen had suspected nothing. Allan had escaped danger unawares, as if he had casually brushed a spider from his neck and then recognized a black widow. He relished his luck. It enhanced and was enhanced by the euphoria of finding Elizabeth. For a while he abounded in a sense of the excellence of his life. He felt an immense gratitude towards Owen for having left that intact. One morning he wrote him a letter:

> . . . how really heartwarming it was to be vindicated by such
> a man as yourself. I want you to know that I value it highly and
> appreciate it deeply. . . .

It never occurred to Allan that he might more reasonably have asked Owen for an apology. Owen himself was dumbfounded. Fulsome praise was being heaped on him by a man whose probity he had implicitly questioned. Owen could hardly have guessed that Allan was lovestruck when he wrote the letter. He did check Allan's dates in *Who's Who* to make sure he wasn't getting senile.

Owen left the letter on his office desk. When he next picked it up, he again found himself wondering why Allan had written it. He was not about to borrow money. He needed no social favors. He was not going into politics. He must have had another reason, an unusual one, one that Owen could not suspect; one perhaps that he should not suspect. Was he hiding something—could Allan Ludlam have something to hide? As the thought came to him, Owen was cheered: an enter-

taining possibility was brightening his bleak world. Sicker than
ever, Phoebe had been treating him contemptuously; his son,
Lewis, had sunk beneath consideration; having dedicated herself to Phoebe, Louisa had no time to spare; his work bored him.
Now he had turned up a minor mystery that did not bore him
at all. Owen was delighted by the prospect that someone from
his milieu had guilty secrets. Would Allan's resemble his own
New London ferry caper? Or would it prove a more intimate
peccadillo?

Intrigued though he was, Owen would probably have forgotten Allan altogether if he hadn't mentioned him to Irene at the
end of the following week. She had heard from him too: "Walter's portrait of Elizabeth was stolen. Allan called to ask if our
insurance still covered it. They hadn't had time to take out their
own."

"I didn't know they owned it," Owen said.

"They bought it last month." Irene explained that she had
recently offered a selection of Walter Trale's best work for sale.
"We sent it up to them early in July."

"When was it stolen?"

"I don't know exactly. Allan phoned me yesterday."

Owen said nothing. He knew that Allan had told Irene at
least one lie. No insurance broker would leave anything so
valuable unprotected for two minutes, certainly not two weeks;
and from Allan, a phone call would have sufficed.

What was Allan up to now? If he *had* insured the Trale
painting, why lie to Irene about it? When Allan spoke to her,
why did he only ask about insurance when he might have
requested information about art thefts, and even counsel? Owen
tried to imagine some undeclared motive behind Allan's call.
He could think of none until an unlikely hypothesis crossed his
mind: could Allan possibly want to make money out of the
theft? Was he trying to collect all the insurance he could, the
gallery's as well as his own?

Owen liked this eventuality. It struck him as crass and faintly lunatic; it reminded him of New London. His curiosity about Allan's secret was rekindled. He began asking himself, why not take a look? To Owen, as a professional, Allan's call to Irene and his claim to have left the painting uninsured made the existence of some kind of secret probable to the point of certainty. On the other hand, why should Owen waste time solving an enigma that did not concern him? He found no reasonable answer to this question, rather a satisfyingly unreasonable one: he would enjoy solving this riddle far more than submitting to the rituals of penitence decreed by Phoebe. Even if in the end he found nothing, where was the harm in that? Surrounded as he was by domestic disappointment, wasting time appealed to him.

He decided to begin by approaching Allan himself. He had a number of social and professional excuses for doing so, of which Allan's letter was the most obvious. On the same afternoon he spoke to Irene, Owen started calling him. Allan had left his office; his home phone did not answer, then or later in the evening. Owen repeated his calls the next morning with no more success. He rang Allan's house upstate. A delicately mocking voice—Elizabeth's—announced that Allan was not expected back "for the foreseeable summer."

Owen was annoyed. The man might as well be deliberately evading him. He changed his plans. Before pursuing Allan further, he would learn everything he could about him. He wrote Allan to acknowledge his letter of thanks and express the hope that they would soon meet. Owen resumed his research, focusing it this time not on the minor question of Morris's insurance policy but on more consequent activities in Allan's past. If he had something to hide, it would very likely concern sums of money greater than those of personal accounts; it would have to do with the commercial insurance in which Allan specialized.

Allan's respect for Owen was soon justified: Owen needed only one coincidence to uncover his trail. He had begun by looking at cases in which his office had worked with Allan's, and as he was probing these records, the *Vico Hazzard* file, which he had had no intention of consulting, fell into his hands. He then remembered that Allan had been involved in that affair.

Vico Hazzard was the name of a medium-sized oil tanker that during a storm in March 1958 had sunk fully loaded in the Bay of Biscay, a hundred miles off the French coast. Or so its owners claimed. The insurers discovered that on the day of the ship's sinking the weather had been generally clement, that only ten minutes had been needed to rescue the entire crew, and that no oil slick had ever been observed at the site of the accident. They rejected the claims, which were only settled after a long judicial fight. (The owners had arguments of their own: the ship's loading papers had been correctly drawn up; no member of the crew would testify to sabotage or negligence; storms come and go swiftly in the Bay of Biscay; oil sometimes stays trapped in sunken tankers.)

Owen reviewed the file. Allan was not listed among the brokers. His firm was nowhere mentioned. Owen asked colleagues who had worked on the case if any remembered Allan's connection with it. Fortunately, one did, although she could not precisely define it—nothing important. Pleased that his memory had not misled him, Owen called a friend at the company that had insured the ship. Could he find the time to track down Allan Ludlam's role in the *Vico Hazzard* case? The man answered, "I can tell you right now. He recommended those sons of bitches to us."

"You're sure?"

"Positive."

"Why didn't Ludlam's office write the policy?"

"He was all for it, or at least he said he was, but his partners decided they'd covered enough tankers."

"How come he was so sure about the owners?"

"They fooled a lot of people, including the judge. Well, maybe they fixed the judge. The case was tried in Panama, naturally."

Had they fixed Allan too? With Maud's small fortune, and the excellent living he made? Perhaps he had an expensive weakness, or a private one—gambling, another woman. Most people exhibited a much more obvious weakness: never having enough. Why not Allan? After all, Owen had postulated such a motive in his phone call to Irene and made it a premise of his inquiry. Owen accepted the implication of the *Vico Hazzard* fraud: Allan had been paid off to recommend dishonest clients to reputable insurers.

Notwithstanding a seemingly permanent hot spell, Owen spent more and more time in the city. His investigation absorbed him, and it soothed the sting of Phoebe's spiteful demands. He went to work early and finished his business by noon. The rest of his days, and soon his evenings as well, were devoted to the pursuit of Allan Ludlam's secret.

In his office Owen examined the files of many cases in which Allan had acted as broker. His conduct appeared consistently irreproachable—hardly a surprise, rather a confirmation that, as with the *Vico Hazzard,* Allan's improprieties took place behind the scenes. Then how could his influence be detected? Owen's enthusiasm briefly faltered as he realized that he was condemned to look for evidence only among frauds that had— at least initially—failed: those that had succeeded had vanished into the history of undisputed claims. Where should he continue his research? He knew enough to eliminate instances where the attempted fraud was too crude or too petty. Even so, assuming that Allan had stayed in the background, Owen still had to choose among the hundreds of cases of industrial fraud perpetrated by brokers other than Allan and his associates. Owen's hope revived when he saw that he could eliminate most cases by applying one criterion: with which brokers would

Allan's recommendation count decisively? Here Owen's expertise served him well—he knew who knew whom.

Eventually Owen reduced his cases to the manageable number of twenty-three. These he examined painstakingly. He exhausted the records in his office and those that had been made
available to the public. In his search for information, he frequently found himself obliged to visit other insurance offices,
where he claimed to be writing a historical article on reinsur-
ance in modern times.

Three cases yielded the evidence Owen needed: the *Vico
Hazzard* itself; the Watling Mining Corporation, whose coal
mine near Etkins, West Virginia, collapsed from an unex-
plained blast in 1957; and Kayser Wineries, Inc., whose vineyards in the mountains behind Soledad were destroyed by late-
spring frost in the early fifties. In each case the insurers had
disallowed the claims advanced by their client because of probable fraud. Although fraud was proved only against Kayser
Wineries, all three companies stood to benefit conspicuously
from the disasters. Smaller tankers like the *Vico Hazzard* had
become unprofitable soon after the closing of the Suez Canal in
1956. Before its destruction, the Watling mine, a marginal one,
had been beset by labor troubles. When it filed its claim, Kayser
Wineries had fallen critically low in cash reserves. The insurance company's investigation of the Watling claim determined
that the explosion had occurred on a Sunday when the mine
was empty, the electricity switched off, and no unusual accumu-
lation of coal gas had been reported. The "frost" in the Kayser
vineyards was shown to be hardly more severe than average
seasonal temperatures: it might have damaged the wood of the
vines, not killed them (two years later, production had returned
to normal). The owners of the *Vico Hazzard,* the Watling
Mining Corporation, and Kayser Wineries had all been recommended to their insurers by Allan Ludlam.

Owen had no material proof that Allan had known of the

frauds or profited from them. If questioned, Allan could rightly insist on his negligible legal responsibility in the three cases. Doubtless he could justify his recommendations. Some unexplored clues momentarily tempted Owen. A year after the explosion, the union official who had represented the Watling miners was summoned by a state committee to explain fifty thousand dollars of exceptional expenditures revealed by an audit of his personal account. Owen wondered if Allan's accounts might not disclose similar anomalies. Owen was gratified to have uncovered Allan's secret. He wasted no time speculating as to why someone so well off would risk his reputation in these illegal undertakings.

In his answer to Allan's letter, Owen had invited him for dinner and proposed as a tentative date the last Thursday in July. Two days before Owen completed his research, Allan called to accept his invitation. Owen suggested that they meet for drinks at his apartment and told him that, knowing their wives were in the country, he had also asked a woman they both knew to share their evening. He hoped Allan didn't mind: "She'll keep us on our toes. Nothing's duller than an all-male club. Sorry I only found one. Right now, ladies are in short supply."

The woman Owen had invited was universally known by her childhood nickname of High Heels. Forty-six and very pretty, she had been married twenty-four years to an uninterested husband for whom she had consoled herself with many lovers, Owen among them. He had not invited her innocently. His affair with her, begun the preceding winter shortly after his Christmas wrangle with Phoebe, had soon ended, not from disaffection but because the lovers decided that they preferred the reliabilities of friendship to the uncertainties of passion. They trusted each other intimately.

At first Owen had not known exactly how High Heels would benefit him. He assumed that the presence of an attractive

woman would put Allan a little off his guard, especially since
he knew her so well (he was related to her by marriage). Not
until his investigation was complete did Owen find a specific job
for her.

When Owen learned that Allan had successfully pursued a
career of preposterous frauds, he began asking himself what
light this might shed on his behavior in regard to the stolen
portrait of Elizabeth. Owen was tempted to see in it the sign of
yet another fraud, albeit a smaller, private one. Why else should
Allan lie to Irene? Owen could not at first see what form such
a fraud might take. Recollecting his own "crime," he had imagined Allan trying to collect insurance from more than one
company. This interpretation presented difficulties. When a
work of art is stolen, it rarely disappears; usually it resurfaces
promptly, to be offered for sale if the thieves lack competence,
more often to become the object of negotiations between them
and the insurers. Allan of course knew this. He would not
expect to be reimbursed if a work as valuable as the portrait
were stolen from him; he would expect to get it back.

This suggested to Owen that the portrait had not been stolen
at all. If Allan wanted insurance money, he must make sure that
the painting never reappeared. What could give him such certainty? The work could be destroyed. Then why disguise the
fact as theft, unless Allan himself had done the destroying? But
Owen could not imagine anyone so money-smart demolishing
a possession whose value would certainly grow. More plausibly,
the portrait had been hidden. The possibility impressed Owen
as perfectly compatible with Allan's behavior: secrecy, after all,
had been a condition of his business frauds from beginning to
end.

Owen knew now what he wanted High Heels to do. While
Allan might, of course, have used any number of hiding places,
Owen suspected that he would prefer one where he could keep
his eye on the portrait. The house upstate could certainly be

excluded: Maud would not be privy to her husband's illegal activities. The city apartment seemed much likelier, since it was primarily used by Allan as a place to stay during his working weeks, and during the summer he had it to himself. High Heels must persuade Allan to take her home with him so that she could learn if the portrait was hidden there.

Owen gave her a partial account of the facts, not mentioning his research or Allan's phone call to Irene, telling her only that the Ludlams claimed that the portrait of Elizabeth had been stolen and that he suspected them of having hidden the painting instead, perhaps in Allan's apartment. He had, he said, become intrigued by their strange behavior. No more than intrigued: he had nothing to gain in the matter.

Owen was not surprised that High Heels unhesitatingly accepted his request; and as Owen had correctly foreseen, Allan was immediately drawn to her. Owen's good judgment, however, was favored far more by what he did not know than by what he knew. When he gave High Heels his account of the missing portrait, he acted with unwitting shrewdness in lumping Maud with Allan. He did not know that High Heels was nursing a years-old grudge against Maud Ludlam and was delighted to catch her out in a suspicious scheme; delighted, as well, to date her husband. Nor could Owen possibly know how sentimentally vulnerable recent events had made Allan. His affair with Elizabeth had humiliated him, Maud had forced him from his own house—he was ripe for consolation. His long acquaintance with High Heels only heightened her attractiveness by removing the barrier of unfamiliarity that had, before Elizabeth, made him shy away so often from sexual adventure.

The evening with Allan and High Heels thus took Owen by surprise. He had planned to coddle his guests into mutual sympathy; he found himself with nothing to do. From the moment they met in his apartment, the two conversed in the liveliest fashion. By the time they sat down in the restaurant, their understanding had started growing into overt complicity. Owen felt almost an outsider at his own dinner. He even wondered, knowing the man's deviousness, if Allan had somehow enlisted High Heels in his cause. Were they now allied against him? What if they were? *He* had nothing to hide, nothing to lose. (The thought had no sooner come to him than he remembered Phoebe, aged eleven, running out of school to meet him.)

After dinner, Allan asked High Heels and Owen to join him for a nightcap. Owen declined and left. Allan timidly asked High Heels where she would like to go—a favorite bar? her place? his? His would do fine. In the taxi she took his hand; they kissed in the elevator; they had barely crossed his threshold when they began making love, the first of three leisurely times.

Their delight in each other had the intensity of ignorance, if not innocence. Allan knew nothing about High Heels's grudge against Maud, or she about his domestic troubles. They applied themselves to slaking a mutual thirst that had naturally and delectably inflamed them, not asking questions, not needing to know. Waking up the following morning, they spent themselves on one another before exchanging a word.

However, once they did start to speak, High Heels eventually said: "What I'd really love is a toasted bagel." She had hesitated to pronounce these words. She knew that when she did, Allan would go out to the nearest deli, and she would search his apartment. What Owen wanted her to do seemed now a little squalid: spying on her new lover might prove as great a betrayal as disappointing her old one. She stuck to her agreement. She had made Allan happy, he still exuded warmth and attentiveness, and she sensed that the attentiveness revealed something other than warmth—an awareness that, no matter how much he liked her, she would never find a place at the center of his life, not even for a season. He paid attention to her now because he might find few other chances to do so; later meetings would still remain exceptional events. Allan was assuming that she knew this as well as he did, and he was not mistaken. She did not mind his so carefully sweetening her own return to "real life"; and she knew she must expect no more of him. She too liked him, and, among other reasons, she liked him because he *would* go away, go back to Maud. She liked him for a good husband, after years with her own bad one; and she couldn't help imagining how her life might have turned out with a man like the one now lying in her arms. The thought flushed her with yearning: a yearning she loathed, brimming with regret, one she had sooner or later to cut short. When Allan proposed English muffins, she preferred the bagel that would take him away from her.

She found the portrait wrapped in a clean sheet, leaning against a wall in a doorless storage space next to the kitchen. She checked the dimensions and appearance and, after restoring her wearied face and body, returned to bed, where Allan found her.

To attest his gratitude, Owen sent High Heels two best seats for *How to Succeed in Business Without Really Trying,* a musical sold out five weeks in advance. For years, Owen had scarcely stretched his wits in business; he had now proved them as sharp as ever. Through his own flair, he had from meager evidence calculated exactly what Allan had done. He did not think of Phoebe for a whole day, he forgot his routine call to Louisa, utterly pervaded by a reassuring glee.

Late in the afternoon, four days afterwards, he kept ringing Allan's home number until he answered. Owen said he was in the neighborhood, could he drop by for a drink? By all means, Allan replied. He'd advise the doorman immediately.

Entering the apartment, Owen savored the coolness—the temperature outside had reached the mid nineties. Allan greeted him jovially, holding a gin-and-tonic in one hand and, with a help-yourself wave of the other, motioning Owen towards the bar: "I've been meaning to call you, damn it. Tonight you be my guest."

"We'll see."

Allan stared at the other man as he mixed his drink. Owen looked serious and alert. "What's up?"

Owen turned to Allan: "I came up here on a false pretense. This is really a business visit. Here's mud." He raised a glass full of chiming cubes.

"Chin chin. Well, we've been doing business for years, in an impersonal way."

"You're telling me. This is between the two of us."

"*Servidor de usted.*"

"You own a painting I'd like to . . . acquire—a portrait by Walter Trale."

"My wife and I own it." Allan walked past Owen to the bar. "I can tell you right now: Maud would never agree to sell."

"I'm not surprised. I saw it only once at Trale's studio, but I could tell it was special. By the way, for openers, do you think I could take a look at it?"

"That might be a little hard to arrange."

"No time like the present."

"You mean here? We'd never keep anything like that in town. A couple of prints, to show where the walls are, and that's about it."

"What are they? I still can't tell China from Japan. Could I see the portrait when I go back upstate?"

"Owen," Allan said with gentle reproach, "did Irene tell you the painting was stolen?" He also asked, "You don't know Elizabeth, do you?"

Allan's voice indicated that the question mattered to him; Owen could not relate it to what he knew. He said, "So what happened?"

"What happened about what?"

"How did it get stolen?"

"*I* don't know what happened. . . ." Allan did not mind playing such games.

"Then what have you done about it? Police? Private detectives? Who's your underwriter?"

"What do you think I should do? Art thefts are tricky."

"Irene was surprised when you asked her about the gallery's insurance."

"Is that why you're here—Irene again? Why should she care?"

"Irene's got nothing to do with my being here."

"Then why do *you* care?"

"I told you. I hope to own the painting."

"But that's out of—" Allan stopped. What was Owen getting at? The other man's eyes looked steadily into his, neither friendly nor unfriendly. "You wouldn't like to talk over dinner? The gin's gone straight to my stomach."

"This shouldn't take long." Owen sat down, crossed his legs, and set his drink on the floor beside him. Allan leaned against the wall, facing him. Owen had vexed him. "Would you mind telling me why we're having this conversation?"

"Sure. I think you made a mistake. You gave yourself away. You want the gallery's insurance to pay for the painting."

Allan suddenly wanted to laugh; he only said, "Wow!"

"I'm serious."

"No." Allan couldn't suppress a grin. He paused. "I don't know where to begin."

"Anyplace. It won't matter."

"I don't even know who insures the gallery—you probably do. I just asked Irene one question. That doesn't mean I'm making plans. What tickles me," Allan went on, "is that what you're accusing me of is how you make your money. You push all your claims to the limit."

"That's right. But only against one insurer for each claim." Owen mentally crossed his fingers, remembering New London. He thought: I should have never told those people about New London.

"I haven't made any claim. The painting is bound to show up. If it's cheap enough, we'll buy it back ourselves, and it probably will be." Allan was looking down at his guest with growing confidence. "If the people who stole it want to haggle, it wouldn't hurt to get the gallery involved. That's why I called Irene."

Because he held the ace of trumps, Owen had not pushed Allan hard. He had nonetheless cornered him. Allan thought he had won: the rosy assurance of his face attested it. He had once felt fear of Owen; his fear had proved groundless. If this time Owen was attacking him openly, he remained as innocent as he had been in writing Morris's policy. Allan could not help showing a slight contempt for Owen for being so mistaken.

At this point, Owen's attitude changed. He had anticipated confronting a colleague with professional irregularities. The irregularities had excited his curiosity more than his disapproval, and he had only expected to show Allan that although he was smart, Owen was smarter. He had imagined wanting the portrait only as a ploy: as a "serious" pretext at first, then as a position from which to press his adversary. Owen now found himself thinking in earnest about getting the painting for himself.

He had begun feeling a need to do more than outwit Allan. He was facing a rich, reputable colleague who for years had defrauded the system he claimed to serve, who now stood beaming with confidence because he had once again gone uncaught. Owen angrily dismissed his first intention of merely showing Allan up: values were at stake. He entertained no doubt at all that he had the moral fitness to mete out the punishment Allan deserved.

"You thought that up just now. I don't believe you. You know why?"

"No, and I'd be very interested—"

"I've been studying your career," Owen interrupted, "I don't mean your legitimate accomplishments, I'm not questioning them. What I mean—what I've learned—is that you're a chronic swindler"—Owen spoke fast enough to cut off any protest—"and you've been damned successful at it. As I see it, though, you have one problem. A swindler who's been born and raised poor knows that if he loses, he loses everything. But someone with your cushy background feels safe, and he starts thinking he really *is* safe. He forgets about the risks. He makes mistakes. Like calling Irene."

If Allan was surprised, he didn't show it: "Owen, tell me what's on your mind. Something you think I did has made for a misunderstanding. Or maybe your interpretation of something I actually did. What's the point?"

"Three names to show you I know. And don't kid yourself— I'll know *you* know I know. In chronological order: Kayser Wineries, Watling Mining, *Vico Hazzard.*"

After a few seconds, not moving from where he stood, his hands behind his back, Allan replied, "Who's arguing? Of course those were mistakes. Why me, though? A lot of other people were involved."

"They were mistakes, and you didn't make them. You let those other people do that. You advised them to."

"I advise all the time. It's part of the business—you know that. Has all your advice been perfect? My own batting average is pretty good—about nine-fifty."

"You bet it is. Remember the Circle C Ranch? They wanted you to double the coverage on their herd. Before recommending them, you made sure there'd been no brucellosis in the county for thirty years. You did your job. How could somebody like you not know the *Vico Hazzard* was sailing empty? Why should you bother with punk outfits like Kayser and Watling unless it was—"

"Look," Allan broke in, "it was investigated."

"It didn't come up roses, either. I know you're covered—you were only counsel. And we're all so busy we never bother much with the past. But I'm on to you, old buddy." Allan said nothing. Owen added: "I'm not interested in making trouble for you, truly. Why should I be? I just want that portrait of Elizabeth. And no, I don't think I know her. I may have met her before the war."

The mention of Elizabeth sickened Allan. Two weeks before, she had been his; at least, he had been hers. He had spat on her feelings by parading his dishonesty in front of her. Perhaps she had revenged herself by telling Owen rather than Maud what she had learned about him. He asked, "So you know about the horse?"

For the only time that evening Owen was baffled. "Does Elizabeth have a horse?"

"Not *that* horse," Allan answered irritably. "You'd better ask the thief about the portrait."

"That's what I'm doing."

Why did Owen care so much about this "theft"? Before tonight, Allan had almost forgotten the story he had made up for Irene. "You mean *I* stole the painting?"

"Listen, I'm getting hungry myself. I'll make you a proposition. I find the painting, I keep it. And I promise not to tell a soul."

Allan still did not understand. Owen emptied his iceless glass, got up, and walked into the kitchen. Allan heard the stretcher being dragged across the tile floor.

"Do I have to unwrap it, or will you take my word?"

Allan lost his temper. For twenty minutes Owen had been preparing to make a fool of him, holding, and withholding, his knowledge that the portrait was there. "You'd better get out."

"You're right. Leave the painting downstairs sometime tomorrow, OK? I'll send a man over. Unless you'd rather I took it now."

"Big joke. Get the hell out of here."

"Ludlam, I understand how you feel. You'd better start understanding how *I* feel. I'm not interested in shooting you down. It'd be messy, and some of your shit would stick to me.

Anyway, I'm not a policeman. I don't give a tiddlywink how you behave. But I can get you, and I will if I have to, because I do mind one thing: every time we guys went to bat for one of your crummy clients we were putting our money and reputation on the line. I risked my ass on account of you. You may never have to pay your debt to society, as they say, but you sure as hell will pay it to me. I'm letting you off cheap—one painting."

At this moment Allan remembered the toasted bagel. He spoke quickly, before dismay seeped into his voice: "Owen, the story about the portrait being stolen—it was an elaborate family joke."

"So what?"

"That's what we're—"

"That was *my* joke. I'm talking about your reputation. As I trust you realize, I am not joking about that."

Allan gave up. He hated to lose; he would hate losing; he could see nothing he might do to avoid it. For once his cleverness had failed him: the roulette wheel had been fixed by a woman he had not doubted for a moment. What he now wanted most in the world was to get Owen out of his apartment. He agreed to the price: "I'll drop it off at the front door on my way to the office."

"Perfect." Owen smiled. "Now, how about dinner? No? I'll be going. Just one thing I'd like to ask you. It's something that's had me wondering ever since I got interested in you—it's probably *why* I got interested in you." Allan stared at the bar. Owen continued: "How come you did it?"

Owen waited patiently for a response. After a while Allan looked up: "Because they're jerks."

"Who is?"

"Everyone is. Not *you,* maybe," Allan hurriedly added. "But most of the others. They're so successful, they make so much money, they have Pucci wives, beach houses, and malt scotch, and they don't have a clue what it's all about. They don't even know there's anything to know. They're sheep."

"But not you."

"You seem to enjoy playing games. Do I have to explain?"

"I only wanted to know. It's an answer. Here's a suggestion: since we're not *all* sheep, you should be prepared to let others do unto you what you'd like them to let you do unto them—I think I got that right." Allan had again lapsed into silence. "Look, for the record, we'll need sale papers. Let's list a price two thousand under whatever it cost you. You'll get a capital deduction—not much, but every little bit helps."

At the door, Owen turned back; Allan was gazing out the window at a rug-sized plot of dirt fourteen stories below, where a forsythia and three evergreen shrubs withered in hot, eternal shade. "You know, Allan, you didn't need to prove anything. You're a better man than you think."

Outside, he entered the sweltering city night. A year ago Phoebe had reported the first signs of her disease, and at the time the news had actually brought him relief.

Allan did not see himself as a man at all, rather as a little boy dreaming his way through some stupid childhood misfortune. He loathed himself for having given up so abjectly. Why was he experiencing such humiliation on account of a painting and a glorified public adjuster? What had happened? He had barely looked inside a cookie jar, and the pantry cupboards had crashed down around him. He had phoned Irene and told her his fib because he expected her to repeat it to Maud; Maud would have been horrified, either because she believed the story or because she knew he was lying—in either case, she would have come after him, and he would have been able to resume his life with her. The stratagem recalled other, more tractable childhood misadventures, the ones he would instigate in order to recapture his mother's attention. A new shoe "lost" would do the trick. He would be scolded and punished and no longer forgotten. This time, however, a detective from the shoe store had arrived unannounced and threatened him with dungeons. It made no sense.

The intensity of his unhappiness nevertheless had its explanation. What sickened him, what squeezed his testicles up into his bowels as though he were leaning over a penthouse ledge, was the memory of High Heels. He could excuse her deceit (she could hardly have foreseen its consequences); but he could not endure having Owen to thank for his night with her. The thought unnerved every part of him, even the anger in his chest. He wished he could call her. She could take pity on him. She had no reason to despise him, not as he despised himself. He felt himself incapable even of speaking to her.

Maud, Elizabeth, High Heels—lost in one July.

Allan expected his anger with Owen to return in force, flooding and ebbing for days, even weeks. He had been too openly disgraced not to resent his attacker. Nevertheless his anger lacked the clear fury of vengefulness or moral outrage, and Allan, without noticing it, soon reconciled himself to his antagonist. Owen had fallen on him without warning, like a natural disaster, impersonally and arbitrarily (Allan never saw his error in writing the letter of thanks); and little by little Owen began to assume the mask of a one-time avenging angel, a fairy-tale comeuppance, a bugaboo, a caricature that even Allan unconsciously recognized as his own invention. At the same time Owen, the real-life businessman, took on a very different, although complementary, role as the audience Allan's spectacular frauds had always lacked.

It was Owen, in this double guise of hobgoblin and witness, who at last allowed Allan to give up his criminal career. The hobgoblin reminded him of the risks he ran; the witness, that he no longer needed recognition. The gelding destroyed on the eighteenth of the month marked the end of Allan's secret life. Later opportunities presented themselves—crop failures on unplanted land, bank-engineered computer "errors." On each occasion he was checked by an invisible figure in his apartment who sat facing him, a melting drink in his hand. An unprejudiced observer might have concluded that Allan had summoned Owen into his life for this very purpose.

That evening, however, Allan wanted only to drive Owen out of his thoughts, preferably by retroactive murder. He stayed home, convinced that elsewhere he would feel even worse. For supper he made himself his next day's breakfast: eggs, toast, tea. Neither scenes from an earthquake in Macedonia nor *The Jack Paar Show* could temper his despondency. He went to bed early, with some magazines, without even a nightcap.

Lewis and Morris

SEPTEMBER 1962-MAY 1963

MORRIS HAD MET LEWIS AT WALTER TRALE'S, LESS THAN a year before his death.

Lewis had lived with his parents for a year and a half after his graduation from college; more accurately, he lived with Louisa, while Owen did his best to ignore him. Although Lewis hardly felt at ease with Louisa, she tended him and forgave his moody ways. Lewis felt at ease with almost no one. He had few friends of either sex and made no attempt to keep those he did have.

He loved and trusted Phoebe. Their father had always favored her, she excelled where he endured; her absolute loyalty to him forestalled all resentment. She was three years younger than Lewis, and his rock. During his tedious months at home, Phoebe never asked him, "What are you doing now? What are you planning to do?" Lewis had answers to these questions; he knew them to be no more than shaming lies. He was doing nothing, and he did not know what he would ever do.

133

Lewis, anything but dull, suffered from an excess of misguided cleverness: he could disparage himself brilliantly in a
matter of seconds. He knew literature, art, the theater, history;
and his knowledge surpassed what a college normally provides.
His knowledge led nowhere, certainly not into the world where
he was supposed to earn a living. Lewis had once gone to work
in the bookstore of his school because he loved handling books
and looked forward to being immersed in them. He was then
instructed to keep careful accounts of merchandise that might
as well have been canned beans. He soon lost interest in his
simple task, failed to master it, and quit after three days. Eight
years later, he was still convinced of his practical incompetence.
College friends familiar with his tastes would suggest modest
ways for him to get started: they knew of jobs as readers in
publishing houses, as gofers in theatrical productions, as care-
takers at galleries. Lewis rejected them all. While he saw that
they might lead to greater things, they sounded both beneath
and beyond him—the bookstore again. Other chums who had
gone on to graduate school urged their choice on him. Lewis
harbored an uneasy scorn for the corporation of scholars, who
seemed as unfit for the world as he. He remained desperate,
lonely, and spoiled.

During his second autumn at home, he read, in an art magazine called *New Worlds,* an article by Morris Romsen on the
painting of Walter Trale. Phoebe, who had been working with
Walter since February, had recommended it to him. Lewis took
it to heart for reasons that had nothing to do with Walter.

Morris began his article: "A fish begins to rot at the head;
the rot in painting begins at the idea of Art." Lewis did not
understand these words. They swept across his mind like an
arm angrily clearing a table of its clutter. Reading on, he could
not tell whether Morris's pronouncements illuminated his subject; he knew they illuminated *him.*

Lewis had had fugitive dreams of writing, soon discredited

and abandoned. Morris was showing him what writing could do. He advanced the notion that creation begins by annihilating typical forms and procedures, especially the illusory "naturalness" of sequence and coherence. Morris did more than state this, he demonstrated it. He made of his essay a minefield that blew itself up as you crossed it. You found yourself again and again on ground not of your choosing, propelled from semantics into psychoanalysis into epistemology into politics. These displacements seemed, rather than willful, grounded in some hidden and persuasive law that had as its purpose to keep bringing the reader back fresh to the subject. Lewis could not explain this effect, or why the article so moved him. When he reread it, doing his best to find fault with it, like a shy and incredulous father poking his newborn child, his first reaction held true, and his reservations were dispelled. He had found something in the world worth doing, after all.

Lewis did not tell Phoebe of his decision to become a writer; he informed her by letter instead. When he had talked to his parents about his new commitment, he had as he spoke lost hold of what he was saying, and enthusiasm could not compensate for vagueness. Louisa had been confused, Owen disgusted (did he expect them to support him forever?). Lewis wanted to make sure Phoebe understood: Morris's article had given him nothing less than a hope of salvation.

My burdens are isolation and a haunted mind. Now I can put the first to work and exorcise the second. Solitude will be my shop. Others will use what I make there, in *their* solitudes—a long-distance community of minds. I'll take the words droning inside my head and make them real—make them into things that strike, or stroke, or puzzle, or disappear. This is something I can actually do. A little something—doctors are more useful, actors communicate better—but buggers can't be choosers. Before, reading was better than not getting out of bed, but how

what I read got written was weirder than Linear A. Enter
Morris Romsen, and shazam.

Phoebe asked, would he like to meet him? She could easily
arrange it. (Already sick, for Lewis she would have rolled naked
in snow.) At Walter's next party, knowing Morris was expected, she asked Walter if she might invite her older brother.
Lewis rejoiced; refused to attend; attended.

The party, which took place on the night of November first,
included almost fifty guests. Phoebe mentioned Lewis to Morris
and quoted one or two passages from his letter. She warned
Lewis when he arrived that Morris might act aloof; he must
forgive him for that. She also told Lewis that Morris suffered
from "a heart condition, as they now call imminent death."

"But he's so *young*. Is that why he looks so sad?"

"He's had it since he was twenty-three. And no, I don't think
so."

Morris surprised Lewis, and not by his aloofness. Lewis's
poor opinion of himself made him expect worse than that, now
more than ever: if choosing to write had exalted him, writing
itself had only made life worse. After an exciting glimpse of
freedom, he found himself still trapped between a pitying
mother and an irritable father. He had written a little poetry
both mannered and crude and kept a self-sniffing diary that
could hardly qualify as a "journal." From Morris he looked
forward at best to an acceptance of the stammering praise that
constituted his only offering.

Because he liked Phoebe, Morris was favorably disposed
towards Lewis. Whatever aloofness he did show sprang entirely
from sexual prudence. He mistrusted his own peculiar inclina-
tions, especially with a younger man whose penchants he knew
nothing about. He openly welcomed Lewis's admiration; and
Lewis, with astonishment, found himself, instead of stammering, conversing almost spontaneously.

They were standing under Elizabeth's portrait. Lewis said, "From what you wrote I'd imagined it different. Maybe that's what you wanted?"

"Ah, so?"

"No? I got something like: one can't really describe *anything*. So you pretend to describe—you use words to make a false replica. Then we're absorbed by the words, not by the illusion of a description. You also defuse reactions that might get in our way. So when we look at the painting there's nothing we expected—none of your false words, none of our false reactions—we have to see it on its own terms?"

"Not *bad*. So what's the point?"

"The point, the point . . . is, what's actually there? You leave the thing intact by giving us what isn't there—?"

"Promise not to tell? They won't get it."

"I don't either—I'm only guessing. I mean, some of the things you say are *wild*. What about: 'Our original heaven is the tempestuous sky of the vagina'?"

"Just more of the same." Morris pointed to the portrait. "Imagine writing about that mouth. Even if you keep it abstract—like 'a mauve horizontal'—people will look and tell themselves, incredible mouth, so mauve, so horizontal. And horizontality means this, and mauve means something else. Goodbye, Miss Mouth. 'Tempestuous sky' gets rid of the vagina, and vice versa, even if the words are still there, doing whatever it is words do. Of course, most people can't even see the print."

"So what about them?"

"Who knows? It's a dull delirium of a world. Lewis, take care of *yourself*. That's plenty for a lifetime, no matter how short."

Morris had called him by name; Lewis did not even notice. Not since childhood, certainly not since Phoebe's birth, had he once forgotten his own feelings. He had never met anyone like Morris, whose self-assured talent was disguised by attentive-

ness, and his endangered heart by distractingly good looks.
Lewis had not expected Morris to be beautiful. He had not
expected to love him.

Later they talked again. Morris had made his rounds; Lewis
had watched him. Not thinking about himself had lightened
Lewis's demeanor and made him agreeable. Morris suggested
they lunch the following week. Lewis silently postponed his
return home and accepted.

"You probably won't approve," Morris told him in parting,
"but I'm going into business with a friend. I'll be buying and
selling paintings."

"A gallery?"

"Out of my apartment."

Lewis was surprised. He did not approve. At their lunch he
said as much: "With your reputation? They'll say you're pro-
moting. Think of your authority now. It's priceless."

"It could work the other way. I put money in something, my
opinion's worth that much more."

"But what *about* your opinions? Isn't a work of art going to
look different when you've invested in it? Even Berenson—"

"*Even?* Be my Duveen! He knew what he was doing—so do
I. I'd like to do my shopping uptown for a change. And I
wouldn't mind collecting a wee bit for myself."

"With your eye? It's a piece of cake."

"Lewis, you're sweet to care, but. Look: there's oceans of
money sloshing around out there. All I want is a beach pail."

"I know. And you're right, I do care. There's a better way."

"You mean," said Morris, waving his glinting Muscadet
through a long bar of smoky sunshine, "I can have caviar *and*
a clean mind?"

"The trouble is the selling part. That's what's compromising.
But if you buy—"

"And *not* sell? Like to pay for lunch?"

"My pleasure. What I'm suggesting is *advising* buyers. There
are dozens of rich people around who want to own new art. It's

the latest ticket to whatever. They also want to look original and do it on the cheap, but they only know what they read in the magazines, and that's not news. So you find them artists on the way up. You help the buyers, you help the artists, you help yourself—you get a commission on each purchase. You don't have to deal. No speculating with your own money. No temptation to promote."

"People want work that other people want, and they don't need me to find it. Know any eager buyers for unknowns? One or two, I daresay—"

"I've got eight." Lewis unfolded a typewritten list and read it out loud. He had pestered the names out of Louisa. "I've talked to three of them—the Dowells, the Liebermans, and the Platts. The Platts were suspicious. The others sound interested."

"You bucking for Eagle Scout, little boy? *I* know you're just being nice, but with some you might pass for a closet schmuck."

"But *you* know I can trust you."

Morris picked up the list and left the check. He liked Lewis. He behaved condescendingly towards him because he was twenty-eight, Lewis twenty-three and young for his years. Morris felt an irresistible craving to curtail the younger man's enthusiasm and to do this by acting hard. Acting hard gave Morris pleasure. Lewis willingly submitted. Such treatment gave *him* pleasure. Morris failed to notice this. Experienced though he was, he still hesitated to believe that anyone sincerely relished punishment, still found his own yearning to inflict it perverse.

Lewis knew only that he would unquestioningly accept whatever Morris said or did. He enjoyed Morris's disdain. Watching his friend pocketing the list touched Lewis more than any thanks. He did not guess that Morris, while showing interest in his proposal, had no intention of giving up his original plan; had he known, he would have admired his duplicity.

Lewis had carefully garnered Morris's occasional remarks

about writing, and on his return home he tried some of them out. Morris recommended imitation as a practice as useful as it was unfashionable. Choose a model, he had said, and copy it. The model will have substance, form, and style. You can imitate all three; you can imitate one or the other; you will probably fail to reproduce any of them, and this inability will point to what you can do, to what usually you are already doing. You will begin discovering your own genius. As his models, Lewis chose a poem by Wallace Stevens, a story by Henry James, an essay by William Empson. He had a wickedly hard time and savored it: the work kept him busy, and full of thoughts of his new friend.

He saw Morris briefly three weeks later. They drank martinis in a bar off Fifth Avenue called Michael's Pub. Lewis reported his attempts to follow Morris's advice about writing. "Advice? I read that in *Mademoiselle,*" the other exclaimed. The riposte, Lewis thought, revealed the essential Morris.

Lewis had to cut the meeting short. He was expected elsewhere. He took a taxi to Second Avenue and Thirty-second Street, walked south two blocks, crossed to the southeast corner, and went into a bar. Scarcely a dozen men sat in its booths—a late place. Lewis passed through a door in the back into a smaller room. Two men by the window nodded to him. Through another door, he reached the building's service elevator and rode three stories up. He entered a loft that occupied the entire floor, now divided crosswise by a black rayon curtain. Six or seven men standing in front of the curtain smiled when they saw him. As he approached, they turned their backs to him and continued their conversation.

"I thought your friend was the one who strangled the bath attendant?"

"Only gossip, I'm afraid. But it taught me wisdom all the same—*never* be jealous of the past."

One man turned to Lewis and said, "Break a leg, Minerva—or shall we do it for you?"

Lewis had visited the loft more than once. Tonight for the first time he would star here: they were going to crucify him.

The elevator regularly swelled the group of men, until the closed space seethed.

Except for some ambiguous episodes at summer camp, Lewis had tried to keep his sexual particularity a secret. He knew that others shared his taste. He had seen proof of it, and, like Morris, hardly believed it; and insofar as his family's world was concerned, he might have gleaned his knowledge from science fiction. If he had examined that world more cunningly, he would have found as many brothers there as elsewhere. Lewis preferred the conviction that giving or receiving pain for pleasure belonged to a furtive milieu. At twenty, on a visit to the city, he had been spotted in the street by an alert big boy and properly cruised and bruised. He had then discovered clandestine gatherings where his taste was the rule. He dreaded these meetings and longed for them. They filled him with implacable sensations and the intangibility of old dreams, and they succeeded in briefly satisfying him with a melancholy peace. He attended them at long, regular intervals. They provided one place where he belonged.

He himself had chosen his part for this warm, overcast late November evening. The announcement of the event had disgusted him, and he had guessed that his disgust only gauged his desire. At a subsequent meeting, the others had shared the disgust, no doubt to encourage him—to shame him. They told Lewis that while he had no right to participate at all, the leading role struck them as too degrading for anyone else to perform. It required the lowest of the low.

He was assured that the performance would be no sham. The crown of thorns had been woven out of rusted barbed wire. He would be whipped with willow fronds peeled and wetted. High above the grungy floor, he would be nailed to the pine-log cross with real nails (needle-thin and hammered home by an expert—

with luck he might escape crippling). A Gem blade set in a bamboo pole would slit his side. The same pole would prod a urine-soaked sponge into his face. The only departure from gospel tradition (aside from a foot-square platform under his feet) was intended to keep him from seeing his tormentors. Why give him that satisfaction? "Don't expect to get gone on those upturned faces, Lulu. A rock like you could pull a real Camille. We'd rather full-focus on your cakes." They would nail him face to the cross.

Like any fledgling performer, Lewis suffered intense stage fright. It proved superfluous: he had nothing to do. Whatever was required of him was done by others. He was stripped, crowned, scourged, and lifted up by gangs of adept males; he could only submit to them, like a swimmer rolled in an endless succession of toppling breakers, or like a little boy with his head held underwater in the vise of a bully's legs. He held his breath until it was punched out of him. He was allowed no respite in his humiliations. On the floor he was pissed on, on the cross screamed at and pelted with bolts, sneakers, stinking pellets. He never had time to think or feel anything except his sensations, to which he surrendered in the certainty that they belonged to him absolutely and lay beyond his choosing. He heard himself sobbing: nothing more than the dross of his consciousness as it soared like a rocket into clouds—clouds of tar steam that choked him and made him drunk. He felt blood run down one hip and leg, not the cutting spear. He wondered if he'd shit. Pine bark chafed his swollen cock.

The voices in the room lowered. Something else was happening. A familiar ladder jolted into place beside him. The twenty-year-old who had so deftly nailed him up was setting pliers to his feet.

"Already?" Lewis moaned.

"Velma's here."

"Huh?"

"The orgy patrol. The vice," hissed the other, addressing his left hand.

Can anyone keep a crucifixion secret? The police had doubted it. (Two of their members attended these meetings.) They decided not to risk indiscriminate revelation; they staged a raid and turned the scandal to their own advantage. The raid was efficiently executed. No one was hurt. Only six of the thirty-four men present escaped to the upper floors, where they were permitted to spend an anxious night before absconding.

The police had tipped off friendly newspapermen. Early editions of the *News* carried a photograph of a nameless young man lying on the loft floor, half naked, somewhat bloody. Louisa's sister and Morris, among others, recognized Lewis.

Lewis had been taken to the emergency ward at Bellevue Hospital. After tending his wounds, the doctors on duty sent him to the psychiatric ward, where he passed a scary night. Word that he had been admitted as a pervert spread quickly. The ward's drunks and psychotics expressed no less scorn for him than his crucifixion audience, and theirs was meant in earnest. The few tired and jaded orderlies promised feeble protection. Although the violence remained verbal, Lewis waited for the morning in terror and, even after he had washed and eaten breakfast, did not da·e sleep, praying fervently and incessantly for the arrival of a doctor who might authorize his release. Shortly before noon, he saw Morris standing among a group of visitors at the end of the ward. Lewis crouched behind his bed.

When Morris found Lewis, he squatted down and tendered him a little plastic shopping bag. Lewis stood up. The bag contained toothbrush and toothpaste, shaving articles, hairbrush, cologne, and a box of Band-Aids.

"I couldn't remember if you smoked—not here, I guess. How's tricks?"

"How did you find me?"

"Your picture's in the paper. Don't worry, it's a terrible likeness. And nobody who'd mind reads the *News* anyway. Phoebe wants to know when she can come and see you. She sends lots of love."

"Phoebe!"

Lewis began to realize that his secret life lay open to the world. Everybody knew, or would know. Morris kept speaking to him matter-of-factly, and in time Lewis noticed the silver lining: Morris cared about him. His coming to Bellevue proved that. Thanking him, Lewis almost cried.

"Any plans?" Morris asked. Lewis knew what he meant: he couldn't go home. "Let me help. Not today, I'm afraid, but come and see me tomorrow evening. We'll, as one says, discuss your future."

Lewis left the hospital two hours later. In the First Avenue lobby he met Louisa, who had just arrived. Her teary consternation made him cringe. He welcomed her first words, however: "I promise you Owen doesn't know. I'll make sure he never does. Please tell me, are you all right?" Lewis's bandaged hands and feet (he was shuffling in heel-less straw slippers) gave him the look of a battle casualty.

"Yes. I'm sorry. Mother, I'm really sorry, but I can't stand being with you right now."

Louisa said she understood, put him in a taxi, promised not to interfere. She made him take the hundred dollars in her handbag. "Promise to call me if you need anything?"

Lewis booked a room at the Chelsea. Next day, making sure his parents had gone out, he fetched his few belongings from their place. At ten that night he arrived at Morris's apartment, which occupied one high-ceilinged floor of a converted brownstone on Cornelia Street. Lewis blushed when Morris embraced him. They sat down in a corner between lofty, slovenly bookcases. A decanter and two glasses had been set out on a low table beside a platter of toast and Roquefort cheese. Morris poured out the wine, one Lewis had never heard of—sweet, French, and with *Venice* in its name. With the wine a warmth of relief and contentment seeped from his throat and stomach to the tips of his toes, to the tip of his nose. He licked the rim of his glass, shutting his eyes. Opening them, he found himself sitting in the same place, naked, with his ankles and wrists bound to his chair. Morris stood in front of him, bare to the waist except for chromium-studded black leather wristbands and a set of brass knuckles on his right hand. When Lewis's eyes met his, Morris said with a grin, "Now, Louisa, I'm going to beat the pie out of you."

First visit: Morris drugs Lewis, strips him, ties him to a chair. He threatens him with brass knuckles (made of metal-painted rubber) and does not use them, finding better things to do. Lewis soon reveals certain weaknesses (others might call them preferences). Barely awake, he says, "Do anything you like, but let me loose. I go crazy if I can't move." Morris draws up an armchair. "Louisa, you're crazy anyway. But I'd love to see what you mean." Lewis begins to cry. Morris taunts him, in accidental slang: "Poor Ella, such a sad route to go! How did a swinging skinner like me pull a dorky trick like Miss Thing. . . ." Lewis interrupts, "Don't talk like that. I'm not a screaming faggot, and neither are you. It makes me puke." Morris: "Poor baby! Did you just step out of a time machine? You can suck my Jewish ass! I'll talk any way I want." Morris harangues him late into the night.

Morris had a surprise for Lewis. On the following day he took him to Thirteenth Street just west of First Avenue and there, three metaled flights up a tenement stairway, led him into a two-room apartment. Although its size forbade even one closet, it had been properly maintained, and its rent was eighty-five dollars.

"Which I'll pay till you find a job," Morris told Lewis, who moved in ten days before Christmas.

The two men saw each other for drinks, for dinner, for openings, for double features; never privately. For nearly two months Morris refused to let Lewis come to his apartment. Lewis's pleadings did nothing to shorten the interval.

Second visit: January 27, 6:00 P.M. When Lewis has undressed, Morris fastens his wrists to his ankles with short-linked metal cuffs. Unable to walk, Lewis hops after Morris at his bidding. A nudge topples him. Morris passes a rope through his arms and legs. Drawn tight through an eye-knot at one of its ends, the rope bunches Lewis's hands and feet, pressing his head against his knees, reducing him to a sack-shaped bundle that Morris drags behind him. In the kitchen, while he readies his dinner, Morris resorts to the jargon Lewis abhors and vents his disillusionment with the practice of sadomasochism, which he is planning to give up: ". . . It may mean short roses for us, but that's show biz. I mean B and D is so gaggy. And where does it all end? In a bug wing, at fat best. Just think—a nice girl like you already getting taken home! *You'll* probably end up popped. I wouldn't actually mind, except playing god must be your dream. No, this one plans to rejoin the fluffs in the vanilla bars. You should, too. It's not so bad. You could always turn out spinach queen. Or why don't you just try going it alone? That's you! I'll give you a fifi-bag to remember me by. . . ." Morris continues his monologue while consuming shrimp, chops, salad, flan, Petit Chablis, and coffee. Afterwards he settles down in his study. Twenty minutes later, Lewis calls from the kitchen. Morris answers the summons with an irritated "Do you mind!" and tapes a wool sock inside Lewis's mouth. Lewis fears he will choke and starts writhing on the floor. "*Must* you be so pigeon-titted?" The cuffs keep clattering. Morris hauls Lewis across the living-room floor. Opening the window, he loops the drag-rope over the top of the railing outside and pulls Lewis upwards until his back barely touches the floor. When the rope is secured to the railing, Lewis is immobilized by his own weight. The window now cannot shut; through it pass bitter gusts and occasional fine snow. Morris returns to his desk.

Lewis had taken a temporary job as night watchman at a factory building in Queens. Afternoons, he haunted off-off-Broadway theaters, where he tried to make himself useful in any capacity that might lead to being hired. Three days after Lewis's second visit, Morris introduced him to Tom, the head lighting man at the City Center Opera. He had agreed to have Lewis apprenticed to him. This meant low pay and invaluable experience. The sudden opportunity intimidated Lewis. Tom coached him patiently, and Morris reassured him during his fits of self-doubt. After such kindness, Lewis could not understand why Morris again barred him from his apartment. He offered to run the most humdrum household errands for his benefactor. Morris remained adamant. For three weeks, Lewis had to content himself with public meetings, knowing that all the while Priscilla frequently visited the lodgings on Cornelia Street.

Third visit: February 14. Books fill every room in Morris's apartment, including the kitchen. Even the back door is hidden by a bookcase. This door is not, however, completely blocked: the lower shelves of the bookcase can swing out to allow passage of upright dogs and crouching humans. Lewis is permitted to return only if he promises henceforth to use this entrance. He is given a key. On Saint Valentine's night he makes his first appearance on his hands and knees, to Morris's satisfaction: "That's fine. *Don't* stand up. Wriggle out of your Peck and Pecks right where you are. You'll have yourself when you see what I've brought you." He hands the naked Lewis a straitjacket. Lewis bursts into tears. Morris snaps, "The party's over," and picks up his overcoat. Lewis begins obediently working his way into the straitjacket; Morris knots the drawstrings. With a short length of nylon cord he attaches

Lewis's left foot to a leg of the kitchen table. He also fits him
with a studded leather cock ring, its points facing inwards.
Morris then pulls up a chair and begins his talk for the evening. He has taken for his subject Lewis's sexual inadequacy.
Morris explains that he has tried to lessen its effect by keeping
Lewis away as long as possible. Now he must speak his mind.
He has never had so boring a lover. He describes the delights
of some earlier affairs, long and short: ". . . One piece of ivy
pie was so righteous! Never been tampered with, and he still
knew twice what you know, Zelda Gooch. . . ." However, he
will not linger over his past. After fifteen minutes, putting on
his coat, he tells Lewis, "I'm out for dinner tonight. You
won't be alone, though. Phoebe's coming to see you. She'll let
herself in." Lewis huddles under the kitchen table. He pisses
on himself.

   After weeks of insistence, Morris pestered Lewis into showing him everything he had written—his poems, his journal, his
imitations. "You'll need one reader at least, and I *am* on your
side, you know." For the first and last time, Morris became a
teacher. He went through Lewis's work with him line by line.
He refused to correct; instead, he invented exercises for Lewis.
He made him rework passages in other styles. (Lewis's "break-
through" took the form of a political polemic rewritten as a love
poem.) Morris took care to do these exercises himself, keeping
no more than a step ahead of his pupil. Little by little he weaned
Lewis from his limitations, his "individuality": favorite words,
repeated sentence rhythms, obsessive metaphors, whatever let
him shy away from the entirety of language (as a novice skier,
preoccupied with his skis, shies from the buoyant steeps that
can give him wings).

   Fourth visit: March 14. Lewis finds Morris with Tom from
the City Center. Morris tells him that Tom will spend the
evening with them. Two long boards are leaning against the
mantelpiece. A small vise is screwed to both ends of each

board. After Lewis has stripped, the men spread-eagle him against the boards and clamp his wrists and ankles in the four vises. Only the loose boards hold him in place; Lewis does not dare stir. Morris and Tom sit down to dinner. They discuss Lewis while they eat. Morris speaks of his hopelessness as a writer; he reads a few hilariously incompetent passages by him out loud. Tom describes him at the theater—slow to learn, manually clumsy, so socially clumsy the entire staff dislikes him (including Tom). After dinner the two men sit together on the sofa in front of Lewis. They start kissing. Lewis falls to the floor, gashing one knee bloodily on the glass coffee table. Morris replaces Lewis's left foot in the vise from which it has slipped. Talking campily and incessantly, he and Tom caress one another. At last they put on their coats and leave. Tom's place, they agree, will be cozier under the circumstances.

The following afternoon, Lewis met Morris at an opening at the Stable Gallery. Morris greeted him exuberantly. He had sent a selection of Lewis's work to one of the editors of *Locus Solus,* a little magazine whose reputation was unrivaled. Three poems had been accepted. "You tell people you're a writer, they say 'Wonderful,' and *always* they ask next, 'And have you published anything?' Now you say yes."

The two pursued their study of writing several hours each week.

Fifth visit: April 15. The worst for Lewis so far. He picks up the evening's "toys": a full-length inflatable rubber suit that constricts its wearer whenever he struggles against it. Lewis climbs three floors of a dilapidated building on lower Varick Street. A small nervous man dumps a bundle in his arms and slams the door in his face. When Lewis crawls through the back door into Morris's apartment, he finds Morris waiting for him, naked except for a gag, a note in his outstretched hand:

Dear Louisa,
   My turn. Put the contraption on me, use the pump to blow
it up, and get out. If you do anything else, or if you come back,
I'll never forgive you.

                                                                    M.

In tears, Lewis complies with his instructions. Afterwards he
goes to a restaurant. He can't eat. He decides to see a movie,
a revival of *Twenty Thousand Leagues Under the Sea*. James
Mason doomed to submarine exile makes him cry so hard he
has to leave. He walks down rainy streets for another hour.
How can Morris's heart survive the constricting suit? He goes
back, crawls once more through the bookcase, and releases his
friend. Morris is panting fearfully. Lewis holds the sweating
body in his arms, murmuring brotherly comfort. Both men
speak words of endearment, and like all of Lewis's visits, the
evening ends in a prolific tenderness that lasts into the next
morning.
   Morris had imagined a prodigious book: for that place and
time, The Book. It was to include fiction as well as criticism,
theory as well as poetry, using the most appropriate medium to
explore each facet of its subject: the finiteness of intellect and
language confronting the infinity of the intuited universe. During the spring weekend they spent with Phoebe in the Hudson
River valley, Morris invited Lewis to collaborate on the project.
They would begin work on May 24, Morris's thirtieth birthday.
The task would take at least three years.
   Sixth visit: May 23. Entering the kitchen on all fours, Lewis
finds Morris busily stirring five plastic basins with a broom
handle. The basins contain black matter, heavy and wet. Morris
hands Lewis the stick. His efforts have left him rather pale. He
now only adds water to the basins while Lewis churns them.
The basins, he learns, are filled with quick-drying cement. At
Morris's bidding, Lewis carries them into the living room and

sets them around the edge of a small area covered with layers of newspaper. Lewis undresses and stands at the center of the area. Using a housepainter's brush, Morris daubs grease over Lewis's head and body. Kneeling down, he then starts covering him in cement, first heaping it generously around his feet and ankles to form a massive base, then applying a half-inch thickness over his limbs, torso, and head. Morris leaves an opening for nose and eyes and with his forefinger jabs a passage into each ear. When he finishes, sweating and breathing hard, Morris is visibly pleased with his crude statue, whose arms stretch out sideways like a scarecrow's, giving it an air both of solidity and of helplessness. While the cement is hardening, Morris goes off to wash and eat dinner. On his return, he tells Lewis to move his arms and legs. Tears and sweat are already dripping from the end of Lewis's nose, and his eyes now wince with effort: he cannot budge. Morris walks back and forth in front of him while delivering his customary monologue of abuse. He has hesitated, he confesses, to tell Lewis the most important thing he will ever say to him. He has spoken already of the repulsion inspired by Lewis's degeneracy, by his lack of sexual talent, by his lack of talent *tout court.* Morris has since realized that everything he has said falls short of the truth: what makes Lewis ultimately repulsive is his intrinsic self. His specific shortcomings only manifest the underlying ugliness, stupidity, and heartlessness that constitute his very being. With growing passion Morris applies his new insight in appalling descriptions of Lewis's physical, mental, and social behavior. Wherever he looks, he can discover only failure and disreputableness. Some might consider his nature something he has no control over, but this makes it no less unbearable: "Even if I don't like reading you the stations, I won't spread jam. So please, Louisa, get it and go. You're a mess, a reject, a patient—I could go on for days. And don't tell me—I have your nose wide open. I'm sorry. Spare me the wet lashes, it's all summer stock. Because the only one you've ever been really strung out on is your own smart self, and you always will be. Think I'm going to stick around and watch the buns drop? And for what—to keep catching my rakes in your zits? Forget it, Dorothy. This is goodbye. Remember one thing, though. No matter what I've said to you, no matter how I've turned you out, the truth is"—Morris's eyes become wet; he turns a surprising shade of red—"the truth is, and I'm singing it out: I lo— . . . " Morris is staring past Lewis as his voice breaks off. Has he stopped because the telephone is ringing? His color veers from red to gray. He turns to lean on the back of a chair, except that no chair is to be found where he leans: he sinks onto his knees before lying face down on the floor. He rolls himself slowly onto his back, looking up at Lewis, who watches his lips form a repeated word *(Nitro, nitro)*, then remain open and still. Morris breathes rapidly, until a moment comes when he does not breathe at all. Lewis shouts into the cement plastered across his mouth. He only makes his own head hum. Panic has started to overcome him when he realizes what has happened: Morris is playing a joke on him. He is deliberately scaring him out of his wits. Lewis's panic turns to rage. Morris has gone too far, inhumanly far. Lewis will never forgive him. Remembering their previous meeting, he knows that Morris may very well lie there half the night. He can only wait, and he is steeling himself for his ordeal when he notices Morris's eyes. They are fixed in an impossible stare. They never blink. Lewis counts sixty seconds, the eyelids do not move. The fly of Morris's shirt lies motionless over his chest and belly. Lewis keeps looking down at his friend. A grieving numbness is expanding through his body. Another minute passes before he thinks: I may be wrong. Perhaps Morris is only stricken, or perhaps if he's dying there's time to save him. Lewis screams another muffled scream, tells himself: Emotion does no good. Figure out how to get free. Earlier, Lewis has noticed a croquet mallet leaning against one of the bookcases. Morris would have used it to crack his shell. The phone is ringing again. Question: what can he use for a mallet? Answer: a fall to the floor. How can I fall when I can't move? However, Lewis can move, if only inside his skin. He can squeeze himself left and right, or front and back. Will this let him shift his weight? Seven feet away to the front and left, on the coffee table where he cut himself, sits the phone. Lewis begins pressing towards it and then away from it, right heel to left toe, left toe to right heel. He begins to sway, minimally. He senses a tapping of the cement base on the floor. His hunch is working. The statue has started to rock. He must not fall backwards, away from the table. He puts all his strength into pushing forwards. The base goes tap-thump, tap-thump. A momentum has been established. A point comes when the backwards swing does not occur. Before falling, Lewis and his carapace balance for three full seconds on the front edge of the base, precious seconds during which he twists hard clockwise, trying to swing his left arm in front of him, and the arm does strike the floor an instant before his head and chest. The cement shatters to the elbow. The phone lies too high to reach. He yanks it by its wire onto the floor and pulls the handset in front of his face. The cement around his head has cracked. With his free hand he loosens a piece over his mouth. Running his finger over the rotary dial to the last hole, he dials zero. He hears an answering voice, barely audible. He calls out Morris's address, begs for help, explains that he is immobilized. He repeats his appeal over and over, long after the operator has connected him with the police. Still speaking into the receiver, he hears someone at the front door. Who is it? Why are they ringing the bell? and knocking? "Break it down!" he starts shouting. The bell still rings. He hasn't noticed the sirens before, several of them. Ringing and knocking stop. The door is being forced, a heavy old oak door equipped with three locks. Lewis has nothing left to do. He begins sinking into a weary, gloomy dullness. With despondent irony he tells himself that Morris will never top this. He is mistaken, in the sense that worse is to come. He is not otherwise mistaken: Morris has bequeathed him a legacy that will perpetuate and compound the experience of his six visits. Their last evening has become a moment of pain that will engender further moments of pain, and these will have to be endured without any hope of Morris's returning, as he had before, from dinner or from Tom's place. In his guise of tormentor Morris will enshroud Lewis's life. Lewis will never want to forget him, and he will have no choice in the matter. A rosary of mourning, shame, and isolation has begun entwining him more finally than thongs and chains. Morris might well in these consequences be completing his last aborted sentence, which Lewis had unhesitatingly grasped in its entirety: "The truth is, I loathe you."

Lewis and Walter

JUNE 1962-JUNE 1963

PRISCILLA LUDLAM ATTENDED THE SAME PROGRESSIVE liberal-arts college as Phoebe, graduating from it, a year after Phoebe left, with a major in art history. For her degree she wrote a commendable bachelor thesis, entitled "The Female Figure in Recent American Art," having as its true subject the work of Walter Trale. (Priscilla's tutor, the same admirer of Walter's work who had taught Phoebe painting, suggested the nominally broader subject to mollify her colleagues in the Fine Arts Department.)

As soon as she had completed her paper, Priscilla wanted Walter to read it. She gave it to Phoebe and asked her to bring it to his attention. It soon occurred to Phoebe that the paper might also interest Lewis, who at the time knew nothing about Walter except what she herself had told him. She sent him a copy.

An account of Walter's early portrait of Elizabeth con-

155

stituted the centerpiece of the thesis. As a teenager Priscilla had heard about the portrait, which Walter had painted in the upstate town where she still lived. Priscilla set out to gather information about its early history. In her thesis she compensated for her limited critical skills with an abundance of anecdote.

Priscilla had sharp wits. At twenty-two, however, her curiosities drew her less to analysis than to the rehearsal of life—to people, to attainment, to the city. She had not majored in art history because she thought herself scholarly or even "artistic": she was interested not so much in art itself as in those who created it. Art came as close to magic as a possession-prone world allowed. What did it take to become a magician? Priscilla's interest was encouraged by the unprecedented glamor, fostered by critics and buyers alike, of new American painting. When her tutor proposed that she spend a year studying Walter Trale, she accepted enthusiastically, because she could at once imagine him as another Pollock or de Kooning. She devoted many hours to staring dutifully at slides of Walter's work. If she came to feel at home with it, she could not be said to have ever understood it. It never touched her, at least not on its own terms. It mattered to her because she saw in it an expression of the artist's life. Her interpretations of the work surreptitiously concealed an imaginary likeness of Walter himself. He was a subject that did touch her; and her delineation of him made Lewis respond to her thesis with idiosyncratic sympathy.

Priscilla described at length the background of the "Portrait of Elizabeth": how Walter, at eighteen a precociously successful painter of racehorses, prize dogs, and cherished pets, was transformed by his meeting with the woman he was soon to portray. Elizabeth had revealed to him the "animal grace and transcendent sexuality" of a woman's beauty. Merely seeing her had initiated the revelation; but according to Priscilla, Elizabeth also intervened actively in Walter's life. She had seen *him*—seen him for what he might become—and through her friendship she had inspired him to become it. By her visionary wisdom Elizabeth made a creator of him. In Priscilla's view, it was not only through her beauty and intelligence that Elizabeth exerted her influence but by fully assuming the role of Woman as muse and genetrix. It was this experience of Elizabeth as absolute Woman that Walter had recorded in his portrait of her.

Priscilla supplied engaging anecdotes to support her claim. Defending her interpretation of the portrait proved harder. If the painting looked inspired, what else did it look like? Certainly not Elizabeth. All biographers explaining art take their wishes as facts. Priscilla made the painting conform to her need, which was to establish in it the presence of *das Ewig-Weibliche* (as, knowing no German, she insistently called it). To her, the gold and white of the face invoked a medieval Madonna. The ocher of the eyes belonged to Athena (or perhaps her owl). The mauve lips stood for mourning (notice that the bared teeth are not smiling)—a demonstrable recollection of the *Pietà*. A mouth-colored mouth with no teeth would probably have suggested to Priscilla the Cumaean Sibyl; plain brown eyes the mortality of autumn leaves; pink cheeks the sacred Rose.

Priscilla never realized that her analysis suffered from self-indulgence, and Lewis did not care. Morris would later teach him what art criticism might achieve. For the time being he was seduced by her account of Walter the man. Priscilla's absolute Woman crystalized Lewis's own feelings; women had always struck him as awesome and inexplicably different. At no age that he could remember had he been close to anyone of the opposite sex, except for Phoebe; and if other women acquired mystery by their remoteness, Phoebe had become no less mysterious through intimacy—her love for him left him perpetually incredulous. Mystery meant an aversion that differed from his hostility towards men. Lewis disliked men because, as one of them, he knew all too well how they functioned. He knew, among other things, how they experienced desire. He was attracted to men because he wanted to rediscover with them this familiar, recognizable desire. Women had unimaginable desires, and one particularly unimaginable sexual desire. He remembered at four watching Phoebe while her diapers were changed and staring at her big button. It looked anything but girlish. Lewis was not bewildered by the vagina, but by the irrelevant and impudent clitoris. He did not want it there. It was the stopper. It meant that women had been fashioned as unpredictable beings, that he could never trust them to behave in an accountable way.

With men, he knew how to provoke the aggressiveness through which he could respond to them. Even here women eluded him. Once, when he was nine, at a family gathering, he called a pretty eleven-year-old cousin a bitch. He knew the insult to be reliably bad because his mother had slapped him when he tried it on her. The cousin laughed gleefully, said he was cute, and pampered him for the rest of the day before withdrawing to Connecticut. They were not to be trusted.

In spite of dating one girl in late adolescence, Lewis's aversion never wavered. Because he kept his true desires hidden, classmates at school and college thought him merely shy, and they frequently introduced him to young ladies both nice and not-nice. He wanted no part of them.

Walter's experience of women, as Priscilla described it, confirmed Lewis's. Walter displayed generosity and ebullience, Lewis pettiness and anxiety; both could agree that in Woman mystery and power abide.

Lewis found a second reason to like Priscilla's thesis: it showed precisely the extent of his difference from Walter. Walter had recognized the power in women and faced it. Through Elizabeth, he had let it into his life. Perhaps he had even mastered it in his art and turned it into a power of his own. Walter was thus an exemplar of all that Lewis could never aspire to.

Lewis often had crushes on the men he admired. A fund of natural affection underlay his habitual mistrust. Because he was frightened by the give-and-take of friendship, Lewis expressed this warmth either by provoking those he liked or by adoring them from a distance. In Walter, Priscilla had supplied him with a new idol.

Lewis confided his admiration to Phoebe, who at once saw in it an opportunity to move him into the living world he was so determined to avoid. When, in early June, he exclaimed over the phone, "What an incredible man!" she replied, "So why don't you visit? See the work yourself."

"I don't mean the work. I mean *him.*"

"So come and see *him.*"

Lewis began commenting on the current heat wave. He heard Phoebe saying to someone at her end, "My big brother thinks you're the cat's pajamas, but he's scared to meet you."

When Walter took the phone, Lewis had fled.

Phoebe did not let him get away. She called back repeatedly to tease, berate, and beg. She even lured him with the unlikely possibility that Lewis might somehow work for Walter. The proposal flustered him at first; soon, however, he began working it into his fantasies, until his fantasies themselves changed. Instead of worship, Lewis began dreaming of servitude. He could put his own inadequacy to good use. He could free Walter from whatever distracted him from his art. He would clean his brushes, wash his skylight, scour his toilet bowl, run errands in Brownsville. He accepted Phoebe's invitation.

In the days preceding his visit, walking through the town under dying elms and heat-wilted maples, or sitting with a book on the porch of the house, or lying in bed late at night, he thought of what his meeting with Walter might bring. He did not want gratitude or recompense. He longed ultimately to become indispensable to Walter. He imagined a career starting as charman and ending as watchdog.

Walter in the flesh only strengthened Lewis's devotion. He

looked his forty-three years and looked them well. A nonchalant alertness pleasantly animated his sprawling features, his wrinkles tempered his obvious candor with an aura of lessons learned. Lewis felt a surge of tenderness when he saw him. This would normally have ensured his protracted silence, but Phoebe kept prodding him to speak.

"It's incredible," he finally told Walter over sizzling shrimp, "how you started your career with such a really profound work."

"Profound? 'Digger III' profound? Sure was a *gloomy* beagle."

"I mean—I *meant* Elizabeth. Your first woman—I mean, the first person you painted was a woman. That's probably significant."

"No shit." Walter had not yet read Priscilla's thesis; Lewis had not yet seen the portrait of Elizabeth.

Phoebe said, "Lewis thinks you're accomplices in misogyny."

"Not misogyny, not really—" ("No, not really!" Phoebe camped) "—but, you know, that power," Lewis hurried on. "It's not that it's bad, just big. You don't want to get in its way."

"That's in the portrait?" Walter asked.

"Why, sure." Lewis looked startled. "I don't have to tell *you.*"

"Tell me anyway."

Lewis discoursed on female unpredictability. He related the incident with his eleven-year-old cousin: "It wasn't as though she was genuinely fond of me. I was used."

"The trouble is," Walter said ruefully, "*they* never seem to realize." He was suffering at the time from a woman's unresponsiveness.

Although Walter liked him, and Lewis was as willing as ever to serve, he was frustrated in his aims by a rudimentary fact:

he was a man. At the studio the next morning, after Walter asked what kind of work he wanted to do for him, Lewis replied, chores—cleaning up, shopping, soaking the beans. "That's no kind of work for you," Walter said. He meant, among other things, that it was woman's work. Walter, who enjoyed chores, might have accepted another woman as helper; when Phoebe cooked dinner for him, he felt that her presence made a difference. A man could only add more of what he knew all too well.

Walter said, not unkindly, that he found Lewis's offer to play housemaid silly. Lewis was scarcely disappointed—he had been schooled, after all, in Owen's harsher ways. He readily withdrew to his first, safe role as worshiper.

Lewis did not see Walter again until the November evening when he met Morris. In the meantime, both their lives had changed. Walter was living with Priscilla; Lewis had been overwhelmed by Morris's article.

Lewis and Priscilla had once known each other well. Six years before, they had had a serious falling out, and they had not seen each other since. Before the November party Priscilla decided to bury the past. She wanted to please Phoebe, and she assumed that in six years Lewis had grown up. When she saw him arrive, she greeted him with a hug. Lewis was surprised and pleased; however, preoccupied as he was with the prospect of meeting Morris, he responded distractedly to Priscilla's welcome. She mentioned hearing from Phoebe that he had liked her thesis. He replied, "Yes, it was really nice. As a matter of fact, for a while it kind of obsessed me. But you've read Morris's piece? *That* says it all, doesn't it?"

Priscilla had worked hard on her thesis. Walter himself had praised it. In those few seconds Lewis squandered his credit with her.

Late that month Lewis was arrested in the crucifixion raid. Although a reader of the *News,* Walter failed to spot the incriminating photograph. Priscilla noticed it and called up Phoebe to check. Phoebe went out for the paper and phoned back to thank Priscilla for letting her know. Interrupting Walter at work, Priscilla told him, "Look what's happened to Phoebe's brother, the poor guy!" She wondered how he'd become involved with such freaks. "They must have given him drugs. Nobody's that screwy."

Lewis often saw Walter that winter in Morris's company. In his behavior towards him Walter showed an amiable lack of concern. He knew that Morris and Lewis had become lovers, a relationship that, according to Priscilla, was "doing wonders—just what Lewis needed to get it together." She sometimes reminded Walter that for Phoebe's sake they should be kind to him. By this time Priscilla had become Morris's business partner.

Walter came to think of Lewis as a "case"—someone not all that sick who you still wished would get better. Inevitably Lewis reminded Walter of Phoebe, whom he was losing to her own "neurosis," and of Morris, whom he respected and rather feared. Lewis was to be tolerated and encouraged and, perhaps, avoided.

Morris died. Public and private accounts of his death were gluttonously sucked up by downtown gossips. Walter knew Lewis too little to resist the vague story that many people eagerly accepted: Morris had not died accidentally, and Lewis had not merely witnessed his death.

Lewis had changed in the half year that followed his arrest. Phoebe's old hopes for him had been essentially fulfilled: if Walter had done nothing for Lewis, Morris had done everything. He had offered Lewis the chance to earn a living, to write professionally, to recognize and express the love he felt; and, overcoming his chronic fearfulness, Lewis had taken that chance. He learned, for a time at least, that fearfulness could not excuse running away. He was proud that he could now handle a lighting console, that he was going to be published, that Morris had adopted him; prouder still of being able to get a job done, of writing for his own increasingly stern taste, of having turned his sexual addiction into a means of loving one man. When Morris died, Lewis clearly saw the fullness his new life had taken on, and how fragile, without Morris, it had now become.

Morris had incidentally altered Lewis's attitude towards Walter. While Morris always praised Walter's painting, he treated the artist himself almost patronizingly—an attitude completely at odds with Lewis's obsequiousness. At one December opening, after Morris had walked away from Walter in mid sentence, Lewis asked him how he could act so cavalierly. "I adore Walter," Morris answered, "but he says absolutely everything that comes into his head. He can be *brainless.*" Lewis said he always listened to Walter because he was so perceptive. Morris interrupted him: "In so-called life he doesn't notice anything, except the visuals." Lewis once again ventured to cite Priscilla's theory of Walter and Woman. "Louisa!" Morris exclaimed to Lewis, who shrank, "that's infantile caca! Even if Miss Priss is right, it's still only Big Momma Rides Again. Most boys feel that way sometime—like you, *n'est-ce pas,* am I not insightful? Walter probably didn't notice—Wonder Woman's name for him was Cadmium Rose. Doesn't mean anything, only words. My words for it were 'tempestuous sky of the vagina,' remember, and *they* don't mean anything either."

"I never asked you—why 'tempestuous'?"

"What's rumbling thunder remind you of? *Basta!*"

Lewis returned to Walter: "You mean good painters can be mediocrities?"

"He's not a mediocrity. I love him—warm as a farmhouse bath on a frosty night. It's only those surfeits of well-meaningness. . . . Maybe it's just been too easy for him. A good shit-dip would have tightened and brightened him. But there's nothing wrong with him. He's just not special."

Lewis began listening to Walter more dispassionately and decided Morris was right. Not knowing he painted, one might have taken him for an affable wholesaler, a well-read truck driver, a debonair postman. Lewis saw that adulating Walter did him an injustice: an extraordinary man can be expected to do extraordinary work; from an ordinary man, such work means that he has transcended his nature. If this notion still smacked of sentimentality, it at least allowed Lewis to transform his idol into someone for whom he felt affinity as well as respect. His own exertions as a writer—small compared to Walter's thirty years' diligence—gave him a sense of comradeship with the older man.

Morris's death cost Lewis his lover, mentor, and closest friend. Within days he learned how alone he had become. Newspaper reports, private rumors even less well informed, were making of him a macabre celebrity. No one seemed sure who had buried whom in cement; either way, the act sounded deranged, if not criminal. The tale of the crucifixion was revived and given wide circulation. Lewis learned that few people knew the truth about him—that he loved Morris, that he wrote, that he worked at the City Center. Many of Phoebe's friends did not know he was her brother. Tom, at least, did not let him down; and the regularity of Lewis's daily stint at the theater sustained him during the weeks that followed Morris's death. However, he valued Tom as his boss. Outside the classroom, he had never worked for anyone; he was now doing a competent job for someone who had trained him well without ever overtly favoring him. Lewis refused to jeopardize their professional relationship by making Tom his confidant.

He knew he needed a confidant. A year before he would have turned to Phoebe; she now lay in a hospital in critical condition. He dreaded facing Morris's sister, Irene. Each time he wondered, who am I going to talk to? he would think, in spite of himself, I have to ask Morris. Grief would then penetrate him, the cold, fleshly grief he had felt when he gazed down at his lover's breathless lips. Phoebe was lost for now, Morris forever. Lewis turned to their common friend.

He had seen and not spoken to Walter at Morris's funeral. On Wednesday, a few days later, he called the studio. Priscilla answered: Walter was busy, was there anything she could do? How was he?

"Same as you. Except you have company."

"Big deal. It's *awful*. There's this hole in my life I keep falling into. . . ."

"I do reruns all the time—I saw it, but I still can't believe it. Listen, when is Walter free?"

"When would you like?"

"Right away! I really need to talk to him."

"Gotcha. I'll tell him."

He gave her the number of a delicatessen that took messages for him.

When Lewis returned late that night, Walter had not called. At the theater, he had heard one of his companions ask another, "Jesus, is he still at large?" The next morning he received a letter from Owen's lawyer. It assured him that his father would assume his legal expenses. Lewis again phoned Walter, and Priscilla said to him, "Lewis! I'm so glad to hear from you. Can you come over tomorrow afternoon?"

"Tomorrow?"

"Darling, it's the best he can do."

The "darling" angered him, more because of his own help-lessness than the intimate concern it implied.

Priscilla *was* concerned: she was doing her best to keep Lewis at bay. Only six months had passed since she had skillfully won a place in Walter's life, and she still considered her position handicapped by youth, inexperience, and a lack of credentials.

Most of Walter's friends had known him for years. All displayed forcefulness or originality or both—even the bums had
clownish charm. Priscilla could not pretend to be "interesting."
Only Walter's attraction to her justified her presence at his side.
She needed to fortify this attachment. She needed to establish
herself at the center of Walter's life, with the rest of the threat-
enii ɉ world kept apart from their private sphere.

Lewis presented no threat. His disgrace served her plans,
however, now that Phoebe and Morris could no longer protect
him. Priscilla had already consigned Lewis in Walter's eyes to
the role of psychic invalid. She now wanted to banish him
conspicuously from their life so as to confirm certain benefits
she would derive from Morris's death.

Walter was feeling intense remorse over Morris. He had
neglected someone to whom he was uniquely indebted. He told
Priscilla he wanted to atone for his neglect by befriending the
dead man's lover. The impulse had so far remained only a wish,
because Walter shrank from seeing Lewis, whom he wanted to
like and didn't and whose strangeness in the wake of Morris's
death had become forbidding. Priscilla knew, however, that
Walter's generosity would win out. Mere aversion was no
match for it.

Priscilla sensed she could turn Walter's remorse to her own
advantage and so delayed Lewis's meeting with him. Lewis had
called back on Friday morning. That afternoon she had been
summoned to appear at the reading of Morris's will. She had
been informed that no legacy in the will approached in value
the life-insurance policy of which she had been named beneficiary. She planned to come home that evening with public proof
that she, not Lewis, had been chosen by Morris as his heir.

Not knowing that the insurance policy proceeded from a
business understanding, Walter reacted as Priscilla had foreseen. She had been consecrated as Morris's intimate. Unmen-
tioned in the will, Lewis was relegated once again to the fringe

of things, a pathetic, suspicious silhouette. That evening, alone with Priscilla, Walter for the first time found the ability to vent the grief he had been withholding. He cried in her arms. Morris became a precious bond between them.

Walter woke Lewis up Saturday morning to briskly excuse himself from their meeting that afternoon. He suggested that Lewis join them for drinks Sunday evening: "We're having a few friends over." Baffled with unfinished dreams, Lewis sleepily accepted. The phone rang again: Phoebe. She was leaving the hospital to catch a train upstate. He asked if he could take her to the station.

"Thanks, but no. I've made such a deal about doing this on my own. I do want to see you. How are you? Better not tell me! *I'm* awful, too. Come home, soon, and we'll hold each other's hands."

Lewis had intended to see Walter alone. He went to the studio that Sunday because he preferred seeing him with others to not seeing him at all. He regretted the visit. Those guests who knew who he was (the others were soon told) treated him with careful nonchalance, pointedly discussing their politics, their diets, their vacations, confronting him with the undisguised curiosity reserved for movie stars and youthful victims of terminal cancer, with one difference: they never touched him, not even an elbow, as though he were threatening them with terrifying contagion. A cheery Priscilla took him aside and earnestly questioned him first about Phoebe, then about his work, and last about his grief, which, she too emphatically insisted, she more than shared. Lewis sadly realized that they were engaged in the conversation he wanted to have with Walter.

Walter behaved like the others. In the features of the man he had chosen to trust, Lewis saw himself registered in terms all too familiar: as pervert and pariah. When he noticed Lewis's gaze, Walter's inane smile almost split his face. Lewis later detected something else. Walter averted his eyes from him as from the thought of Morris, of Morris-as-corpse. Lewis had become a carrier of mortality as well as disease. (That suspended look reminded him of someone else, someone he could not then recall.)

Lewis wondered what Priscilla had told Walter about him. Why was she so set on keeping them apart? He was about to ask her (what could he lose?) when a great weariness settled on him. It had arisen, as well as from disappointment, from the sorrow that for ten days had followed him like a childhood dog; he had spent all his courage tending it. He looked at Walter once more. The openness of the face contracted into studied blankness. Lewis left.

He met Walter and Priscilla by chance the next morning, on the corner of Carmine and Bleecker Streets—Priscilla still cheery, Walter silent, standing behind her, contemplating Lewis with the appalled eyes that identified him as doom made flesh. As he was replying to something Priscilla had said, Lewis recognized that familiar expression: it was the way Owen always looked at him. Lewis's understanding of the couple he faced began to change. He lost track of what he was saying to Priscilla. His scalp prickled with sweat.

"What's wrong?" Priscilla asked.

Lewis lied, "I just remembered talking to Morris once on this corner." He kept staring at Walter. "You know how his being dead—you forget it for five seconds, and something brings it back—don't you, Priss? *You* know what an incredible man he was."

Thirty-seven years before, Walter had sat down conclusively on his little sister's best celluloid doll. Since that time, no one had ever looked at him as she had then, as Lewis was looking at him now. The aversion drained out of him; he reverted to his considerate, vulnerable self. Lewis did not notice this because of the tears of rage in his eyes.

He walked away. He did not see them again until early September.

Every year during the hot midsummer drought, on the hills overlooking the French Riviera, hundreds of acres of pine and cork oak are laid waste by fire. At the end of one arid July, a thirty-year-old schoolteacher, passing a spot where underbrush had begun burning, got out of his car to observe the spreading flames. Other drivers saw him, assumed that he had started the fire, and reported him to the police. He was arrested. Overnight he provided the outlet for a nation's frustrated anger. Although he was cleared of the charge against him, to him this hardly mattered. Six years later he declared that for the rest of his life, no matter what he did, he would be remembered as the "Arsonist of Provence."

From the behavior of Walter's guests, from the remark overheard at the theater, from the exaggerated discretion of the countermen at his delicatessen, from Owen's coldly dutiful letter, from Phoebe's pity, from the telephone calls of junk journalists, from the silence of acquaintances, Lewis knew that he was similarly condemned. For years the mention of his name, his appearance in a room, could only recall King Koncrete or whatever tag stuck to him best. How many books would he have to write to obliterate his scandalous fame? Would he have to write them under another name? (Morris had said that Lewis Lewison was so good it sounded made up.) To read in Walter's face this squalid verdict hurt more than he could endure. Why had he blamed Priscilla? She had her old reasons for mistrusting him. Walter should have known better.

Lewis's situation excruciated him because he could see no end to it. Phoebe might console him at home; elsewhere he had no prospect of support or even sufferance, not if someone like Walter repudiated him. Lewis's awareness that his pain would last, that its unfairness would not modify its persistence, urgently demanded comforting: he needed someone to blame. Throughout his life he had always blamed himself for the failures that, loving mortification as he did, he had in truth often provoked. Now he chose to blame someone else. He hated his pain, most of all when he recollected his happiness with Morris. He turned this hatred against Walter. Kind and candid, Morris's friend and Phoebe's, Walter should have known better. His blindness excluded forgiveness, and Lewis did not forgive him. Three months later, after the portrait of Elizabeth was brought home from the hospital, Lewis immediately noticed its disappearance and discovered that his father had destroyed it. He spoke to no one of what he had learned. Walter must be the first to know; Lewis must tell him. He waited until they met at another funeral to enact this small revenge.

Louisa and Lewis

1938-1963

$\mathcal{S}$ EEING LEWIS IN TROUBLE HELD NO NOVELTY FOR LOUISA. Since infancy he had schooled her in disaster.

When the Lewisons decided to have a child, Owen, although claiming to want a boy, was disappointed by Lewis. Soon afterwards he began saying how sad it was to be an only child, as he had been. Three years later, at Phoebe's birth, Owen saw his true desire satisfied. He devoted himself to her thereafter. Lewis was left to Louisa.

Lewis had already made her suffer. During her second pregnancy he had been afflicted with intermittent fevers that came and went without reason. He might be playing in his room late in the afternoon; Louisa would hear him whimpering and find him flushed and breathless. By nightfall his temperature would reach a hundred, sometimes rising to a hundred and four during the night. Doctors offered baffled diagnoses and prescribed aspirin and orange juice. As long as the fever lasted his head and body ached, he slept fitfully, he threw up most of what he ate. Louisa stayed in his room night and day, cooling him with wet sponges, reading stories, singing songs, talking until she ran out of words.

After three days the fever would abate, leaving Lewis weak and testy. Louisa knew that, at two, he could not be expected to acknowledge her care of him; she was nevertheless pained to find herself blamed for his miseries: "I hurt when *you're* there." Sometimes he would cry when she appeared at his bedside.

Louisa expected to feel surpassing love for a firstborn son. What love she felt was regularly distracted by the conviction that Lewis had come into the world with a nature she would never understand. Louisa found males strange—she even liked their strangeness, at a distance. Owen had proved a special case. Before they married, he had clearly wanted her, and Louisa did not mind that he wanted her in part for her good name and connections: she accepted his suit wholeheartedly, and her commitment to his career after their marriage maintained their mutual trust. Other men bewildered her. She found them full of abstract generosity and practical unkindness, broad-minded towards the world (and their dogs), impatiently suspicious of individuals who disturbed their opinions. Louisa may have been blinkered by the memory of her father, a big, brusque man who had died when she was five, leaving her family poor and herself haunted by a strong, elusive presence.

Even tiny, Lewis looked to her like another mysterious male. Her sense of incomprehension, and its attendant fear of motherly incompetence, made her swear to keep doing her best by him. Failures only renewed her dedication. As a result, her life with him was punctuated with "I must" and "if only." Whatever happened, she must, she must sustain him; and if only, if only she hadn't behaved in this or that way, what had happened might not have; and if only it hadn't happened, Lewis might be different. She never thought, "If only *he* hadn't," no doubt suspecting that such thinking had as its logical *terminus a quo:* if only he hadn't been born.

Fearfulness made Louisa vulnerable. Lewis learned that by demanding and blaming he could get the better of her. He learned, too, that if he could lure her into a shameful business with him, she would forgive him anything. He sensed that Louisa would always protect him from Owen.

At the age of three he discovered how to make a shameful business of his genitals. With tantrums threatened or indulged, he would force Louisa to stay with him when he was in bed or in the bathroom and squeeze his penis in a special, reassuring way. A year later, by then too "reasonable" for such games, he would harry her with questions about his member: "Will it snap off when it's stiff? Momma, promise to tell me if I'm supposed to snap it off?" Until he was almost ten, he would get up at night in tears if she had not come in to secure the bath mitt in which he lodged his penis while he slept.

These tactics reduced Louisa to impotence. She complied with them, concealed them from Owen, and at last found herself depending on them. They became her most reliable evidence that Lewis trusted her and that she could comfort him.

When Lewis was eleven, the Lewisons rented a summer house upstate, in the neighborhood where they would eventually settle. Friends with children of Lewis's age made a place for him on picnics and swimming parties, and after a few days Lewis began bicycling into the summer haze to join his new acquaintances. One day he stayed home. He sat until evening on the porch steps. After that, he never again left the house of his own accord. He spent his afternoons reading comics or hunting through the unfamiliar library for "grown-up" books. On weekends he kept to his room, out of Owen's sight. His gloominess troubled Louisa less than his utter loss of insolence. He offered to help her around the house. He behaved almost gently with her.

One morning, having dispatched him to riding school, Louisa searched Lewis's room. In the bottom drawer of his commode, twenty-two stacked issues of *Action Comics* concealed a sheet of blue-lined paper on which a doggerel poem had been penciled. Three quatrains followed its title, printed in capital letters: TO LEWIS WHO WE LOVE TO HATE. The last quatrain read:

> We think you'd be better off dead, get it?
> Cause you're really sick in the head, get it?
> You think you're sharp as a tack, get it?
> But you're really crazy as a *bat,* get it?

Louisa restored the page to its cache. When Lewis came home, she asked if he had had any problems with his new friends; he fell bitterly silent. Louisa spoke to other parents, who made necessary inquiries. She soon found out what had happened.

A few days before he began his solitary life, Lewis had asked all the boys he knew to meet him at one of their houses. Early in the afternoon, carrying a wicker hamper, he had joined a dozen ten- to twelve-year-olds in the mortifying heat of a third-floor attic.

Lewis had tried to initiate the meeting with a speech about "friendship and courage." No one listened, and he quickly proceeded to the main event. Opening the hamper, he turned it upside down, shook it hard, and kept shaking it until, twenty seconds later, a small bat emerged, soon followed by another. The two bats spent some time fluttering among the tumbling, shouting boys before settling on the darker side of a corner rafter. By then the group had evacuated the attic. Only one ten-year-old remained. He had retreated sobbing to a spot behind a queen post where he still sat clutching his knees, watching incredulously as Lewis, his hands sheathed in electrician's gloves, calmly plucked the bats from their refuge and returned them to the hamper. (Two days before, Lewis, in his own attic, had devoted three turbulent hours to techniques of bat catching.)

When he came downstairs, grinning with pride, Lewis found his group dispersing. Two or three boys whom he addressed replied with scant, nervous words before biking hurriedly away. He had plainly produced an effect; he did not worry what sort of effect until the poem was dropped anonymously into the Lewison mailbox. As far as Lewis was concerned, summer had ended. No boy would now dare to be known as his friend. Lewis felt that he had been cruelly mistreated. He had only wanted to impress the others. Having succeeded in that, he hoped (this he barely admitted to himself) that he might propose to his admiring friends that they all confirm their companionship by masturbating together. It was this half-secret, not-unsociable wish that had inspired him. It did not merit ostracism.

When she learned about the bats, Louisa told herself that the author of the poem was not far off the mark: if not insane, Lewis seemed certifiably strange. He frightened her by what he had done, and no less by his perfect secrecy. Except for borrowing the hamper, he had given her no clue about his undertaking. She could not console him—she was unsure of what he might do in return. Above all, she longed to recover his trust.

Lewis gave her the chance to do so before the summer was over. He went alone into town one morning (something he was forbidden to do) and came back with a foulard by Hermès as a present for her. Suspicious, Louisa asked where he had found the money to pay for it. Lewis told several lies, all of them transparent. He was almost relieved when he had to admit to stealing the scarf.

Louisa lost her temper. To one of her upbringing, shoplifting was the first slippery step to armed robbery and hatchet murders. She slapped Lewis hard—the last time she ever did so. He yelled, "I did it for *you!*" and ran away in tears. Louisa realized that he had in his devious way confided in her. She must not lose him.

She followed him outside, where he had hidden between two lush snowball bushes. The slap had worked. He fell into her arms, sobbing, "I'm sorry, I'm sorry." If she had been less shocked by his thieving, Louisa would have cried too. She hugged him as long as he let her. They walked twice around the house together, her hands on his shoulders. She explained that she must take the scarf back. She would look at other scarves, slip it among them, pretend to choose his, and pay for it; she could then keep his present. She made Lewis promise never to steal again and, if he did, to tell her at once. She did not mention his father.

In this manner Lewis implicated his mother in the first of many thefts, making her his ally against Owen, against a world both respectable and hostile, against his own ordinary yearnings. Her involvement enabled him to steal with zest. He knew that if the worst happened, she would suffer the consequences. Sometimes the worst did happen; and whenever he was caught, Louisa duly appeared to soft-soap the store owner, or floor manager, or policeman. Neither mother nor son ever acknowledged that they felt happiest together after these dramas.

Thieving brought Lewis another advantage: possessions. He learned that by threatening to steal an expensive object he could, once he convinced her that he craved it, make Louisa give him enough money to buy it. (He sometimes stole it anyway.) Cultural items like books and classical records best suited this blackmail, and Lewis assembled a library and a record collection remarkable for one his age. On his own, he acquired, among other things, two hundred and ten packages of chewing gum, a hundred and sixty-nine Tootsie Rolls, ninety-eight bananas, oranges, and apples, seventy-six pens and pencils, eighteen neckties, seven bottles of French perfume (although three were open samples), and five six-packs. His grandest failures included a top hat at Tripler's and a multipurpose electric tool kit at Sears; his proudest triumphs, a small dress sword filched under the malevolent eyes of a Third Avenue pawnbroker and a first edition of *Madame Bovary*, which he spent twenty harrowing minutes slowly shifting from the depths of Brentano's, rack by rack, until, reaching the sidewalk of Fifth Avenue, he made a four-block dash with it into obscurity.

He told Louisa about most of his thefts, only neglecting to mention those too trifling to outrage her. He ultimately sought outrage rather than complicity, and he discovered after two years that his achievements left him dissatisfied, because Louisa invariably proved kind. Lewis had a secret hope and fear: that Louisa, at last turning against him, would inflict the punishment he deserved—leave him to the police, send him to a military academy, tell Owen. Louisa's governing rule, however, was to keep her crazy boy within eyeshot. She did not really care what he did, as long as he stayed hers—hers to watch, to listen to, to mollify, to save from his craziness. She scolded, complained, threatened, and always bought him off. After weeks of argument, she let him keep *Madame Bovary*. (He had made a rare choice, and she hated Brentano's.) Where Lewis was concerned, the observant Owen noticed nothing.

In Lewis's eyes, each kindness of Louisa's reshaped her into a likeness of the Connecticut cousin who had loved him for his rudeness; each kindness made her less dependable. In this he judged her unfairly (Louisa was consistency itself) and resented her sincerely: she had abdicated her parental function of providing pain.

After four years, their complicity ended.

The Lewisons continued to vacation upstate in spite of Lewis's unhappy summer. In time his unhappiness waned. The bats passed into half-spooky, half-glamorous legend. One day in July, when he was fifteen, members of an unfamiliar gang noticed the solitary Lewison boy and decided to adopt him. Fearing trickery, Lewis acted petulant and unresponsive. The others laughed at him and said they needed a good sorehead. Even when Lewis had come to enjoy these funny companions, he never left himself unprepared for some cruel joke they might be playing on him.

One of the gang, a girl a year younger than Lewis, openly pursued him. She persisted in spite of his overt mistrust of her. She biked at his side, let him dunk her when they went swimming, and retrieved his nasty comments good-naturedly ("Just because I like you, Groucho, doesn't make me all bad"). One evening, while they sat together at the movies, she rested her head on his shoulder. An hour later Lewis kissed her. He pressed his jaws against hers, not feeling much, excited by the idea of kissing. He knew he should try for more.

Behind his parents' house lay a farm, whose barn he had often explored. Lewis brought the girl there two days later. Piled to the tie beams with new hay, the high building was deserted, as he knew it would be at four o'clock on a steamy August afternoon. They settled in a corner, night-black after the summer sunlight, and embraced between a cliff of hay and a tar-scented wall. Lewis kissed her harder and harder. After a while she let him squeeze her small breasts, then asked to go outside. Lewis held her. She complained. He did not know what to do. She would not let him touch her elsewhere, she wouldn't touch him. He wrestled her to the ground and lay on top of her, rubbing against her, trying to pull down her shorts, poking inside them. The girl tried to bite him. Both were gasping and sweating in that close corner. Dust from ancient harvests, roused from the barn floor, drifted into their nostrils and eyes. Lewis went on thrashing against her, unwilling to stop. The girl began sniveling. She was frightened: no light, seemingly less and less air, Lewis hurting her with his elbows and hips. She took a deep breath to scream and choked on dry hay-dust,

coughing wretchedly. She shit in her pants. Lewis smelled it.
The girl had begun to utter faint spasmodic cries when he ran
away.

Louisa was standing in front of the barn door. She had
noticed the two bicycles while walking by. Lewis did not speak
to her as he mounted his bicycle to sprint off through the
cornfields. Louisa found the girl inside the barn and brought
her to the house to bathe and change. She made tea and talked
to her. Louisa had no problems with women, whatever their
age. She soothed the girl. Learning what had happened, she
spoke of her chronic difficulties with Lewis. The girl had grown
calm, almost content with their secrets by the time Louisa
drove her home.

Louisa found Lewis waiting for her when she returned. He
was wet-eyed with impatience. Once he knew that she had
talked with the girl, he would not let her speak, fitfully splutter-
ing forth his resentment: his life was none of her business, she
should stay out of it, for good. . . . He ran off the porch,
slamming the screen door with a bouncy clatter.

Louisa understood that the violence choking him did not
represent shame for his assault. The girl had told her, "He
didn't really do anything, but he got so wild trying." She had
felt in danger less of rape than of Lewis's incapacity for it. He
was ashamed to have his mother know this. He wanted never
to face her again.

He stuck to his aversion and kept beyond Louisa's reach. He
stopped speaking to her about stealing (in truth, he stole no
more). In the years that followed he clung fiercely to an absurd
position: he was helpless to prevent his parents from condition-
ing his life, and at the same time they had nothing to do with
him. Louisa supposed that he would have given up eating if he
had thought it put him in her debt. Lewis claimed that he owed
his parents nothing, and that they owed him everything in
compensation for the circumstances to which they condemned

him. Louisa's concern and affection demonstrated only minimal decency, nothing to her credit and no help to him. How could she help him in his pursuit of philosophical consistency, political integrity, or whatever other distant goal he had most recently set himself?

For eight years, Louisa depended on Phoebe for information about her son. She respected her children's intimacy. Fearful of weakening it, she never pressed her daughter to tell more than she volunteered; so her knowledge remained limited while her anxiety grew large. She worried about Lewis's social life (he never brought a friend home); about his love life (she thought he was homosexual—was he at least homosexual?); about his future (bleak); about his relations with his father. His life offered her little not to worry about. He seemed locked inside himself—a place that he enjoyed no more than any other.

If, month after month, Louisa kept speculating about her son, she never guessed at his career as a practicing masochist. The crucifixion raid devastated what trust she still had in her own insight and gave her anxiety something real to gnaw on. After she rushed to Lewis's side and he fled from her, she began spending much of her time in the city. She was determined to stay near him, hovering just out of his sight, hoping that she could stave off the next catastrophe. She feared for his life.

Morris's friendship with Lewis dismayed her because the more Lewis saw Morris, the less he saw Phoebe, and the less Louisa knew about him. She wanted to believe Phoebe's assertion that Morris was working miracles on Lewis's behalf. To Louisa, however, the crucifixion had proved her son insane, and she did not see how anyone could change that. Morris might have reassured her if she had approached him; Lewis's unpredictable reactions made her afraid to risk that. She went on worrying about Lewis, rarely seeing him, pleased when she knew what he was doing, disheartened when she didn't, her imagination then inflating itself with volatile, inaccurate terrors.

One evening in late May, getting out of a taxi in front of the Washington Square apartment house where she was dining, Louisa saw Phoebe walking by. Heading for Macdougal Street, Phoebe did not look at Louisa or turn at the sound of her name. Anyone except Louisa would have been concerned for Phoebe; Louisa thought, what has happened to Lewis? When she called her an hour later and Phoebe failed to answer, she knew that something awful had happened. Louisa bravely telephoned Morris. At first his number did not answer either; it then rang busy for a full ten minutes. Louisa left her dinner and hurried across Sixth Avenue to Cornelia Street. At the door of Morris's building she pushed intercom buzzers until she found a tenant willing to let her in. She climbed the two flights to the apartment and began ringing the bell. A voice resounded far inside— perhaps shouting, she thought; she couldn't make out the words. She kept ringing and knocking. The man who had let her in came down for a look, a woman in a gym suit appeared on the stairs below. They think I'm bonkers, Louisa thought, but I'm doing the right thing.

The voice inside kept calling out. No one came to open the door. Outside she heard a siren approaching, a second and a third, each swelling to soprano frenzy before declining in a long, laggard wail. Downstairs the building door opened to thudding feet. She was surrounded by cops and unhatted firemen. Exquisitely, they lifted her to one side, then attacked Morris's door with an ax, a sledgehammer, and two crowbars. When it sprang from its hinges, Louisa was trembling with dread and eagerness.

She quickly got inside. Two objects lay on the living-room floor in a litter of newspapers: Morris's body and a long shattered stone, which four firemen promptly surrounded, chipping carefully at its black fragments. Louisa bent over Morris. He looked distracted, did not answer her, seemed not to breathe. She knew what to do. She began blowing air through the parted lips.

A policeman pulled Louisa away, led her to the large, wide-open window, and held her there. She started to lose control and swore loudly. She twisted her head around and saw Lewis lying among chunks of black stone. She screamed. Two white-suited males forced her onto a stretcher and strapped her to it; another man adroitly needled a vein in her left forearm. Louisa woke up in a hospital room on the East Side.

She was still drowsy when, late the following morning, a visitor was announced. She was surprised to see Lewis: "You're all right? It's darling of you to come here. Wherever here may be."

"You need someone to sign you out—this is the nut ward. Phoebe's on her way, but I thought I'd speed things up."

"*Thank* you. How is Morris?" Louisa asked—a lying question. She knew she'd breathed into a dead mouth.

"He had a heart attack. He died right in front of me."

"Lewis, I'm so . . ." Tears were rising fast.

"What the fuck were you doing there?"

"I didn't know . . . Phoebe wouldn't talk to me." She sniffled into a bouquet of Kleenex. "I'm sorry. It was hard enough for you without my . . . Thank you for coming, I don't deserve it. I *am* sorry."

"You don't deserve it, and you're not why I'm here."

"You said, so I could get out?"

"I'm trying to contain the damage. I hope you leave the hospital, go home, and shut up. Let's say you don't answer the phone for a week."

She recognized Lewis's manner, not its present motive: "Lewis, I just don't understand."

"Remember the policemen at Morris's last night? Policemen like to file reports. Some hotshot young prosecutor with a flea up his ass held a press conference this morning. He made, shall we say, selective use of the reports. There was Morris, there was me, somebody was buried in cement, but he didn't say who, just 'one of the parties.' And, big surprise, a certain Mrs. Lewison

Irene and Walter

MAY - AUGUST 1962

B ECAUSE HIS SHOWS AT THE KRAMER GALLERY MADE WAL-
ter Trale famous, many assumed that Irene Kramer had discovered him. In fact he came to her late, less than a year before
Morris died, with almost thirty years of painting behind him.

Irene had heard of him long before and had seen his paintings in group shows and in private collections. She had never
found an opportunity to assess his work as a whole.

Although Irene was only thirty-four when she opened her
gallery uptown, she had been selling art for twelve years, ever
since she had finished four terms of art history at the New
School—all the formal training she was to have. She had paid
her way doing part-time secretarial work. Her father, who had
started as an usher and who owned six movie theaters when he
retired, might have paid for studies in law or medicine or business; to him, art dealing meant high risks and uncertain returns.
He underestimated his daughter: Irene could have succeeded in

almost any career she chose. She had intelligence and ambition, and she usually knew what she wanted. (She had, as well, a diminutive, perfectly restrained hourglass figure and a pretty face to which wide brown eyes could sometimes lend a melting beauty.)

While at the New School Irene met Mark Kramer, ten years her senior, a prosperous public accountant with a weakness for high culture. He persuaded her to leave the Bronx. From their brief marriage she learned that the sexual sincerity of the male may have capture and imprisonment as its covert goal. Mark soon wanted her staying at home being her wonderful self, not caring if that self demanded more. After her second year of study, Irene went to work as an assistant at Martha Jackson's. This meant not going with Mark to Europe, to the Bahamas, to Sun Valley. She could see little point in this, he in that. When they were divorced, in 1952, she told him, "Don't pay me alimony, give me a lump sum. We'll both benefit." His calculations proved her right. He borrowed the money she wanted. He felt so grateful that for five years he paid her rent.

Irene began buying paintings, which she sold from her apartment. She chiefly handled Europeans—Americans then were still condemned to being either too famous (and too expensive) or unknown. Since she had to recoup her investments in the short term, she left discovering the undiscovered till later. She struck some profitable deals; notably, in her first year, the purchase for six thousand dollars of twenty-two Klee gouaches (a year later she sold two of them for the same amount). It took her five years to establish herself as a reliable dealer, with access to works she wanted to sell and customers on whom she could depend. She then opened a small gallery on Sixth Avenue south of Fifty-sixth Street, financing it with her personal collection as collateral. The gallery barely sustained itself commercially, but it brought her into the public eye, and she made an enviable reputation for herself through her farsighted choice of painters.

(Irene claimed that a good dealer had to know how to "buy potential"—had to know how to see, in paintings actually looked at, work not yet imagined even by the artist himself.) In the fall of 1961, when she gathered twenty of her best clients and presented her plan for a new and larger gallery, they backed her without hesitation.

Morris's essay on Walter appeared in *New Worlds* the following May. He had already urged Irene to sign on this painter whose talent had been proved and who had not yet become fashionable. Irene had taken her younger brother seriously and also a little skeptically—she had seen his earlier enthusiasms wax and wane. When Morris's article was published and acclaimed (it was chosen for that year's *Trends in American Painting*), Irene decided to take a careful look at Walter's work.

What she had seen of it she admired, and if she had avoided it professionally, that had to do with commerce, not art. Walter wore his originality strangely; he was a master in disguise, even if he wore the disguise of a master. He could not be classed as an abstractionist, even when he most resembled one. His figuration had a disturbing offhand look, with none of the starkness of Hopper and Sheeler or the stylization of Lichtenstein. Now that Irene had started her new gallery, Walter's eccentricity ceased to be an obstacle. She had originally become a dealer to encourage new art. She could now do so.

Because she liked Walter's work, Irene had imagined that she already knew it, forgetting that an occasional painting provides poor insight into an artist's universe. Irene spent a week assembling in her mind a complete Trale retrospective and found herself increasingly fascinated the more she saw. She started at Walter's gallery, then visited collectors, including those with work from his animal years, and concluded her tour at his studio. Walter had kept for himself over a hundred paintings and at least a thousand drawings, many of them among his best. Irene spent a long afternoon in their midst. When she was done, she knew that she had discovered a world that revealed more than talent and intelligence and imagination. Walter's originality resembled that of original sin. He had reinvented the act of painting itself.

Walter kept away during Irene's visit, letting Phoebe play hostess. The two women spoke little. Irene was absorbed in her study; Phoebe knew better than to distract her. As she left, Irene said, "He's better than anything I can say about him. I'll be in touch soon."

Walter had never cared much for public success, which he'd already known as a boy. He had never lacked confidence in his abilities. For twenty-five years he had been satisfied with earning enough to pay for his big studio and the parties he liked to throw in it. Now his attitude was changing. Morris's article had affected him too. The art market was starting to boom. Painters half his worth were selling for twice his price. If his time was to come, he wanted it to be now. Irene had opportunely appeared. Phoebe's account of her visit exhilarated him.

He waited for news. None came. He phoned her gallery. She was busy. She did not return his call. Three days later, he called again. Irene was out. "Walter *who?*" her secretary inquired. Next morning Irene did phone and made matters worse. Her careful praise of his work sounded like a checklist of routine compliments. She mysteriously concluded that this was not the moment to talk business: "I can't explain why. You can probably guess."

Walter could not possibly guess. In her enthusiasm Irene had made the familiar mistake of assuming that the man was as clever as the artist. Her remarks aimed at efficacy and discretion; to Walter, after ten days of silence, they signified indifference. He reacted morosely. His thrill of expectation grew sour with disappointment. With resentment as well: he felt his good will had been abused.

Walter found an explanation for this injustice when he stopped at his gallery the following day. His dealer was out—

not surprising at two o'clock in the afternoon. The surprise was that he was lunching with Irene. Walter was informed by the admiring young assistant that they were meeting for the third time. "It's all about you, isn't it?" She would not tell him more. Walter jumped to a conclusion founded wholly on suspicion: the two dealers were conspiring against him. Irene knew that in her gallery his work would fetch higher prices. She had not signed him on because she was planning to buy his paintings from his present dealer and resell them. The two dealers would split her markup. Since Walter would be no better off than before, they were keeping him in the dark.

As he paced along dank, warm streets that afternoon, these thoughts kindled Walter's mind with ever-brightening hostility. At home, he called his dealer, who only said, "*You're* asking *me* what's happening?" Walter never considered that the other man's curtness might be justified. It simply confirmed his suspicions and enabled him to savor in earnest his role as intended victim.

He decided to let his enemies complacently elaborate their scheme. His pleasure in wrecking it would be all the greater. His patience proved short-lived. A few days later an elderly friend from his *animalier* days took him out to lunch uptown. As Walter sat down, he saw Irene and Morris at a table on the far side of the restaurant. Throughout the meal he observed them busily conversing, so engrossed with one another they did not notice him until they were leaving. Morris then waved connivingly; Irene blushed as she smiled at him. As well she might: Walter saw at once that the conspiracy to exploit him had broadened. The critic who had rediscovered his work would now promote it and so merit a wedge of pie. And they hadn't even bothered to shake hands with him! Their nonchalance made Walter especially bitter. He refrained from venting his outrage to his lunch companion only by silently deciding to intervene.

As he walked the fifty-two blocks to his studio, he realized that Morris's complicity aggrieved him most. He scarcely knew Irene; perhaps she had a tougher character than he'd imagined. He knew his dealer well enough. Walter liked in him above all his pleasant lack of ambition; if Irene had proposed an easy way to make money, he might understandably be tempted. Walter felt passionate respect for Morris. He thought him bright, eloquent, fervently committed to a rare idea of art held by few artists and fewer critics. Because of this commitment, Morris's essay on his work had convinced Walter that they shared an intense if impersonal affinity. Walter had been understood; he had been assigned the place he deserved, at the dark, sharp point of invention. That Morris could exploit what he had so intimately perceived jarred Walter painfully.

He called Morris and suggested that he come to the studio at ten-thirty the next morning. The suggestion had the ring of a summons. Morris deferentially ignored the tone and accepted.

Having overheard the phone call, Phoebe asked Walter what was wrong. For the first time he related his fantasy to someone else. As he spoke, he reminded her of Lewis, at age eight, on the verge of a fit. Wondering how many cocktails had preceded lunch, she did not dare speak her mind.

In the morning, she found Walter still sheathed in glum determination. Letting Morris in, Phoebe gave him a trouble-in-paradise look that pinched the smooth space between his brows. Walter mutely motioned him to a chair by the dining table, which had been cleared of everything except the telephone. Facing Morris across the table, Walter solemnly lifted the handset and dialed.

"Gavin Breitbart, please, Walter Trale calling," he declared, adding in ominous sotto voce, "My lawyer." He cleared his throat: "Gavin?" Standing painfully straight, he began delivering into the mouthpiece a long statement obviously, if inadequately, rehearsed. His voice reminded Morris of someone from the past—Senator Claghorn?

" . . . a very grave breach of professional ethics, which I want you to start proceedings in the matter. . . ."

Walter stared belligerently at Morris while he listed his grievances: Irene's duplicity, her conspiracy with his dealer, her plan to include Morris as a highbrow publicity agent.

Listening to him, Phoebe wished she had gone to New Mexico. Morris was emerging from perplexity into half-credulous mirth. No one could have taken Walter seriously if self-righteousness were not so crassly distorting his benevolent mug. When Morris heard himself personally implicated, he bent over and cut the connection: "Stop. Stop before they come and cart you off. What have you been sniffing—Drāno?" Walter scowled. Phoebe stared at her toes. Morris went on: "Listen, maestro, Irene wants you in her shop. She didn't like cutting out your dealer, so she offered him a percentage for the next couple of years."

"Exactly."

"No, not exactly. It's out of her pocket."

"Says who?"

"She does." (The phone rang: "Oh, Gavin . . . Later, OK?") "Your dealer's a piggy. He keeps upping the ante. She even thought of making him a partner. But that's finished."

"How come?"

"No contract, I believe. Irene got fed up. *He* suggested cutting your share, you know. She says screw him."

"Yeah, and not just him."

"Walter, can't you grasp that she's mad for you? Look, I knew something was up, so I told her to drop in. You'll see."

"That's what *you* say. Why don't you admit you're in cahoots? I saw you the other day. What are you, lovers?"

"As I live and bleed! *A,* I'm queer. *B,* she's my sister."

"Kramer?" Walter leaned one thigh against the table.

"Her ex."

The doorbell rang. Phoebe admitted Irene. Morris said to

Walter, "Don't forget Gavin. He may have an emergency patrol on the way."

"OK—he*llo,*" Walter said to Irene, "something I have to clear up." He was reddening. A moment later he was telling his lawyer, "It was a mistake. Forget it. It doesn't matter—no, the name *doesn't* matter. Listen to me. Well . . . Kramer." Lowering his voice, he turned his back to the others. They stood there politely hushed, except for Phoebe, prey to the giggles. "Look, I'm not alone . . ." Walter's voice petered out. He glanced at the others—Irene patiently watching him, Morris shaking his head, Phoebe red with restraint. He hung up. "Coffee? Beer?" He ran both hands through his hair. Irene gazed at him in nascent consternation. Walter was breaking into a sweat. "Irene, there's something I think—"

"Not a word!" Morris interrupted. "We'll never tell, will we, Phoebe? Not for lox and bagels!" Phoebe nodded as she wiped her eyes.

Irene said, "Mr. Trale, Morris thought this might be a good time to see you. Phoebe's told you how extraordinary I think your work is? I apologize for having taken so long to find that out. I'd love to show you—I'd like to give you *two* shows, back to back. A retrospective first, then new work. I can do well by you, I promise. I don't have to be told that you'll do well by me. Just having you under my roof would be a blessing."

She had spoken plainly and earnestly. Her low voice soothed Walter. He gulped her words down like lemonade in a hot spell. He made a few appreciative noises until he was again overcome by an awareness of his folly and began shaking his head in retrospective consternation. When he next looked at Irene, he realized that she was still speaking to him:

" . . . No? *You'd* rather?"

"I'm sorry—"

Morris reminded him, "Walter, it's *over.* "

Irene resumed: "What I was suggesting is, I've been having

trouble with your curmudgeon of a dealer, but if *you* agree, I can certainly come to terms. I can take care of all that, if you like."

"Great!" Walter replied. He stared at her as though he had rediscovered his beloved elephant. The bell again rang, and Phoebe went to the door: Priscilla stood there, thesis in hand.

Walter never even saw her. He went on staring at Irene, who was turning the faintest shade of pink. It occurred to him that she might like to sit down. "Coffee? Beer? Please don't call me Mr. Trale. It makes me feel older."

"You *are* older, Walter," Irene replied, with a most agreeable chuckle. She was pleased to have secured this fine painter, pleased that he was so likable—a nice, big baby. "Thanks, I can't stay—I don't *want* to stay, because I'm going to your gallery right now and settle things. I'm making sure you don't get away from me."

"Who'd ever think of doing that?"

Morris and Phoebe might have been in Manitoba. Walter was immersed in his abrupt conviction that Irene should take complete charge of him. "I'll come with you. The three of us can work it out together."

Morris said, "Leave it to the pros. You'll just work up a froth."

Irene remained silent. Her smile—warm, faintly condescending—was filling Walter with concupiscent awe. "You're right," he agreed, at once asking Irene: "So I'll see you later?"

"I'll phone you as quick as I can."

"No, I mean *see* you. How about dinner?"

Phoebe shook her head. Even Lewis at four had never sounded so demanding. "Say please!" she whispered. Irene's smile widened; Morris pursed his lips.

Walter refused to be distracted: "What *about* dinner?"

"Walter," Morris chided, "this isn't Schenectady."

"What? Well—tomorrow? How about—"

"All right," said Irene. "The day *after* tomorrow. Meet me at the gallery at seven." Morris reflected that she had found a humane way of liberating them all.

Two days later, Walter arrived at the Kramer Gallery early, a bouquet of sweet william in one hand. Irene told him, "I'm pooped. Can we have a drink here and go straight to dinner? I reserved at the Polo Lounge, in the Westbury. Ever eat there? You'll love it, although not necessarily the food, but you'll need a tie. I bought you this"—a strip of raw blue silk.

Walter formed no opinion of the restaurant. When not perfunctorily swallowing food, he sat with one forearm thrust across the table and the other perched on the back of the banquette, staring at Irene. She herself sat upright and still, folding her hands between courses, glancing sideways at Walter with smiles of affectionate amusement. At first, for his sake, she had tried to smile less—she smiled as though watching a doddering colt. He didn't mind.

Walter was doing his best to be adorable. He hurriedly drank enough to break down his own reticence. He laughed often; tears sprang to his eyes readily when a thought moved him; he disparaged and praised himself without affectation; he listened to Irene's words with conspicuous attention. Walter wanted to know Irene almost as greedily as he wanted her to know him. He failed to see that she knew him already, that he could do nothing to make her like him more.

She did not mind his courting her, although his method seemed startlingly direct, like a puppy rolling over to have its belly scratched. Colts and puppies made for fondness, not desire. She decided that disappointing him no less directly would prove the greatest kindness. When he reached over to stroke her arm, she tartly exclaimed, "You're not going to make a pass at me!"

Walter's eyes shone with relief. She had been the one to broach the hot, imminent subject. "Baby, I've never wanted anyone so much!"

She saw that it would take more than hints to discourage him. "You'll get over it, Mr. Trale! I may not have many rules, but there's one that I swear by: never go to bed with an artist. *Certainly* not one of mine."

"And every rule has its exception, right?"

"Not after seven years. My God, if Norman Bluhm ever thought I was seeing you—" Walter laughed. Irene saw that she would have to speak more bluntly: "You don't interest me sexually. Not at all. And I like you. If you have enough sense to understand that, we can have a nice time."

"Maybe you'll change your mind. I can wait." He hardly seemed willing to wait. For the rest of dinner he refused to talk about anything else. Irene finally heaved a great sigh of exasperation (Walter thought: I'm getting to her) and said, "Let's move out of here."

"I'll ask for the check."

"It's been taken care of."

"I invited *you*—"

"In my league, the dealer does the inviting. Where would you like to go?"

"Wherever you say."

"Your place?"

"Yes," Walter gasped.

"It's on my way. I'll drop you." She did not forget the sweet william.

Irene refused to date Walter again. She soon learned that this decision was putting her freedom and perhaps her career in jeopardy. Walter visited the gallery once a day, sometimes twice. He phoned her morning, noon, night, and in between. He tirelessly restated his longing and shared all his thoughts and feelings, which new love was delivering daily by the gross.

Irene agreed to another dinner if Walter would leave her in peace. Their evening together turned out better than she dared hope, even though it took place in Walter's studio, even though they spent it alone. (The other hypothetical guests never appeared; Phoebe vamoosed between drinks and the cleaning woman's jambalaya.) It happened that when Walter turned on the oven, the pilot light had gone out. Lowering a match towards the burner, he ignited a soft explosion that frizzled his forward scalp and reduced his eyebrows to stubble. He thereupon withdrew into a mortified sulk, as obstinate as his lustful state and far less obnoxious.

On another evening Irene even let him take her home. She first subjected him to a demanding social round: a gallery opening, two cocktail parties, a long, late supper together. Only then, after Walter had drunk more than any stag's fill, did Irene maliciously invite him to her apartment. Walter, beaming like a prize student, didn't know what he should do with his diploma and had two more double scotches to find out. He woke up the next morning on the sofa with a friendly note pinned to his shirt instructing him in the use of Irene's coffee maker.

Walter tricked the gallery receptionist into revealing that Irene was to spend the following weekend in a resort town upstate. He followed her there but could not track her down, and in consequence he found no pleasure in a place full of old friends and memories—he stayed with Mr. Pruell, one of his first patrons; here, twenty-six years before, Elizabeth had transformed his life. Monday, in the city once again, Irene refused to relinquish her secret: "We all need a place to hide. Except you, I suppose."

Irene told him she would be busy through the coming week. Walter took the news calmly. He had a plan. Irene loved classical music; a highly touted performance of the Verdi *Requiem* was to take place at Tanglewood the following Saturday; Walter would ask Irene to drive up for it. He first had to reserve accommodations. Pleasurably furnished adjoining rooms were not easily found in that season. Fortunately, a family canceled at an inn in West Stockbridge.

Irene accepted his proposal. "What a great idea! We'll stay

at the Broffs' in Lenox." Walter mentioned the inn. "Save your bread. No, wait: let me check if there's an extra bed. They'll always find a corner for me." The Broffs were full up.

They arrived in Lenox at noon. At the Broffs', Walter verified the presence of three houseguests. Lunch turned into a winy meal attended by four more guests, after which the entire party removed early to Tanglewood, where they claimed a swath of field directly in front of the shed and settled on rugs and blankets spread out in a profusion worthy of a Caucasian tribe. Walter sat down next to Irene.

A couple of his neighbors stretched out on their backs. Walter followed their example. It was a cool, sunny day. He listened languidly to the gossip around him. When the talk stopped, he sat up to join in the applause for the musicians and then once more lay down. Summer sun warmed him from his crown to his soles. Soon the sound of voices and instruments began surging over him gently, like banks of warm fog. He paid little attention to the music: he had come here for Irene. He took care nevertheless to prevent his vagrant mind from deluding him into sleep. Sleep felt as tempting as a mud-bed to a hippopotamus, and he would not disappoint her so childishly.

His thoughts pursued images of a landscape consisting entirely of her. Today she had seduced him once again. Behind saucer-large mauve lenses her eyes glinted like birds vanishing through a screen of leaves. Her small, ripe body chided his attention under billows of buff and beige. He ached to unwrap her. He began an enjoyable game: imagining her body, he let quiet passages of music suggest an unveiling of it, louder ones still closer involvements. The sun warmed his delectations.

He was swimming through warm and enchanted seas like a happy, solitary seal; and he hardly felt a quiver of surprise when he sensed something like a responsive caress, as though the point of his pleasure had been dreamily handled.

He recalled where he was and opened his eyes. A cashmere

shawl Irene had been carrying lay across his hips, in the shape of a fore-Alp. Irene herself sat gazing intently towards the performers as they stormed into the *Dies irae*. Her fingers were locked tightly together, she had decisively sucked her faintly trembling lower lip between her teeth.

Walter loudly groaned. Surely he had reached an age when he could keep his fly buttoned? He briefly longed for a dagger or an icepick to plunge into his chest. With death not readily available, he resorted to flight. Gathering as he rose the shawl around his impenitent erection, he started racing across the sunlit expanse, thick with human obstacles that he skirted with immediate expertise, like an ace slalomist or broken-field runner. He did not slow down until he had reached the city and his own studio.

For several mornings he woke up to spasms of shame, as though shame were a cat poised to leap onto his belly the moment he emerged from sleep. He did not leave his studio until Tuesday. When, early that afternoon, he appeared at the Kramer Gallery, Irene led him straight into her office. Closing the door behind her, she sat down on a leather couch and motioned Walter to sit next to her. As she observed his thunder-head countenance, she found herself smiling once again.

"I thought I'd better bring this back."

Irene accepted the shawl. "What happened to you?"

"Oh, nothing. I just wanted to die. I still do."

"Why did you run away? No one minded. *Au contraire,* we all found you very impressive."

Walter looked up at her. If it pained him to have his anguish made fun of, Irene's forgiving him offered delicious solace. He managed a small laugh. "It was all for you, you know." He looked helplessly into her brown eyes. She said nothing. He unzipped his jeans and pulled forth a now wizened penis. "It still is. It's all yours."

Irene blushed and went on smiling. "Oh, my dear!" She

shook her head. Walter took her right hand and laid his member in its palm, where it rested still as a mouse. "My dear!" she said again. "So small, so sweet!" Bending over, she brushed her lips across it, with the faint smack of a childhood kiss. Someone knocked at the door. Walter made way for business.

That evening Irene disappeared. For four weeks, almost until the end of August, she could be found neither at work nor at home. Walter pestered her friends, in vain; not even his own friends would help him, not even Phoebe.

In early August he learned that Irene was staying at a secret retreat upstate. He learned no more than that. Irene remained safe with Louisa, the old and still-dear friend who had promised to shelter her for as long as was necessary from her distracted suitor.

Priscilla and Walter

JUNE 1962-APRIL 1963

PRISCILLA WAS FIFTEEN WHEN SHE FIRST HEARD OF
Walter. Old Mr. Pruell was showing her portraits of horses he'd
owned. He spoke of the man who painted them with a warmth
that made Priscilla curious.

"He was about your age. A natural."

"Does he still paint horses?"

"He's still painting. He makes a living at it. A nice man."

"Does he still paint horses?"

"No, he doesn't. He'd have been a millionaire. But he wanted
to be a success as a, well, regular painter. It wasn't easy for him.
Funny: he could manage stallions or rabbits, but give him a
plate of apples, or a human being, and he didn't know where
to start. Elizabeth changed all that."

Of course Priscilla wanted to hear about Elizabeth.

"She was a few years older than Walter, and very sharp.
Attractive, too—big and handsome and graceful as a cat. She

loved horses. Walter met her at the track one day, and I think he thought she was part horse. By the second race they were thick as thieves. Just good friends, though, they never went— they never fell in love. She had exactly what he needed—she was a *human* animal. She posed for him every day for the next week or two. He must have done dozens of sketches, and finally he painted her portrait in oils."

Priscilla found the anecdote irresistibly romantic, even if Elizabeth and Walter had remained just friends. During the years that followed, she often asked family friends about them; and she had accumulated considerable lore by the time her professor of art history in college told her that Walter was destined for fame. Priscilla's teacher, who had already nourished Phoebe's interest in Walter, differed radically in her attitudes from the well-to-do families among which Priscilla had grown up. That Walter should be admired both by her and, for instance, by Mr. Pruell lent weight to Priscilla's sentimental fascination with him. Walter migrated from a world of fantasy and elderly reminiscence into that of flesh-and-blood heroes, among basketball stars, actors, and presidential candidates. Priscilla agreed to make him the subject of her senior thesis.

Learning and thinking about Walter almost convinced Priscilla that she already knew him. (She would later enjoy claiming that her thesis had brought them together.) As her knowledge of his work increased, she consistently translated it into terms she could call her own. Priscilla treated paintings like doors: she wanted to know what lay behind them. She sensed the power in Walter's art, and she could not accept that its source might be evident in the paint itself. It was to be found, she thought, in some extraordinary experience that the painting expressed. Thus she developed her theory of Walter and Woman.

Priscilla expected her thesis to bring her access to Walter. Her expectation was strengthened when Phoebe became Walter's assistant. Even if she and Phoebe were not close friends, they had known each other since childhood, they had gone to the same college, and as young women starting out in the world they were disposed to helping one another. With Phoebe as go-between, Priscilla looked forward to meeting Walter without delay.

Priscilla called Phoebe up soon after her graduation. Phoebe said that she would gladly give Walter "The Female Figure in Recent American Art." Priscilla should drop it off at her studio the following Tuesday. Priscilla asked, couldn't she give it to Walter herself? When was he usually home? What was he like? Was Phoebe having an affair with him? Phoebe told her, "I can't invite you in right away. One of my jobs is keeping people out. Wait till he reads it, then I'll fix something up."

Priscilla did not want to wait. One morning she showed up with her thesis at Walter's studio, where Walter was busy falling in love with Irene.

Priscilla apologized to Phoebe later that day, deploring her own ruse so frankly that she made Phoebe laugh. Priscilla knew better than to try again. Soon afterwards a new way of approaching Walter presented itself.

Going back to her parents' home upstate, Priscilla learned that Walter was visiting nearby. He had come only for the weekend, and he left Mr. Pruell's before she could catch him. She felt certain, however, that if he came back, she could instigate a meeting.

In August Walter returned for two weeks. Priscilla told Maud and Allan that she wanted to meet him, and they agreed to get her invited to any social events Walter might attend. Three such events occurred. At the first, Walter failed to appear. At the second, she spotted him across a crowded expanse of lawn; he had gone before she could reach him. At the third, she accosted him promptly, with a mutual friend to introduce them. Priscilla was wearing a dress of clinging silk jersey, its

pale ground stamped with bold geometrical figures that enhanced the gentler lines of her young body. Walter looked
briefly at the dress. When he raised his eyes, they stared
through hers as towards some distant thing—the ghost of Irene.
He spoke to Priscilla distractedly.

She was more disillusioned than disappointed. Priscilla knew
she pleased men; Walter's lack of response made her doubt not
herself but him. She had never imagined that the Genius might
be a jerk. She dismissed her interest in him as adolescent day-
dreaming.

Summer ended—Priscilla's last long student vacation. She
looked back on it without regret. In early September she visited
the city, staying at her parents' apartment. She declared that
she had come to look for work, although privately she felt
uncertain what kind of work she might profitably attempt.

One evening, after a day of listless job hunting, she stopped
at the Westbury for a drink. In the Polo Lounge, settled in a
raised enclosure some distance from the windows, she observed
through their high panes the allegretto traffic of Madison Avenue. It was almost eight o'clock. First lights winked on in the
slowly fading dusk. The men passing by still wore jackets of
pale gabardine or seersucker, the women chemises of crisp
linen, earth-brown or olive-green. Priscilla shivered with yearning for the city around her, a yearning to belong. What part
could she ever hope to play in this alluring, forbidding world?
From the table next to hers a male voice unexpectedly addressed her: "It's magic out there, isn't it?"

Priscilla had been enjoying her solitary gin-and-tonic. Purs-
ing her lips, she turned a look of definitive contempt on her
neighbor, who was Walter. No line of her expression wavered
as she recognized him. He did not recognize her. He winced
under the look and continued to smile and even speak. "It sort
of makes the locals look good."

She stared at him disdainfully before returning her gaze to

the street. "The 'locals' look great to me. You're not one of us,
I presume?"

"Well, I've lived here forever. Originally, I'm from Schenectady."

"From Schenectady? How interesting! I've never met anyone
from Schenectady. I imagined nobody in Schenectady ever got
away—except maybe to Albany."

"It wasn't so bad. It was a long time ago."

"I can see that. Some things, though, you just never can grow
out of."

Six weeks of frustration had started to blunt Walter's longing
for Irene. On her return, she had called him to discuss his
forthcoming shows and nothing else. She refused even to acknowledge that she had gone into hiding because of him. He
could not so much as apologize. Irene had locked the door on
their private past.

Tonight, coming back to the setting where he had declared
his passion for her, he was commemorating something he knew
had ended, indulging a melancholy that was not without self-
disdain. Watching Priscilla, he became acutely aware that for
almost three months he had slept alone.

"Care to freshen that?" he asked.

"Tanqueray and tonic. Schweppes, please." She sucked on
gravelish ice. She had yet to smile.

He ordered their drinks—her second, his fourth. They
drank. He offered her dinner. She accepted, on the condition
that they stay at their separate tables: "It's cooler that way."
When he started to introduce himself, she interrupted, "No
names! No *last* names. What's the point, for one meal?" She
refused to hear what kind of work he did: "Can't men understand? The pleasure with strangers is leaving that stuff out."
She was holding names and "that stuff" as her trumps. She
considered Walter as he leaned into that cool space between
them, revving himself up.

By coffee she allowed herself a little gentleness. "Thanks for the treat. I'm not all barbs, you know. It's just that most men . . ." She then asked him his last name. The question thrilled Walter; it implied that she might see him again. At his answer, Priscilla released like a glittering fan the full smile she had withheld all evening. She reached towards Walter and grasped his left hand in both of hers. Even to her, the gesture seemed impulsive; she blushed appropriately.

When she in turn told him her name, his response surpassed her hopes. He had read her thesis twice. Priscilla's theory of Woman and the Artist may have made bad criticism, but it had allowed Walter to recognize himself—"discover himself," as he put it.

Some males claim to dislike women, others to like them, but all share an original, undying fear. Every man is irrationally and overwhelmingly convinced that woman, having created him, can destroy him as well. Men are all sexual bigots. The distinction between dislike and like only separates those who resist women's power by attacking them from those who try to exorcise it through adoration and submission. Walter belonged to the adoring class. Priscilla had inadvertently caught his feelings when she described Woman as a Muse who could transform him. Gratified already by Priscilla's insight, he would have been delighted to be speaking to her even if he had not been suffering from loneliness, even without her stimulating display of coldness.

Three minutes after Priscilla had spoken her name, Walter invited her to see his new work. She said she'd love to. A taxi took them to the studio, where she stayed the night.

Once again Priscilla judged Walter accurately. Knowing that with her almost-beginner's experience she could hardly surprise him sexually, she divined that the gratification Walter most wanted was the gratification he might give *her*. She let herself be gratified, let herself pass again and again, with outspoken delight, from readiness to passion to affectionate gratitude. Priscilla did not have to feign. She did not like boys her age, who always seemed intent on proving something. Even if Walter was older than any previous lover, she had no reluctance to overcome. She had only to confound her animal and her personal desires. She wanted Walter, and wanted him to want her. This need expressed itself in profusions of pleasure. The next morning, Walter shyly invited her to stay on.

Priscilla accepted, with some anxiety. She had idealized Walter, schemed to meet him, given him up as a loss. Now she had possessed him after a single encounter. She scarcely knew what sort of prize she had won, and she moved in with little idea of what to do next. When she told her parents, Maud acted astounded and concerned, Allan astounded and hurt. Priscilla listened to them patiently (she had already transferred her clothes, books, and records to Walter's studio). Certain words of her mother's concentrated her own preoccupation: plainly an attachment so hurriedly formed could be no less hurriedly ended. How, if she wanted to, could she make sure her new life would last?

Priscilla had no doubt that for the present her strongest asset was Walter's heaven-sent desire, his desire for *her* desire. During that first night with him she had discovered, almost accidentally, a powerful way to express her excitement. She had begun talking out loud while he was caressing her and felt his fingers and tongue quicken as she did so. Afterwards, remembering the effect, she spoke at greater length, as roughly as she could: "My cunt never felt so hot, darling, I'm turning to jam inside, put another finger in, yes, baby, and in my ass, too, how did you know. . . ." Her talking turned into a fond harangue, a running commentary suitable for some blind voyeur with an insatiable craving for detail. To Walter, her words magnified their acts with impersonal erotic grandeur, and he was never less than shocked to hear them issue from this expensively educated young mouth. They made the mouth and the body breathing through it all the more desirable, and the voice itself was an almost threatening sound, one that demanded stilling. This became Walter's delectable task, at which he never failed.

Walter's first weeks with Priscilla followed one another in a stagger of satisfaction. He made her his one and only drug. Priscilla grew more confident. Years before, however, she had noticed how different from their ecstatic beginnings marriages became, after two years, or one year, or three months. She knew that while the contractual solemnity of marriage (real even when taken lightly) might dampen enthusiasm, it also provided a barrier to ending a relationship casually. No such barrier protected her. She would need more than passion to keep him. Priscilla decided to go on playing the self-possessed woman Walter had met in the Polo Lounge. She demanded, she refused, she disagreed. She knew she was acting. Even if she made her part convincing by insisting on it, she never forgot how vulnerable she remained. Out of bed, she had nothing to offer that Walter could use. She had brains and energy, in a city stocked with efficient women. Her family's connections were rapidly losing their allure now that Walter had reached the verge of fame. She almost regretted having money of her own, since Walter might have enjoyed supporting her. Undeniably, she possessed youth and good looks; they were not enough. (Sadly, perhaps inevitably, Priscilla in her accounting ignored what to both Walter and herself mattered supremely: she liked him better than anyone she had ever known.)

Her anxiety was sharpened by the success of Walter's first show at the Kramer Gallery, a large, well-chosen retrospective. She gauged the extent of that success by the almost smug contentment of the guests at the opening. They knew they were witnessing a rare conjunction of history and current taste. Women in shantung pantsuits, men in cashmere jackets and silver-buckled moccasins, after a minute or two spent in

rememberable conversation with Walter, descended avidly on
Irene, whom some of them actually knew. She could have
auctioned the show for three times its stated price. As she had
foreseen, she and Walter were doing well by one another; and
that day she perhaps deserved to outshine him. She had hung
on her walls paintings that had long been accessible, making
their private value public. Priscilla felt towards her an admiration almost free of envy. Irene had achieved all that she herself
might aspire to. She was the masterly intermediary. At that
moment Irene's power impressed Priscilla as even more compelling than Walter's genius.

That power frightened Priscilla. Walter had loved Irene
(mightn't he still?), and she was making him famous. She
treated Priscilla with a plain politeness suggesting that the
young woman might someday soon be gone. After their first
meeting Priscilla was convinced that Irene had penetrated all
her ambitions and doubts. Priscilla asked her if she had read her
thesis. Irene answered, "I read it, and I liked it—I love good
gossip. I wouldn't push your line downtown, though. They're
all into Schapiro and Greenberg." She added, not unkindly,
"You might try reading them."

Priscilla's fear revealed what she needed. It led her to imagine a day when she might offend Irene, who would promptly
destroy her in Walter's eyes. (In truth, the two women mis-
judged each other. Priscilla thought too much of Irene's influence, Irene too little of Priscilla's pluck.) Priscilla saw that she
must find someone Walter trusted who would side with her in
a crisis.

She had hoped to make Phoebe such an ally. Priscilla had
taken pains to anticipate any resentment her intrusion might
have provoked, consulting Phoebe systematically about household matters, staying out of sight when she was working with
Walter, reiterating her admiration of Phoebe's painting. Phoebe
may have been surprised to find Priscilla at the studio on that

mid-September morning, but she accepted her at once; and her
ready acceptance finally discouraged Priscilla from enlisting
her. Phoebe manifested no disapproval of Priscilla, and no
approval either. She responded to Priscilla's advances amiably
and with indifference. Phoebe was preoccupied with her own
life and her burgeoning disease. She did not care whether Priscilla stayed or left.

Morris visited Walter shortly before the retrospective
opened. Priscilla had read his article in the summer issue of *New
Worlds;* it had left her more bewildered than enlightened. Walter reassured her: no one would ever understand him as she had,
"but this is about something different—where the work's going,
not where it's coming from." She kept a wary distance from
Morris when they met.

Morris was Irene's brother—a fact, ominous at first, that
eventually brought her Morris's friendship. At the opening, she
saw him standing alone in front of a Manet-inspired "Canoeing
Couple," staring disdainfully at the crowd around Irene. She
went up to him: "Looks like a smasheroo."

"Mmm."

"You must be pleased."

"I am. But what a roadhog!"

"You think so? I feel Walter's happy staying in the background."

"I didn't mean *Walter.* Oh, why do I have such a wildly
jealous nature? But you, little princess, have every right to
kvell."

Priscilla clasped the revelation to her. Clever Morris had a
foible. He was not "wildly jealous," except of Irene.

A week later she had a chance to exploit this discovery.
Morris phoned: could he stop by and see them? Come right
over, Priscilla told him. Morris found her alone and untypically
morose. He asked what was wrong. Her first evasions stimu-
lated his curiosity. Apologetically, she admitted to being wor-

ried about his sister. She was a brilliant dealer, Walter was
happy with her, and there was something wrong. She wasn't
sure what. Perhaps Irene had only guessed that Walter was
great, without really understanding him. In a way, and not
intentionally, she was exploiting him. "You know she's selling
'Spruce Fox' to Chase Manhattan? It ought to be in the Whit-
ney."

In fact the building's architects had only made an offer for
the painting; it had not been sold. Her half-lie, however, only
sharpened her point, which had touched Morris. Even as he
disagreed, gently assuring her that Walter was in good hands,
he told himself that she was right. He advised Priscilla to keep
her doubts to herself. Walter entered, and the three of them
talked of other things.

If Priscilla did not again mention Irene to Morris, she took
care to cultivate the sympathy she knew he felt for her. He had
been pleased to be confided in, pleased to give advice. She asked
for more. She phoned him for critiques of Walter's friends.
When they met at social gatherings, she begged a few minutes
of him to be taught what Stella or Judd was trying to do. She
consulted him about where to buy the best smoked salmon
below Fourteenth Street. She paid extraordinary attention to
everything he said. Irene aside, not since childhood had any
woman so fussed over him; and Priscilla had wit and looks and
youth. How could he resist?

Over a lunch Morris said to her, "You may be right about
Irene." Priscilla bit her tongue to keep from grinning. She had
been waiting in strenuous silence for these words.

"Do you think I'm good for Walter?"

"You're better than good." Morris was joking, Priscilla saw
her goal within reach. She had her ally.

She still needed a treaty of alliance. Like Walter's loving her,
Morris's liking her could be ended by a whim. She needed a
partnership of acts and facts.

Soon after, she asked him why he had never made money

from his expertise. "Do you really like doing the spadework and seeing people cash in on it?" He replied that he liked his freedom. He could work when he wanted and sleep till noon. The prospect of dealing with framers, shippers, and accountants hardly appealed to him. "*I* could do all that," Priscilla said. Why should she bother? "To know what you know. I've got to learn about *something.*"

She lured him with young painters excited by the prospect of his sponsorship and with works that looked like sure bargains. After a week he confessed to being interested. He consented to a trial run.

Priscilla then took a critical step. She suggested to Morris that, given his competence and his high commitment, he should consider handling some of Walter's work. "Irene would never agree," he objected; "*Walter* would never agree." Priscilla said, "Let me try."

Walter had become a minor celebrity. Three glossy monthlies were scheduling articles on him. Museums were showing interest. Phoebe half-seriously proposed that he hire a social secretary. Elated by the public attention, Walter knew how to protect himself in private. His success never impinged on his attachment to Priscilla, and he even associated it with her advent: the unexpected happiness she had given him seemed to have expanded into the excitements of fame. Whatever he was doing, he remained peripherally aware throughout each day of the unharvested vocalizing with which she would rapturously conclude it.

Artists and their dealers are sure to have occasional misunderstandings. For Walter, any disagreement with Irene tapped a reserve of passion that his affair with Priscilla had not quite emptied. In November Irene sold "The Prepared Piano," one of his favorite paintings, to a collector in Des Moines. Walter was appalled: "He'll stick it in his silo, and it'll never be seen again."

That evening Priscilla suggested to Walter that such trouble should be avoided. Did he have to entrust all his paintings to one person? Walter replied that as he kept so many for himself, he felt obliged to give Irene the rest. Still, he agreed with Priscilla "in theory."

This gave Priscilla an opening. She had not yet told Walter that Morris had become a dealer. She broke the news the next day. Morris was exactly what Walter needed: a friend who understood his work, and who would never be irresponsible about selling it.

Maybe, Walter said; but what about Irene? When Priscilla again brought up the subject, he said Morris was a great idea, except that Irene would be dead set against it. Priscilla asked, What if she agreed? Why, said Walter, it's a great idea.

Priscilla made an appointment to see Irene. She knew what she had to do. Irene had no reason to share Walter's success with anyone, not even her brother. Priscilla would have to disguise the nature of the understanding between Walter and Morris—she would have to lie. If the truth came out later, Irene would know who had misled her. Priscilla accepted the risk because she had so far been winning. She had successfully courted Morris, she had held on to Walter, both men had accepted her plan. If carrying it out meant lying, she would lie and cope with the consequences when they occurred. If caught, she would claim that she had been misunderstood by Irene, or by Walter, or both. She might have to fight. She would have a position to fight for.

Priscilla reassured herself by declaring her problem to be essentially semantic. If I can find the right terms, Walter will think my proposal one thing, Irene something else. How will they talk when they discuss it? What words will they use? What questions will they ask? Certain words, like *sell,* could wreck her plans. "Irene, Morris has just sold my 'Last Duchess.' " The probability of such a statement made her shudder. She experienced moments of extreme doubt. She drew up lists of all

the words that might serve in discussions of commercial trans-
actions. So many other words could replace the coarseness of
buy and *sell: manage, handle, look after, take care of* . . .
Weren't such words the very ones Walter and Irene would use?
The proposal had sprung from a tense situation; it was bound
to remain slightly embarrassing to them and so encourage eu-
phemism. Priscilla chose to trust her luck and her lists. She
could monitor Walter's communications with Irene well
enough to anticipate danger.

She prepared a version of her proposal to accommodate, for
Irene's hearing, whatever Morris and Walter might say. Arriving at the Kramer Gallery for her appointment, she felt a new
confidence: she was representing Walter professionally.

Priscilla told Irene that Walter deeply regretted their disagreement over "The Prepared Piano." He felt that neither he
nor Irene should be blamed for what had happened. Couldn't
such misunderstandings be averted by asking a third party to
act as arbiter in the case of special paintings? He was proposing
her brother for this role. What did Irene think? Morris's discre-
tionary power would affect them only rarely. . . .

"Morris would be perfect," Irene interrupted. "I'd been hoping he'd do the same for me."

Priscilla did not understand this remark. "Walter will be—"

"He didn't need my approval. I wish the darling would grasp
that I'm working for *him.*" Irene paused. "Why didn't he talk
to me himself?"

"Because," Priscilla promptly answered, "he was embarrassed about your fight. So I agreed to stand in." Feeling like
a pro, she decided to gamble her stake forthwith: "If you called
him now, he'd love it." She watched Irene dial their number.

" . . . so I'm not good enough for you, Mr. Trale?" Irene said.
"You need a *man* to look after you. . . ."

She was smiling when she hung up. So was Priscilla as she
went out the gallery door.

"I made it sort of ambiguous," she ambiguously told Morris. "You'll be 'making decisions' about certain paintings. She got the message."

"Miss Priss, you're a star. May I wonder why?"

"I told you—to pick your elegant brains."

"Be my guest. Just one tiny *nasty* reason to console me?"

"I want Walter, you know that. It's tough out there for a brat like me."

"Sho 'nuff. And something to show Mummy and Daddy, too?"

"Oh, maybe. It should keep Maud out of my hair."

Priscilla was to receive more tangible rewards. Morris insisted she be paid money for work done; her willingness to help him for nothing merely reflected the condescension typical of her class. He offered her a percentage of the sales she prepared. She agreed to this. In time she pointed out how dependent this had made her. She had begun earning appreciable amounts of money, and he had recently been having some cardiac "discomfort": "Don't you go and die on me, I've still got lots more to learn! And you know I'm not employable, except by you. Without you, I'm nobody."

He said nothing at the time. A few days later he mentioned taking out a life-insurance policy that named her as his beneficiary. Priscilla burst into tears. Morris gave her one of his rare hugs. "Dear Priss, think how ecstatic I'd feel bankrolling you from the void!"

In her conquest of Morris, Priscilla perhaps achieved her most impressive exploit. Intelligent, cynical, mistrustful of women, he let a little shiksa win his confidence by sheer will. He had justified adopting her by her charm, her loyalty, her usefulness, hardly noticing her strangeness to him, and how strangely he himself had yielded to her bizarre determination.

Priscilla's dealings with Irene impressed Walter, reinforcing his attraction to her with an element of respect. When she asked for work to bring to Morris, he found it hard to say no to her. Although she did not ask often (in the end, Morris never sold any of his paintings), the works sometimes mattered greatly to him, if only because they were new. Priscilla fought him tenaciously on these occasions, making his consent both an instrument and measure of her strength. Hadn't he promised her? Couldn't he trust her? Didn't he love her? Each victory left her a little surer of her place in Walter's life; and as if to prove that place supreme, she challenged herself to convince him that he should give Morris the portrait of Elizabeth. It took all her prowess, and a little over a week, to wear down his refusal, resistance, reluctance. One morning she got up to find the portrait gone from the studio wall and standing by the front door, wrapped in a plastic sheet. For the first time since her arrival in September, Priscilla felt that she could call the city in which she lived her own.

Walter undoubtedly loved Priscilla, and he may have even enjoyed giving in to her. If he was annoyed at having to relinquish certain paintings, he lived too actively, and such losses came too rarely, for him to worry for long; and he was, after all, helping Morris. He saw the portrait of Elizabeth, however, as his primordial, self-made totem; as Priscilla herself had once written, not only his but him. Early that morning, he had remembered Phoebe's brilliantly faithful copy. She had painted it as a labor of love, love for him and for his work. She would not mind if he used it for a while to defend himself. While Priscilla slept, Walter, having put the original out of sight, left the copy where she would surely find it. She jubilantly transported it to Morris's before the day was out.

Irene and Morris

1945-1963

E VEN BEFORE HIS LOVER'S DEATH, PRISCILLA HAD CAUSED Lewis pain. He had become morbidly jealous of her for having persuaded Morris to sell paintings. When playing the tormentor, Morris never failed to describe Priscilla's long and frequent visits to his apartment, which Lewis was allowed to enter barely once a month. Lewis thus pieced together the story of their unlikely friendship. He incidentally learned about Morris's lifelong relationship with Irene.

A week before Morris and Lewis met, Irene asked her brother to become artistic adviser to the Kramer Gallery. She had considered her offer carefully. The possibility had first occurred to her when her study of Walter's work had allowed her to admire the range and depth of her brother's insights. If Irene hesitated to hire him, it was only because she mistrusted her prejudices in his favor, and not only as her brother: as the person she had always loved most.

Irene approached Morris tactfully. She made it clear that she was not acting out of sisterly kindness. She emphasized that he would receive a good salary as well as a commission on sales, and that he could set his own schedule. She explained how deliberately she had made her choice. For months she had felt the need of bringing in an adviser. She had eliminated several eminent prospects—Rosenberg and Hess would have seen a threat to their independence in being associated with a gallery; Greenberg had tied himself up with the Rubin gang. She had concluded that Morris suited her perfectly, even if he was her brother. If the fact might harm him in the opinions of some, she had decided that such opinions belonged to fools. She would not settle for less than the best.

Irene's tact expressed both her esteem and her affection. For perhaps the first time, she was acting towards Morris without a trace of solicitude. She was recognizing him as her equal, not in intelligence (she had known that for years), but as an adult in charge of his own life. Irene had sometimes doubted that she would ever know this happiness. She had been watching over Morris since he was twelve.

Their parents were almost forty when Morris was born, six years after Irene; they were in their fifties when he reached adolescence. They had difficulty understanding their moody son, and he them. Irene became close to her brother when she began mediating the family stalemates that more and more frequently punctuated his teenage years. She had always liked Morris, and her liking developed into love as she came to recognize him as a gifted, erratic boy.

If Irene helped reconcile him to his life at home, she could do little for him in school, where in spite of her coaching his work remained mediocre. During Morris's freshman year of high school, she began to be seconded by a powerful confederate: a history teacher called Arnold Loewenberg. This scholarly Austrian, whose studies had been long interrupted by the Anschluss and the war and who was only now finishing his doctoral dissertation, perceived beneath Morris's indifference to study a passionate and talented mind, which he set out to raise to its proper level. He befriended the boy, introducing him to the pleasures of painting and music, lending him records and books of reproductions, telling him stories of life in Europe, where history lay all around you and works of art were recognized as emblems of that history. Almost in passing he showed Morris how to work—how to analyze what he read, how to organize what he wrote. Mr. Loewenberg also demanded exceptional results of his pupil: first that he become the best in his class, afterwards that he meet the standards of a *Gymnasium* or *lycée*. After a while Mr. Loewenberg began giving Morris failing grades whenever his work fell short of these standards, and Morris's other teachers followed his lead, with varying and sufficient severity—a benevolent conspiracy that turned Morris into a prizewinning student by the end of the year.

Arnold Loewenberg and Irene became friends. He provided her with valuable advice during her days as a student of art history and invaluable encouragement at the start of her career; even so, she felt most indebted to him for adopting Morris. "You must never forget," he once told her, "that he is an intellectual"—he pronounced the word with lip-smacking emphasis—"perhaps will he someday become an extraordinary one, but in a land of greed and ball games he will of course experience hardships." From him she drew confidence that she was not tending a talented misfit.

Morris was strange, and enjoyed being strange. Unlike Lewis, he never suffered from friendlessness and related despairs. He judged his fellows shrewdly, knowing how to make them admire or fear or befriend him. At heart he kept distant, relishing distance as a privilege; and this, more than anything, worried Irene. She foresaw him doomed to the bitterness of the unloving.

The summer following Morris's first year with Mr. Loewenberg, his parents rented a cottage on Kiamesha Lake. Irene sometimes came for a weekend. One Friday she was given an unexpected ride and arrived in the country several hours early. It was mid afternoon. Her parents had gone out. Standing in the empty house, she heard Morris's voice. She looked for him outside, then in the garage, where she did not at first see him, because she found herself face to face with someone else: Morris's younger friend Irwin Hall, dressed in his undershorts. His hands had been tied behind his back with wire; he was standing on tiptoe, so as not to be choked by the noose of thin white rope strung from a joist above his head. As Irene, sustaining Irwin with one arm, began loosening the rope, she heard Morris laugh and saw him standing in the shadows by the wall.

"Don't worry, pardner," he said, "just my big sister."

The rope came free. Irene exclaimed, "You guys are wacko. Morris, get his hands untied."

Panting slightly, Irwin said, "We were playing." The noose had chafed a stripe under his chin. His cropped blond hair set off the liquid, greenish-brown eyes cheerfully turned towards his friend.

Irene blurted angrily at Morris, "You're a goddamned creep."

Normally fearful of her, he only grinned: "You don't know it, Irene, but this man's dangerous." He was rocking from side to side with excitement. Irene unfastened the wire.

Afterwards Morris explained to her that all his friends played "outlaw and sheriff." Several months later, in the attic of their house in the Bronx, she found a mail-order kit hidden under a jumble of old cartons. It included leather-and-chrome thongs, two whips, and a zipper gag. The implements looked new. They had never been used. Morris had ordered the kit, like the magazine in which it had been advertised, to nourish fantasies, not acts. Acts frightened him. Irene's reaction in the garage confirmed what he had already surmised: kit and magazine might belong to the public domain, his desires were still abnormal. They shocked him as they might have his father. After Irwin, he kept them to himself for two years. He then occasionally picked up a boy downtown and let his fancies free.

Once he mistook his prey and was himself beaten up. The damage proved hard to conceal, especially from an affectionate sister. Irene was again dismayed, less because of his sexual bent (she knew that sadomasochism was hardly "abnormal") than by a fear that it would reinforce his essential remoteness. She decided to encourage him forcefully in the activity to which, having proved his merits, he might be best tempted to commit himself; and with Arnold Loewenberg still her willing abettor, she persuaded Morris during his last year in high school to start seriously preparing for a scholarly future. Luckily, such a future had a special attraction for him: it inspired consternation in his parents. They feared it would permanently estrange their son. They could not, however, deny him the higher education so often proclaimed as one of their goals; and they were comforted when, of the colleges that accepted him, Morris chose NYU in preference to Harvard and Chicago. The choice would keep him closer to home, they felt, foolishly estimating in miles the distance between the Bronx and Washington Square.

Two years later Morris began majoring in art history. Irene played no part in this decision, which was initiated by a reading of Hegel's *Aesthetics:* art appealed to Morris as a historical register of society's metaphysical struggles. Irene continued nonetheless to influence his development. She had by now completed her studies, completed her marriage, begun her professional career. She introduced Morris, full of old theory and practice, to art that was local and fresh and to a society of artists still poor and unpublicized, bustling with experiment, with debate, with a sense of urgency worthy of a futures market. Morris was forced to confront his studies with present realities. He thrived.

That Morris should go to graduate school seemed obvious to everyone except his father, who said he should come home and manage the movie theaters, and his mother, who said he should just come home. Irene helped Morris win a scholarship and find a part-time job. She counseled him in his dealings with their parents. He won their approval at last and began his graduate studies at Columbia in the fall of 1954. He would have earned his doctorate in three or four years if his progress had not been arrested by an unexpected and serious heart attack.

Morris spent much of the next two years in hospitals. Times between confinements came to seem like vacations: for him, the reality that mattered was engendered by medical routines, by administered survival procedures. Morris's parents paid whatever the best care cost. Irene made sure he did get the best, in moments of crisis calling on specialists from other hospitals, from other cities. Irene saw Morris through tests and through days of waiting for their results, and through weeks when he was instructed to "do nothing but rest." She made him keep studying. She arranged for him to take examinations and write papers months late. When he was tempted to use his illness as an excuse for giving up, she did not let him forget the joy he found in the exercise of his gifts. Thanks to her, over the course of four and a half difficult years, he did much more than survive.

During this time Morris learned to think for himself. Now that he repeatedly had to face the possibility of dying, his studies took on new relevance. Because he might never see this drawing again, he looked at it with uncompromising attention. Words he heard or read or wrote reverberated like final declarations. He did not give up his philosophical bias, but he began looking at works of art less as symptoms of cultural history and more as individual actions. This change in his attitude did not concern subject matter, or symbolic values, or even form in any general sense. As far as he was concerned, the "individual actions" that interested him were always rendered in terms of appearance—touch, grain, and tone. Morris became uncannily sympathetic to contemporary art; as though the threat of death had cleansed his eyes of all that kept him from seeing it as its declared self: an enterprise dedicated to shifting the center of art to the surface of its medium, where it properly belonged. When he discovered Walter's painting, he knew how to do it justice.

The change in Morris was hidden from Irene by the unevenness of his life. She noticed the events of particular days: how he slept, what he ate and didn't eat, the strength of his voice, the hints for the future in his doctors' pronouncements. Like a mother with her child, she relegated questions other than those of health to some hypothetical future time. She wanted Morris to endure the least pain, his nights to pass restfully, his recovery to be assured. After relapses had brought her many moments of hopelessness, his seemingly unending convalescence ended at last, and he finally recovered. Her devotion had been rewarded. In the meantime she had lost touch with him. Her brilliant younger brother had turned into someone to be nursed. Having encouraged the development of his powers, she came to doubt their importance, thankful to have him alive.

His article on Walter astounded her. Morris had cultivated her surprise, telling her nothing about it, not even mentioning his study of Walter, whose work he had first seen while finishing his dissertation on Lewis Eilshemius. As soon as it appeared, Morris brought Irene his first copy of *New Worlds*—a gesture that made it clear whom his essay was intended to please. Not even he had foreseen the delight it gave her. It so absorbed her that she had to keep reminding herself who had written it. The later approval of Morris's fellow critics strengthened her conviction that even if one article did not make an oeuvre, Morris had fulfilled his promise. Irene continued to wake up thinking about him, but with jubilation now, not dread.

In opening her uptown gallery, Irene knew that her career

was at stake. Although she did not doubt her own capacities, she had often imagined during the first months of her venture having a counselor who could share the pressure of crises and in calmer times encourage her initiatives. She now asked herself, who could be fitter than Morris for such a role? He had endured crises of terrifying proportions. He had led her to Walter and to her success with him. She asked him to become her collaborator.

A month earlier Morris would probably have accepted her offer. He had loved Irene since childhood; he possibly owed her his life. Her response to his essay had satisfied him gloriously, and he recognized her subsequent adoption of Walter as an acknowledgment of his acumen. Against these bonds, however, were arrayed darker feelings no less tenacious. Irene was someone he had always been obliged to admire. She had been bigger, then older, always a model at home and at school. Even his debts to her confined him. As his protector, his mentor, and finally his guardian, she had proved herself strong and good; Morris had been condemned to strangeness, perversion, and sickness. The strong have the privilege of giving. The weak remain dependent and grateful. But was Irene really the stronger? Who had done the surviving?

When Priscilla insinuated that Irene was exploiting Walter, her words spread through Morris like a stain. Irene was exploiting him, too. He had discovered Walter, and she was turning the profit. When Irene made her proposal to him a few weeks later, it occurred to him that working for her would restore his old dependency in a new guise. Priscilla had shown him that he could make money on his own doing precisely what Irene wanted from him. Forgetting his success and his promise, playing the resentful orphan instead, he declined her offer.

Initially this refusal did not surprise Irene: she understood the reticence a big sister might inspire. She did her best to mitigate it. She invited Morris to set his own terms. She enlisted outsiders to plead her cause. Her efforts only hardened his position. (Robert Rosenblum declared that trying to change Morris's mind was like pushing gin at an AA convention.) He avoided Irene and her emissaries. A week and a half later, when Priscilla announced that Walter wanted Morris as *his* adviser, Irene gave up.

Even then Morris kept his distance from her, although she never again referred to her offer. He sometimes did; once to remark, in the worst faith, that even Lewis condemned her idea. Irene came to think of Lewis as an enemy.

At Morris's death, Irene cried all the more bitterly for the estrangement that had preceded it. She blamed herself harshly for it.

One morning in early June, Lewis met Priscilla and Walter on Carmine Street, and his disappointment in the painter turned to disgust. He went to see Irene that afternoon. Hoping to get rid of him, she met him in the gallery lobby. Lewis told her he knew the truth about Walter's business understanding with Morris. So did she, she replied. You don't, Lewis insisted. Irene said that she was too busy to argue; if he didn't agree, that was his problem. (She could hardly bear looking at him. He might have killed her brother.) Lewis lost his temper: "It's *your* fucking problem."

Irene left him standing there. Later she began wondering what might lie behind his outburst. When he called to apologize, she agreed to meet him again the next day.

This time Lewis showed patience. He told her about his affair with Morris, saying in conclusion, "I loved him more than I'll ever love anybody, and I know you did too." She asked him how Morris had died. Lewis supplied every painful detail. He then returned to the subject he had broached the day before: "Priscilla set up this deal—"

"Not really. It was Walter's idea."

"It wasn't. I thought you knew *that.* Morris would anyway decide which paintings of Walter's to sell—"

"Which *not* to sell."

Lewis explained the arrangement. Still bewildered, Irene was reluctant to understand. Lewis suggested they visit Morris's apartment. She could see for herself.

"It's impounded. We have to get a permit."

"*I* don't. How about Sunday night?"

Lewis had the key to Morris's back door, concealed by its bookcases from the police. Irene and Lewis crept through it, each with a flashlight.

Morris had hung Walter's five paintings in his bedroom. The portrait of Elizabeth faced the bed. Lewis went off to look for a sales list. Returning, he found Irene exploring the portrait with her mobile beam. Darkness hid her face; her voice revealed a changed mood. Lewis thought of his mother when he'd given her the stolen scarf. He shivered.

"Morris would never have sold—" he began.

"Of course he wouldn't."

"Even Priscilla—"

"Oh, Priscilla!" She paused. "As they say, the course of true love is paved with good intentions. . . . Let's get these things out of here."

"The paintings? *Now?*"

"What else? When else?"

Later that night, Irene justified her preposterous, no doubt illegal, ploy: if Walter was selling these paintings, she was contractually bound to help him. She spoke with the resolution of solid outrage.

On Tuesday Irene began discreetly offering Walter's paintings to reliable customers from out of town. On Friday Maud bought the portrait of Elizabeth. Three other paintings were sold before the end of July, the last on August first. Irene then phoned Walter to tell him what she had done.

She did not blame him for his role, or excuse herself. She thought that probably he would angrily announce that he was leaving her gallery. He only sounded perplexed. Hadn't Priscilla told her about the deal with Morris? Hadn't Irene called him to say she approved? "Look," he said, "basically it was so Morris could make some money. Is that so terrible? He certainly deserved it."

"I agree. Now, tell me, *cher coeur,* how did Priscilla deserve it? Oh, no, spare me the sordid details. . . ." Irene was finally grasping the truth.

"Priscilla?"

"There's something I'd like to know: what did she say I'd agreed to?"

"Every so often Morris would sell a painting of mine."

"To me she *never* said anything about selling—just giving you advice. Of course I know he was selling other work and splitting the proceeds with her." Walter's silence filled up her pause. "You know he and Priscilla went halves?" Another pause. "Ask her."

"She's away for the day."

"I'm sure she can explain it all. Still, I'd listen to her very carefully. You don't happen to own a tape recorder?"

Walter asked who had bought the portrait of Elizabeth. Irene began feeling remorse. She had behaved unfairly to Walter, who had only acted foolishly, not betrayed her. However, she had not behaved unfairly to Priscilla.

Walter was not thinking of Priscilla, not yet. After Irene hung up, he at once called Maud and told her that the real "Portrait of Elizabeth" had remained in his hands.

Pauline and Maud

SUMMER 1938

MAUD LUDLAM ONCE TOLD ELIZABETH THAT SHE'D HAD
two children: her daughter, Priscilla, and her sister, Pauline.

Their mother had died when Maud was eleven and Pauline
five. Afterwards, their father retained the best governesses for
their care. When governesses began losing authority, Maud
gradually turned into a foster mother. By then she had emerged
from the worst of adolescence. She liked her role.

She also liked Pauline, who was sweet-tempered and zany,
with whims that she clung to indomitably. From the age of
three until her first brush with a policeman she went swimming
bottomless, clad only in a strikingly superfluous bra. At six she
started taking riding lessons; for her first horse show, she was
given English riding togs, which she wore happily enough,
except for the boots: if she dressed up, she said, it was going to
be heels or nothing. For years she startled judges by riding in
black cap, black coat, white shirt and stock tie, jodhpurs, and

high-heeled dress shoes (usually Maud's, padded with cotton). When Pauline was eleven, an elegant Chinese guest of her father's showed her how to handle chopsticks: thenceforth she refused to eat with anything else, carrying her own stainless-steel pair wherever she went, using it, to the stupefaction of one and all, to neatly dissect thick pies and steaks.

Pauline's quirks sometimes embarrassed others, never Maud. She admired Pauline's spunk. Far less daring herself, she aspired merely to pass unnoticed. Her mother's death had bequeathed her a chronic doubt as to her own reality.

Like a coach training a natural athlete, Maud encouraged Pauline through puberty into young womanhood. The sisters enjoyed themselves, Pauline dashing around, Maud feeling useful as her loyal supervisor. Close though they were, they showed tolerance rather than understanding towards one another. They often said they should do more together—go to Europe, for instance.

Their father, Paul Dunlap, had had a long career as a sensible investment counselor. He had increased tenfold the small capital inherited from their grandfather, a real-estate developer in Buffalo. He had speculated on America's entry into the Great War, foreseen the postwar boom, guessed at the crash. He retired a millionaire.

After his wife's death, Paul Dunlap for several years gave up family life. Later, impressed by Maud's grades and her seriousness, he began confiding in her. Pauline stood outside adult concerns, with all the charm, and all the impertinence, of the household cocker.

Paul Dunlap established his preference for Maud in practice and in writ. He taught her what he had learned as an investor, or tried to—Maud had earned her good marks in literature and languages, not economics. When he gave her money so she could learn about handling large sums, Maud only learned that large sums made her long for professional advice. She did not see that her father, muttering vague praises of primogeniture, intended to leave her nine-tenths of his estate. He was making her the head of the family.

Pauline was not instructed in money matters. From Maud she gradually found out that she would have little control of the family fortunes, while Maud would have a great deal. After their father's death, Maud and one professional trustee became responsible for Pauline's capital. Pauline told herself, better Maud than some fathead at the bank. The disproportion of their inheritance did not distress her. It did not affect her life: Maud gave her the money she so happily continued to spend, and she readily acquiesced to Maud's suggestion that, to enhance Pauline's "eligibility," they pretend that their father had left them equally rich.

Maud had qualms. She asked Allan if he couldn't devise a way of evening their fortunes; Allan told her that it was clearly impossible. For the time being, Maud knew, problems existed only in her conscience. She nevertheless could not forget that a wall of almost a million prewar dollars had been raised between them and that it might someday prove more rugged than sisterly scrupulousness and trust.

In the shadow of that wall, Pauline had already changed. She had stopped growing up. Now twenty-two, she once again began deferring to Maud as she had at fifteen. By the time summer came, Maud felt as though she had been depressingly consigned to an older generation. Pauline came to her for every kind of advice. She refused to buy clothes without her, refused to wear them without her blessing: whenever she left the house, she would exhibit herself to Maud with a cheery "How do I look?" that for all its apparent impulsiveness soon became an ineluctable rite. Like any dutiful young girl, Pauline provided Maud with unasked-for, meticulous accounts of all she did; and she flattered her (Maud could find no nicer word) with equally needless attentions, with notes and even little gifts of flowers or

a book, on every faintly memorable occasion in Maud's life—
the day their mother died, the day she first met Allan, the day
her next period was due. Maud groaned inwardly at each of
these tributes, never daring to tell Pauline how much they
saddened her. She had once courted their father in similar
fashion, until one day he firmly stopped her: "It's love insurance. Save yourself the trouble. You've got mine."

Pauline had Maud's love and must have known it. What she
wanted, what she feared losing, was permission to go on playing
as she always had. She did not want to talk or think about
money that Maud had and she hadn't, just as she averted her
eyes whenever she drove past the treeless, set-back, economy-
size supermarket that had wrecked the alignment of their
town's main street. She was determined to pretend that nothing
had changed.

Her attitude reinforced Maud's own reluctance to set matters
straight, as Allan kept urging her to do: Pauline would not live
with them much longer, she must start taking care of herself.
Maud protested, "I'm part of the problem. How can I help her
solve it?"—a good excuse for doing nothing.

Early in July, in this summer of her twenty-third year, a few
weeks after graduating from Wellesley, Pauline met Oliver
Pruell. He began taking her out. Ten days later Pauline rose
early to catch her sister at breakfast:

"He's giving me a big rush. I guess he's serious. He's infuriat-
ingly proper."

"That's not necessarily bad."

"Two years out of college, and risqué means holding hands?"

"He's not a fairy?"

"No. Maybe. I have a feeling he 'knows' I'm rich."

"What's his name?"

"May I keep that one secret from you? He's from a good
family. He works on Wall Street, too. If he's not after my
charms, though, he must want . . . Maud, how can I tell?"

Maud considered herself a poor counselor concerning men; during her adult life she had known only one intimately. She had met Allan three years earlier. They had quickly fomented a friendly complicity: her self-doubt found a perfect complement in his assurance. They had "had fun," going to the theater, dancing late. He had proposed to her as though he were doing her a favor he enjoyed. Her friends warned her that he was thinking of her wealth to come. Her father disagreed, and she, knowing Allan, knew better. She was a little surprised when, three weeks after they had moved into their well-appointed East Side apartment, she found the bill for the rent on her desk. Allan took for granted that she would pay for that, for their trips, for their box at the Met if she wanted it, while he assumed the cost of their cars and his clubs. Maud hardly minded, because Allan was otherwise proving the best of husbands. From their courtship Maud had expected that he would last as a companion; and he had. She had not expected passion. Months passed, and Allan came home to her every evening like a sailor on liberty. Maud found herself in love with him.

(Later, when the war abducted Allan to the Pacific and she turned a horrifying thirty, Maud took a lover. Or rather he took her; or rather he did *not* take her. A slightly impoverished Baltimorean, of exquisite extraction and no less exquisite sensibilities, began pursuing her ardently. At last she yielded. Maud wanted to be confirmed in her bodily beauty; she got homage of a more speculative kind. Michael, capable of satisfying her, explained that he treasured that consummation so highly that only marriage could properly enshrine it. He knew her true worth—he had a friend at her bank, as she learned before showing him the door.)

Maud gave her sister evasive counsel.

A month later, Pauline was ensnared by the losing streak into which Oliver and the martingale had lured her. She owed her beau six hundred and thirty-five dollars, as well as her virginity. She decided to earn the money and asked Maud to help her find a job. She said she wanted to work: "Anything. Selling Fuller Brushes. I'm a disgrace as it is."

Maud was pleased. She foresaw wonderful benefits in Pauline's decision. She might discover the value of money (by which Maud somehow meant its irrelevance). She might earn, if not her living, at least her rent. She might leave Maud and *her* money behind her.

Maud sent Pauline to one of her oldest friends, a man of wealth and local influence, the president of "The Association" (the Association for the Improvement of the Breed of Thoroughbred Horses). Maud had failed to observe that Pauline had taken his son as her constant companion. She could not guess that it was because of this young man that she wanted to earn money.

Mr. Pruell, however, had often noticed Oliver and Pauline together, most recently sharing a bag of chips as they sauntered under the high elms of Broadway. He agreed to see Pauline (who told herself that, after all, a job was a job), but he had no interest in finding her work. He wanted her to look after his son. He confided his concern for him; he showed her Oliver's erotic hymns to Elizabeth. She fell definitively in love.

She wanted to marry. Oliver said they couldn't afford it. Pauline decided to involve her sister. She intercepted her on her way out to dinner.

"Did you get your job?" Maud asked her cheerfully.

"I love Mr. Pruell—I never really knew him."

"He's a dream, isn't he?"

"I'm dating Oliver Pruell—the one I told you about a month ago? It's serious?" The questions in Pauline's voice invited Maud's approval.

"How wonderful!" Maud answered, in dismay. How could she not have known?

The next morning she learned that she had no companions

in ignorance: her "discreet inquiries" about Oliver became comic as each of her friends volunteered straight-to-the-point evaluations at the mention of his name. According to most, he was handsome, polished, very much a Pruell, less admired than liked, no rogue—not one to marry a girl for her money, not with his expectations. Not absolutely reliable: two years ago, after a summer-long affair with Elizabeth, he had ditched her.

Pauline again spoke to Maud. She wanted Oliver to marry her. ("Of course I'm not pregnant!" "But you're sleeping with him?" "It was like pulling hen's teeth, but yes.") Although "mad about her," Oliver thought it greater madness to live on his present salary.

"He says wait till I'm twenty-five—till I 'come into my own,' as he puts it."

"How patient of him!"

As Maud feared, the problem rapidly got worse. Allan went back to the city the next day. With no invitation to rescue her, Maud dined with Pauline, who promptly asked her: "Can I talk about Oliver?"

"Will it help?"

"Something wrong with him?"

"Don't be silly."

"He says it's no dice." Maud wondered why this could not reasonably end the matter; however, they would not then be having this conversation. Pauline went on, "It wouldn't take much to change his mind, I think. Or do I mean 'I don't think'?"

"Are you sure he wants to marry you?"

"Oh, yes. He swears he'd marry me if only—" Pauline stopped.

"So there's a bill of particulars?"

"Oh, Maud, *he* promised me and *I* looked for the answers. I thought that maybe—"

"Could you explain the appeal of someone who insists on more money?"

"I should never have put it that way. Anyway, we *have* the money, don't we?"

"That's hardly the point."

"What *is* the point of having money if you can't use it to get what you want? You always said I should be happy."

"*That's* the point. And after all," Maud continued, knowing she could not ward off Pauline indefinitely, "what could we do?"

"If I got my share now, that would help—even if it's not as much as he thinks."

"It's impossible. Legally, I mean. You must know that."

"Sure. So what if I took my share out of what you have, and I pay it back to you at nine-oh-five A.M. on my twenty-fifth birthday?"

"I can't."

"You say you never know what to do with it all. And think: from now on I wouldn't cost you another penny."

"It isn't up to me. It's Daddy's money—"

"Oh, come on!"

"He *cared* about what happened to it. I don't like what he decided, but I *promised* I'd respect it. Even if I didn't, you know most of my money is in trust, and I'm only one trustee. It wouldn't work. I can't go against his wishes. Not to mention his will."

"Darling, who knows what he'd think now? Why don't you stop using a dead man to hide behind? If you disapprove of Oliver, just say so."

"It's not hiding. I'm responsible—that's the way the money was left to us. I wish *you* had it. My disapproving of Oliver has nothing to do with it."

"You see? That's why you're talking this junk. You wish I had the money! Do you think you'd have gotten Allan without it, with your big feet?"

Pauline left the table. The front door presently slammed. In the living room Maud refilled her glass with the dregs of shaken martinis. Sitting down, she told herself: I mustn't let her think such things about me. The glass sloshed in her hand. She had been blindsided by Pauline's attack.

She came down early in the morning to wait for her sister. Maud said to her that she had forgotten something they could do. The house in the city had been left to Maud outright. It was now rented. If Pauline wanted it, the tenants could be moved out by the spring.

Since the night before, she added, she had realized that she could ask to have the allowance from Pauline's trust fund increased, even doubled.

Pauline accepted. While she was pleased to have more income of her own, she reckoned it was the handsome corner house on Sutton Square that would appease Oliver.

During the night her feelings towards Maud had undergone considerable change. After rushing outside, she had promptly divested herself of her years of submissiveness; and like a snake in springtime, resentment had at once raised its sullen head. Again and again she angrily reminded herself of the unfairness of her position. She was as clever as Maud, she was prettier, and she was so much poorer! She would never have let *her* sister suffer from an old man's whim.

By morning, practice had hardened her indignation. When Maud made her offer, Pauline found it less than her due. Maud's concessions chiefly gratified her by putting Maud permanently in the wrong.

Soon afterwards, before the engagement was announced, Maud chose to travel. The season was ending, and she had time before the wedding to make a long-postponed excursion to Europe. Offended by her departure, Pauline let her resentment flourish. If Maud had stayed, even an angry sister might have noticed that she only wanted peace for herself. Instead, Maud allowed Pauline to turn her into a kind of witch. The happiness of Pauline's engagement, the publicity of her marriage, glittered against a dark background of indifference and betrayal.

Or, if Maud had stayed, Pauline might at least have been able to vent her resentment. Maud would have suffered and survived, and Pauline's anger would have expired into acceptance, if not understanding. Maud left. For many years Pauline saw as little of her as she could, altogether avoiding the familiarity that had so long sustained her. Her indignation had nowhere to go except into a sodden pit of recollection and foreboding, where it lay, impotent and alive, year after year, waiting to emerge on some marvelous day of wrath—a brooding existence, exuding ropy feelers of revenge.

Or, if Pauline's happiness with Oliver had lasted, her rancor might have simply been forgotten. Pauline never interested Oliver except as a prize. He soon neglected her. He discouraged her from working, from having children—when he learned the truth about her inheritance, he declared that in such difficult times children cost more than they could comfortably afford.

So Pauline's resentment lived on, a ponderous beast dormant in its gloomy trough. Twenty-five years after her marriage, her friend Owen Lewison told her one evening that Allan and Maud, for reasons unknown to him, had sequestered a valuable painting by Walter Trale, improbably claiming that it had been stolen. He asked Pauline to find out if the picture had been hidden in Allan's apartment. "High Heels" accepted, with a vengeance, with no illusions about her task: she would seduce Maud's husband and implicate her sister in a dubious scheme. Her night with Allan, however, left her dissatisfied. She liked him more than she wanted to; and this inexplicably reawakened her age-old attachment to Maud. She was confused. She told herself that sleeping with Allan could not be counted as revenge if her sister did not know about it.

She must pay her a visit and make sure she knew what had happened.

The beast had come forth from its pit. In the light of day, it looked less like a dragon than like a lost lamb.

Maud and Priscilla
1940-1963

MAUD, NO FOOL, DID NOT REGRET THAT SHE HAD MONEY
to be liked for. She hoped, less shrewdly, that it might inspire
in others tolerance for her ordinary self. She did not like talking
about money, because the subject made her feel foolish, and her
foolishness made her cringe for her father's sake. She had
learned so little from him, and forgotten so much. Maud had
tried managing the far from negligible sums her father had left
her outright. She had even had conspicuous successes: in 1938,
she added oil stocks to her portfolio after they had shrunk to
half their value and before their precipitous rise. Her pre-
science, however, was invariably based on irrelevant facts. She
had, for instance, no inkling of the oil industry's forthcoming
boom, only observed that its stocks provided a higher yield than
her other securities. She made costly mistakes, such as missing
a chance to buy early into natural gas. After the third such
mistake, she abandoned investment policy to her advisers.

Her withdrawal from finance sadly recalled to Maud her

father's long efforts to train her. A difficult master, he had taught her by examples from which few rules could be drawn; and the prime rule read: in money matters, do not look for rules. While she had believed everything he said, her belief was grounded in faith, not understanding. In resisting Pauline's demands, she had, exceptionally, acted with a reasonable conviction: she could accept as plain good sense her father's dictum that fortunes should be kept intact. Declaring this to sentimental Pauline would have sounded like rank hypocrisy; so Maud had taken refuge, with lesser hypocrisy, in the letter of her father's intentions.

In promising to carry out these intentions, Maud implicitly subjected her future offspring to the rule that had favored her over Pauline: one of them would inherit the bulk of her fortune. As it turned out, Maud had only one child.

When Priscilla came of age, Maud told herself, I know too much and too little about money, but at least I know something. I might have done worse. Priscilla should find out what money can do. Of course, Maud could not teach her. On the other hand, if efficient Priscilla had inherited her grandfather's flair, simply using money might be training enough.

Maud had mostly let Priscilla solve her own problems since, from infancy, she had proved so much better at it. All the same, Maud had looked after her conscientiously. Tempted though she may have been to leave her clever daughter to her own devices, she realized that even the cleverest child cannot foresee the measles or the injustice of lower mathematics. She provided Priscilla with the elements of a healthy life, she found good doctors to supervise her growth, at school she persuaded sympathetic teachers to monitor her progress. Otherwise, Maud simply kept herself available, although she hardly knew why. At eleven Priscilla had her appendix removed. Maud sat with her through her recovery, noticing ruefully that it was Priscilla who kept *her* cheered up.

Diffident Maud enjoyed having a bright, athletic, sociable

daughter. She had what many parents strive for: a child who surpasses them. Maud's own successes always struck her as due to luck, like her timely purchase of oil stock, or too secret to qualify as achievements. Her house, even her garden belonged to this domain of secrecy. Allan pleaded with her to show them to the world; Maud insisted on keeping them in the family.

Behind the house there had once stretched an acre and a half of lawn, conventionally hedged and planted with a few unsurprising trees. Within this space Maud plotted an arrangement of outdoor rooms, cunningly varied and juxtaposed. One room was shaded for sunny days, its neighbor wide open to the skies; some were planted by color (white, blue, rose); others flowered according to the seasons, from the primrose-speckled spring oval walled with high rhododendrons to the autumn rectangle, which was bordered with a multitude of chrysanthemums set against severely clipped hedges of golden-leaving beech. She favored old-fashioned plants—lilies, dahlias, Portland roses; syringa, deutzia, sweet shrub—perhaps because at the heart of all her design lay a simple experience of her girlhood. One day in May, playing hide-and-seek at her Massachusetts cousins', she had concealed herself between two ancient lilac bushes in full bloom. For a long minute she saw the world through their sun-fretted clusters, half suffocating in their heady stench. At the farthest corner of her garden she raised a small room that to her justified the rest: a perfect square of lilac hedges, trimmed along their sides and growing freely at their tops, each May modulating around their perimeter through every imaginable gradation of blossom, from wine-red to palest mauve and back again, the transitions tempered by flowers of the white lilac with which the other bushes were interspersed. Only Allan and Priscilla ever accompanied Maud there; and, of course, John. John had come to work as handyman for her father and stayed on. Not because of loyalty to the family or a predilection for gardening: the intensity Maud brought to her tasks inspired him with a lasting enthusiasm of his own. Except for Allan, no one knew her as he did.

Outside her private world, Maud had rarely experienced the special satisfaction of seeing what she wanted and getting it. Weather permitting, Priscilla did nothing else. One day her fourth-grade teacher called her a dunce; two weeks later she moved to the top of her class. At eleven she saw a movie with Sonja Henie; by the end of the winter she was competing as a figure skater. She successfully pursued popularity, even at boarding school, where she showed a tendency to collect boyfriends. Her classmates forgave her because hers were too old for them.

Any parents would have taken pride in her. For Allan, with his busy career, pride sufficed. Maud, with much less to do, wished she'd had a live mother whose example she could follow. While Priscilla's successes reassured her, Maud suspected that whatever her upbringing Priscilla would have become a prodigious achiever. A pang of regret sometimes transfixed her when she thought of her daughter: had she ever been truly useful to her?

Priscilla showed self-reliance from the time she could crawl. She saw the world as a nest of probable satisfactions. Obstacles like her fourth-grade teacher pointed towards bigger opportunities. Only once had she known complete helplessness. When she was fourteen, during her summer vacation, she had made friends with Lewis Lewison. Drawn to him by his unlikeness to other boys and by a shyness close to surliness, she had given up her hefty eighteen-year-olds to pursue him. At last he kissed her, and on one hot afternoon took her into the empty barn behind his parents' house, where he came to grips with her strong, skinny body, and with his own. Her resistance to his assault enraged him less than his inability to carry it through, which made him wild as he lay on her, rubbing against her flesh like a child trapped in a closet and banging the door. She had been terrified and, finding herself trapped, had lost control of herself.

Lewis ran off. Louisa found, washed, and consoled her. She promised to attend to Lewis and urged Priscilla to speak to her mother. Priscilla agreed. Maud would certainly show compassion, and Priscilla's "accident," if childish, had been provoked by grown-up business. She could talk to Maud as an equal.

Priscilla was less sure of this when she saw her mother. Maud appeared in the door of the house and looked at Priscilla with a not unfamiliar, not unaffectionate, not unwary look: Tell me everything is fine, it said, and I'll go away.

Priscilla was sitting alone in the front room. She had never done this. Perplexed, Maud stood still in the doorway: "I think I'll have some tea."

"Want me to make it?"

"That would be lovely. Darjeeling, please."

"I saw Lewis this afternoon."

"What a lucky boy! How does Gene feel about your leaving him for a fifteen-year-old? *I* saw Phoebe. As far as I could tell, she was teaching her counselors knots."

"I'd have done better going on that trip with her."

Maud put down two teacups and closed the cabinet doors. She groped for words that would invite Priscilla to go on, and succeeded in not finding them. Irritation with what she could not say made her voice tremble: "You should have a brand-new sleeping bag, at least." She laughed foolishly to cover the tremor.

Priscilla laughed too and squeezed Maud's arm. "It's no problem. The other guys will take me whenever I want. Show me what you're wearing tonight?"

They drank their tea. Maud never heard about Lewis in the barn.

As a rule, Priscilla confided in Maud. She told her all a mother might want to know. In delicate matters she often spoke after the fact, leaving Maud with foregone conclusions. When, a few months after her college graduation, Priscilla announced her liaison with Walter, Maud was not surprised that she had already moved in with him. As usual, she had to like it or lump it.

Maud missed Priscilla during the following winter. She missed what they had never had together. It seemed to Maud that her daughter had grown up in one brief flurry of yesterdays, while she was gazing out the window at an Adirondack sunset. Maud had borne her; Priscilla had grown up without her. She could do little about that now.

She could do something. She remembered her father (oh, with him things *had* happened, she had been mixed up with him, she had hung on his words and arms), she remembered her father's determination to train her. If nothing else, she could at least teach Priscilla that money was an opportunity to be mastered. Priscilla might then emerge from the blindness that afflicted Maud and Pauline. Maud knew that, like the moon in the sky or the trees in the woods, money surrounded them too naturally to ever be thought about. Maud could not blame Priscilla if she "didn't really care" about money—she never asked her to go out at night to make sure the moon was shining and the trees growing. Such things looked after themselves. Even Allan, who himself knew and cared about money, showed no anxiety concerning Priscilla: "She's fortunate *not* to have to worry. That's what 'fortune' means. She'll learn when the time comes."

Allan's opinion was wasted on Maud. She brooded over the problem on melancholy winter days. She finally came up with a scheme. She could hardly influence Priscilla directly. She must create a foregone conclusion of her own: a situation where Priscilla would be obliged to use money and make decisions about it.

Maud conceived her project in early May, when spring was

warming belatedly the upper reaches of the Hudson. Several weeks later, she went to her bank in the city and put it into effect. She gave instructions to have twenty thousand dollars transferred yearly to Priscilla for the next ten years. Priscilla could spend the income; she could only invest the capital. She would *have* to invest it.

As she made these arrangements, Maud thought less and less about Priscilla and more and more intently of her dead father. When she had done her part, she asked the bank officials to inform Priscilla. The scheme should be presented to her as the working out of an old covenant. Maud told herself she should spare Priscilla the nuisance of feeling grateful. She had performed her duty in the manner of an invisible guardian, as an agent of impersonal benevolence.

These mildly insane precautions at once aroused Priscilla's suspicions. She recognized Maud's hand. Priscilla recalled that one afternoon when she was nine she had returned from school two hours late and found her mother conferring on the terrace with a policeman. The next day Maud had a television set (then new and rare) installed in Priscilla's bedroom: a bribe never to come home late again. Priscilla thought, I have now committed a bohemian cohabitation, and Mama is bribing me to give it up. That much Priscilla could understand. But the scale of the gesture! Giving away two hundred thousand dollars suggested motives less generous—a tax break, for instance. Priscilla did not mind. She simply wanted to know.

The early summer had been vexing to her. Dedicated to her partnership with Morris, she had not sold anything since his death—their paintings had all been impounded in the dead man's apartment. She hoped eventually to recover them, at least those by Walter; after all, no one else knew about them. With such a stock, and with Morris's life insurance as working capital, she could look forward to the future. Meanwhile, she had to abide the slow course of the law. She had little else to do. Walter spent his days hard at work. Most of her friends had gone away. When the bank told her of Maud's scheme, she decided to get out of the city and unearth her mother's secret. She phoned Maud to announce her arrival on August first in time for lunch.

Priscilla's call surprised Maud only passingly. She had suspected that her precautions would prove wishful. Initially resigned to her visit, by the time Priscilla arrived Maud had come to resent it. Elizabeth had distressed her by leaving for the day. Later, Allan had called to make a disagreeable confession. Watching her daughter emerge from a taxi and stride buoyantly towards the house, she shuddered. My God, she's like Pauline.

On the shady west porch the women settled into upholstered white wicker armchairs. Declining a drink, noticing that her mother's glass was filled with green chartreuse, Priscilla tilted her chair forward, sat pertly upright, and declared her thanks: whatever Maud's reasons, Priscilla was stunned by her kindness. She spoke at length, underscoring her gratitude.

Maud did not respond. She appeared hardly to be listening. Something, Priscilla thought, is unusually wrong. She nevertheless kept up a cheerful monologue. She talked enthusiastically about her life with Walter. "I see, I see," Maud at last interrupted, only then referring to the pretext of her daughter's visit: "They made everything clear in the letter, didn't they? They put everything in the letter?"

"Yes, the letter was absolutely clear. They put everything in it, Mama, except you."

"Oh, me—" Maud sighed, waving to a ghost beyond the lawn.

"I came here for you."

"You're sweet, but you know, I only had to go through the motions—hardly worth taking credit for."

"But you deserve credit. As for going through the motions— Mama, isn't your elbow getting a little sore?"

"What do you mean?" Maud wrily answered. "It's only my seventeenth drink."

"Can you tell me one thing? Is it Allan?"

"He spoke to *you* about it?"

Allan had called Maud earlier. Fearful she would learn about the doomed gelding he had helped insure, he had described his part in the business. Although Maud did not fully understand him, Allan's discomfiture became painfully apparent to her.

"He didn't speak to me. Someone saw them," Priscilla explained. "I'm sorry, Mama. Who would have dreamed it of Aunt Paw?"

Even unwily Maud had the sense not to budge. She sipped her chartreuse and stared through the beetle-butted screen: "Tell me what you know."

"Oh, 'know'! When was it, the night before last, a friend driving across Sixty-third Street had to stop behind a taxi, and she saw Papa and Aunt Pauline get out together, outside the apartment. They were acting—" Maud had risen and started crossing the porch. She tripped over a board as smooth as any other. "Oh, Mama!"

Maud was stumbling with humiliation. Not because of what she was hearing: because she was hearing it from her daughter. She felt outraged by Priscilla's presence, and losing her balance didn't help. She kept silent.

"Mama! It's no fun, but it won't matter. Papa adores you and always will." She barely paused. "You don't have to drink brandy before lunch."

"It's not brandy. I was up at five, and I had my lunch at eleven," Maud declared. Her own anger bewildered her.

"OK, Mama."

Maud squeezed her crystal snifter so hard that it splintered. "Damn you!" she blurted, meaning to say, Damn it.

Priscilla stared at her eagerly. "It's awful seeing you—"

"So why bother coming? I've been so much better since— hah!" Maud chose to steam rather than explain.

"Mama," Priscilla went on, her voice dropping a minor third, "I can't enjoy your becoming a lush."

"Is that what you came here to tell me?"

"I came here, and it *is* a long ride, to tell you—I've already said it. Or maybe you weren't listening."

"Of course I was. I'm glad you're pleased."

"Aren't *you* pleased? I thought my coming up might mean something to you. I didn't know you'd just been 'going through the motions'—as usual."

"Anyway, enjoy the money." Maud had cut her left little finger.

"Mama, you're such a dope!"

"Is there something wrong with enjoying money?"

"Shit! Why do I sit here talking to this flop? Listen, I just inherited a hundred thousand dollars. Not to mention what I've made on my own, you'll be glad to know."

"I *am* pleased. You never said a word—"

"I've been selling paintings. I've been working with Morris Romsen—you know, the critic. Walter Trale gave us an option on his best paintings."

"Not all of them, surely. He didn't give you the portrait of Elizabeth."

"Oh, yes, he did."

"How funny. I bought it last month, and not from you, Miss Kahnweiler."

"What are you talking about?"

"I mean that I bought—that five or six weeks ago Allan and I bought Walter Trale's 'Portrait of Elizabeth' from Irene Kramer. I can't show it to you because your father's taken it elsewhere. Give him a call."

Wasting no time in conjectures as to how Irene had recovered the portrait (she was Morris's sister and heir, after all), Priscilla made silent calculations. She could get back to the city by six; that afternoon an opening was scheduled at the Kramer Gallery. Her father could wait. She had to see Irene.

"Mama, can you drive me to the station?"

"Ask John. He's out in back. I'm going to have a little lie-down."

At two-thirty Maud called her bank in the city to cancel her scheme. She had completed her new instructions and was about to hang up when unforeseen grief overcame her. She asked the bank official to wait and muffled the phone while her sobs subsided. She then said, "Disregard what I told you. Don't change anything, except for one thing. Change the name of the beneficiary. Please delete 'Priscilla Ludlam' and write in 'Pauline Pruell.' Née Dunlap. Send the papers for me to sign as soon as you can."

Maud and Elizabeth

JULY - SEPTEMBER 1963

"   . . . One week," maud was shouting precisely, "what's a week in a lifetime?"

No less loudly, no less deliberately, Elizabeth answered, "A lifetime? And you still want that milktoast?"

"That's for me to decide!" Maud cried (quickly whispering, "He's coming downstairs").

"(Nice going.) It's him or the portrait, you can't have both!"

"You're disgusting!"

"It's my portrait, isn't it?"

"*Of* you—hardly yours!"

"Cut the crap, Mrs. Miniver. I need something to show for my week. (Where *is* he?)"

"(I'll go look.)"

Tiptoeing out, Maud at once noticed that the portrait of Elizabeth was missing from the library, where for a week it had stood unpacked and unhung. After looking into the music

room, the den, and the dining room—all empty—she rejoined
Elizabeth. Together they watched Allan, encumbered with the
painting, walking to the station wagon that he had parked on
the public road.

"I was sure he'd come charging in."

"What was that phone call?" Maud asked.

Until today, Maud had not seen Elizabeth since the year
before she married, and she had forgotten ever meeting her. She
would not have recognized her name if, a year ago, she had not
read her daughter's thesis on Walter Trale. Its account of his
friendship with Elizabeth touched her because they had met in
this very town, where Maud had been summering with her
family. She vividly recalled the evening parties where men wore
white double-breasted dinner jackets and women organdy and
organza. She had gone swimming that summer in a new elastic,
white-belted bathing suit, and she had become engaged to Allan
(when he proposed, she had on high-waisted, pleated slacks,
with a lawn kerchief over her hair). Her father was still alive,
Pauline still her happy protégée. She remembered Walter, then
only a boy, younger even than Pauline, his talent all the more
glamorous for his youth, so that he was lionized by the horse-
and-dog set. Maud felt less sure about Elizabeth. An image
came back to her of someone beautiful and a little "wild,"
someone she could not place with certainty; someone in an
older crowd who had disappeared after a few years; someone
with the bright precarious youth of those not altogether young.
What had that woman now become? (Like Maud, Elizabeth
must be past fifty. What had she herself become? What had she
done to attain this once-faraway age?)

During the months that followed her reading of Priscilla's
account, Maud sometimes remembered to ask acquaintances
about Elizabeth. Their answers whetted her curiosity. Elizabeth
had married a Brazilian—or was it a Lebanese?—millionaire.
She had married a carpet salesman from Topeka. She had

remained single. No man could win her. No decent man would
have her. She had turned into an alcoholic, or a drug addict,
or a nymphomaniac. Hadn't she proclaimed herself a lesbian?
Purest rumor—a rumor probably started by Elizabeth herself,
after she had gone into business. Career women often find it best
not to marry. Elizabeth had had a brilliant career. Not as a
businesswoman: as an actress. Or perhaps as an artist. Remember those banged bronze monsters in Brasilia, or were those the
Brazilian's first wife's? Elizabeth had done none of those things.
She had disappeared. She had come to nothing.

In June, on a visit to the city, Maud stopped at the Kramer
Gallery. Irene, whom she had known for years, confided that
she was offering rare paintings by Walter Trale to her best
customers. Among them was the portrait of Elizabeth H.;
Maud asked to see it and scrutinized it for the symptoms of
Walter's fabled passion. She looked for Elizabeth as well, who
only veiled herself in fresh mystery. Recognizing a windfall,
Maud bought the painting on the spot. Her burgeoning fascination with Elizabeth left her, she felt, little choice. The fascination continued to grow.

It occurred to Maud, a few days later, to question Irene
about Elizabeth herself. Irene said: ask Barrington Pruell.
Louisa Lewison had once told her that he and Elizabeth kept
in touch.

Maud thought that likely. Old Mr. Pruell had befriended
Elizabeth in those early years. On the morning of July tenth she
paid him a visit.

Maud and Mr. Pruell had a longstanding friendship. After
her mother's death, Maud had turned to him for support. He
knew her father well and understood, if he did not condone, his
withdrawal from domestic life. He did his best to explain Mr.
Dunlap's behavior to his young friend, and he encouraged her
to keep up her grades and take good care of Pauline. Maud had
trusted him. After her marriage they saw each other less. Maud

frequented Allan's friends, city people, business people; publicly, at least, Mr. Pruell belonged to the horse-and-dog world. They now took each other for granted. When they met at parties, they hugged, exchanged "news," promised to meet privately, and never did.

When Maud announced the reason for her visit, Mr. Pruell said, "It's your lucky day. No point my telling you about Elizabeth. She's coming to lunch."

"She's here?"

"She arrived last week. Stay and see for yourself."

Maud phoned Allan to tell him that she would be out for the day. She begged Mr. Pruell to talk to her about his friend: "I'd like to be the tiniest bit prepared."

Mr. Pruell laughed. "Ask *her*. You'll have more fun."

Elizabeth called to say she couldn't come after all.

Although Mr. Pruell promised to arrange another meeting, Maud felt a disappointment verging on anger. She felt betrayed. It was then that she realized she had been nourishing a small passion, one for which she could find no name. She knew that it included a trace of envy. What had made Elizabeth so different? How had she won friends like Walter Trale and Barrington Pruell and left in her wake the enticing confusion of her reputations? Elizabeth's failure to appear for lunch clinched Maud's obsession with her. She made up her mind that they would meet.

The next days brought Maud only frustration. She learned where Elizabeth was staying, what friends she saw, which parties she would attend. If Maud had called Elizabeth at her hotel, she could have met her in a day; but without a plausible excuse she was embarrassed to approach her. She did not hesitate, however, to get herself invited to every social event in town. And wherever Maud went, Elizabeth did not appear. After a while, Maud began wondering if the woman wasn't avoiding her. (She could imagine no reason for this. Elizabeth could hardly guess that she was being perversely pursued.) Without getting even a glimpse of her prey, Maud consumed a surfeit of olives and jellied ham and enough drinks to afflict even her seasoned metabolism.

After four days, she grew so discouraged that she actually gave up all hope of knowing Elizabeth. They were, she still felt, linked by destiny: but their destiny was to never meet—"a conjunction of their minds, an opposition of their stars." One morning—the fifteenth of July—she picked up her phone and broke her engagements for the day. At eleven o'clock, after trotting into the driveway, dismounting, and tethering her bay mare to a convenient birch, an unfamiliar red-haired woman in riding cap and jodhpurs walked up to Maud's front door and rang the bell.

To Elizabeth, an hour later, watching Allan drive off, Maud declared, "If anything happens to that picture, I'll roast him."

"In the meantime, why not settle for the original?" Elizabeth slipped her arm into Maud's.

Maud took five seconds to understand. "You don't mean you want to *stay* here?"

"I'd love to. If you don't trust my friendly sentiments, I can honestly confess that I'm broke. Bone poor till September sixth. So it would also help."

"I do love to be useful—how did you guess?"

"Allan told me, of course."

"But you do see—"

"We can always finesse the drama. Although I'm pretty much stuck with it in any case."

"How come?"

"Allan was a discreet visitor but a frequent one. The help at the Adelphi are turning sort of frosty. It's hardly your problem, I know—"

"I suppose not. Then why *do* I feel responsible? I guess I'd rather be on your side than theirs."

"If it's not fun, I'll disappear. I promise. Instantly."

Maud surprised Elizabeth, who had called on her out of impulse, although not without a reason: she had heard that Maud was trying to meet her. Allan had described Maud to her misleadingly. Instead of a devoted homebody, Elizabeth discovered a woman whose clean-edged prettiness had been sweetly softened by the faint wrinkling of years. Her disconsolate politeness inspired Elizabeth with an intense longing to make her giggle.

Until Allan's back-door entry, the two women had talked like schoolmates making up for half a lifetime's separation. Maud soon discovered what they had in common. When she brought up Allan, Elizabeth could not help committing a pause; which Maud of course noticed.

She had thought that Allan might be having an affair. For a week he had acted towards her with distracted impatience; he had also twice brought her home voluptuous masses of her favorite Jeanne Charmet dahlias. What this behavior might signify she had inferred from the solicitous phone calls of not-very-dear friends. When Elizabeth brightly followed her pause with talk of certain attractive men she'd just met, naming names and detailing qualities, Maud interrupted: "Aha! *That's* what my girlfriends haven't been telling me. There's another woman, and it's you!"

Maud recognized something like relief in her voice: as if she were thinking, If he had to cheat, better her than someone else.

Blushing wildly, Elizabeth said, "I won't say, 'If only I'd known—.' I *am* glad we're talking to one another."

"But I've been chasing you for days!"

Elizabeth smiled. "You see why you never caught up?"

"You mean you were running away?"

"No. I was meeting Allan. I'd plan to go to the McCollums' from five to seven, then Allan would call to say he could get away from five to seven—"

"Because of course *I* was going to the McCollums' from five to seven, because *you* were."

"So I would call Mrs. McCollum, or anyway not go."

"The first time was Barrington Pruell's lunch?"

"*You* were the dear old friend so anxious to meet me? Oh, no! You do get it?"

"Yes, I do." Maud felt stupid. Elizabeth was overwhelming her.

Elizabeth leaned across the coffee table and took Maud's hands. "I *didn't* know. I only learned you were looking for me two days ago." Maud glanced up warily. "I never schedule things. Actually, coming here was my horse's idea."

Maud sighed. "I can see how funny it is, my making it possible . . ."

"What's funnier is us, right now." Elizabeth paused. "I'm sorry you wasted all that time. But so what? New game today." Maud smiled as if to say: You're very kind. "Look at it this way: thanks to Allan, we're friends."

Maud gazed into Elizabeth's eyes, thinking, What can I lose? They heard Allan treading carefully through the kitchen. Familiar with house sounds, Maud reported his movements. Elizabeth said she had to phone the stable—her mare was overdue. When she lifted the handset, she clapped her hand over the speaker and for several minutes kept the receiver at her ear. After hanging up, she said to Maud, "Let's blow his mind."

"You mean *shoot* him?"

"No, sweetie pie. Just wow him." Elizabeth proposed a portentous dialogue for Allan to overhear; they thereupon performed it with operatic gravity and gusto.

Maud told Elizabeth she was welcome to stay. Elizabeth thanked her with an embrace. Now she must ride her mare home. "She's probably girdled the birch."

"The 'ladies of the forest' grow like weeds here. It's expendable."

"I hope you like to ride."

Raising her eyes in woeful ecstasy, Maud answered, "Oh, Elizabeth, it's out of the question. Horses don't like me. Or I don't understand them."

"You never met the right horses. Come on out. This one's a dream."

Maud moaned and followed. On the lawn Elizabeth introduced her to the mare, Fatima. The two greeted each other genteelly, if noncommittally. Elizabeth ambled away into summer haze.

She moved in the following day. She told Maud she had everything she needed. "Enough for a week is enough for a summer. Not that I'll stay *that* long." Maud didn't think she'd mind. She had missed her already.

That morning Allan called Maud to ask her if Elizabeth had said anything "about a horse." Maud cut the conversation short. Allan had run away; he could stay away.

In the evening Elizabeth suggested that they go into town for cocktails. Maud demurred: "How about drinks on the porch? I recommend it highly. I do it all the time."

"You haven't been out in two days."

"But I love it here." Maud was reluctant to be seen with her husband's lover.

"So do I. But soon? I've missed some promising bars."

Safe for the night, Maud acquiesced.

The previous morning, from the moment she began eavesdropping on the telephone, Elizabeth had been sure that Allan knew she was listening. He had played the tough guy for her, bringing their brief story to a pitiful end. She said to Maud, "I couldn't quite make it out. He has a devious side, you know."

"You mean," Maud said belligerently, "last week was only the tip of the Venusberg?"

"I don't think so. I've known womanizers (and they have their attractions), but not Allan. Definitely not. He's had a successful career, hasn't he?"

"Very." Perplexed, Maud dropped the subject.

Elizabeth asked, "Whose bedroom is the one next to mine?"

"My daughter Priscilla's. Or it used to be."

"Did I tell you I met her at Walter Trale's? She's sharp. She knew so much about me I almost felt my age. Whatever that may be."

Maud told Elizabeth about her recent largesse towards Priscilla, explaining, "So she'll know *something* about money." She reddened, remembering her friend's "bone-poorness."

"I bet she makes a fortune with it."

Maud drove Elizabeth to the stables the next morning. She had agreed to accompany her if she could just sit and watch. She enjoyed seeing Elizabeth take her mount through its paces: animal and rider looked equally content. After unsaddling, Elizabeth introduced Maud to a few more horses. Maud conceded that with Elizabeth next to her she might, someday, give one of them a try. As they were leaving, a man arrived from the racetrack with a depressing tale about a destroyed gelding.

That night, after dinner, they chose to read. Even though the light was weakening, they sat on the west piazza, their reading glasses perched on their nose tips, reluctant to forsake the evening sky behind the panoply of blackening hills. After ten minutes Maud heaved a sigh of delight. Elizabeth closed her book expectantly. "Well—" Maud said and read aloud:

An extreme languor had settled on him, he felt weakened with the cessation of her grasp. . . . He heard himself quote:

" 'Since when we stand side by side!' " His voice trembled.

"Ah yes!" came in her deep tones: "The beautiful lines . . . They're true. We must part. In this world . . ." They seemed to her lovely and mournful words to say; heavenly to have them to say, vibratingly, arousing all sorts of images. Macmaster, mournfully too, said:

"We must wait." He added fiercely: "But tonight, at dusk!"

He imagined the dusk under the yew hedge. A shining motor drew up in the sunlight under the window.

"Yes! Yes!" she said. "There's a little white gate from the lane." She imagined their interview of passion and mournfulness amongst dim objects half seen. So much of glamour she could allow herself.

Afterwards he must come to the house to ask after her health and they would walk side by side on the lawn, publicly, in the warm light, talking of indifferent but beautiful poetries, a little wearily, but with what currents electrifying and passing between their flesh. . . . And then: long, circumspect years. . . .

"Were the Edwardians ever more neatly skewered? Perhaps they were Georgians by then."

"It's dazzling. How about this?"

I finished my cigarette and lit another. The minutes dragged by. Horns tooted and grunted on the boulevard. A big red interurban car rumbled past. A traffic light gonged. The blonde leaned on her elbow and cupped a hand over her eyes and stared at me behind it. The partition door opened and the tall bird with the cane slid out. He had another wrapped parcel, the shape of a large book. He went over to the desk and paid money. He left as he had come, walking on the balls of his feet, breathing with his mouth open, giving me a sharp side glance as he passed.

I got to my feet, tipped my hat to the blonde and went out after him. He walked west, swinging his cane in a small tight arc just above his right shoe. He was easy to follow. His coat was cut from a rather loud piece of horse robe with shoulders so wide that his neck stuck up out of it like a celery stalk and his head wobbled on it as he walked. We went a block and a half. At the Highland Avenue traffic signal I pulled up beside him and let him see me. . . .

The western light had shrunk to a band of dark green. Maud asked, "What was in the parcel?"

A few days later, Maud consented to ride. At the stables, tucking her slacks into a pair of borrowed boots, she adjured Elizabeth, "You're responsible!"

"Tell that to the horse."

Faced with a beast like an overstuffed pony, Maud was driven to confess that she had once had "endless" riding lessons. Elizabeth chided her for a sneak. "I have the know-how," Maud explained, "it's the performance that gives me the willies. Jumping especially," she incautiously added.

Maud was then assigned a proper horse. For an hour and a half she walked, trotted, and cantered around the ring behind Elizabeth, who at last led her onto the infield grass, on which stood three jumps of whitewashed wood. Elizabeth dismounted and set the bar of the lowest jump at barely a foot above the ground. She led Maud over it at an easy lope. She repeated the procedure with the bar at two feet. Setting it at three, she saw Maud's knees clench on her saddle and thought, she's afraid of taking a spill.

Elizabeth decided to show Maud that she had no cause for fright. When she took the jump herself, she nonchalantly slipped out of her stirrups and slid off her mount onto the turf. Intent on making her fall look natural, she distractedly caught her right foot on the pommel and landed on her capless head. Maud, right behind her, was so unsettled by the mishap that she forgot her own anxiety and took the jump smoothly. Propped on one elbow, Elizabeth cheered.

On their way home, Elizabeth invited Maud to a bar on Broadway. Maud never went to bars. She would again have refused if surviving an hour on horseback hadn't drained her power to resist. Entering the P's-and-Q's, she nervously inquired, "You know this crowd?" She dreaded meeting people she knew, and not meeting people she knew, and meeting people she didn't know. She was reminded of childhood visits to her father's office, full of strange men in shirt-sleeves. She drank too fast and had to pee twice in half an hour. When they left she felt sweaty and sick.

Elizabeth ignored Maud's discomforts. At six-thirty the next evening, appearing in a pale-yellow voile blouse that wreathed over a white sheath skirt, she proposed going back into town. Maud gazed at her admiringly and shook her head: "You go on without me."

"It wouldn't be the same."

"You saw what happened yesterday. I'd rather get sozzled at home."

"How come?"

"I don't like being stared at by strangers."

"It's half the fun. Especially if you give them something to stare at. What about that green Norell shift?"

"Why not a bathing suit?"

"You'd be surprised. Most of them never notice you—you 'one,' not you Maud."

"And the other half? You said 'half the fun'?"

"Staring, just like you said. Or anyway looking. It's pleasant to watch other people. That's what they invented bars for—pleasure."

As they drove to the Boots 'n' Saddles, Maud vowed to remember those words. It was true that, once seated, they attracted scant attention.

Maud talked about Allan: "He sounded eager to come home. I think he should stew in his juice. I have no desire to pass the sponge. Not right away."

"You mean me?"

"I'm glad it *was* you. I still don't like it."

"If you think he needs to squirm, he can manage that by himself."

"Tell me about his devious side."

"How should I know?"

"Why did you ask about his career?"

"I've come to a conclusion about men: they're usually nuts. I'm not sure about this horse business, but it sounds like he's playing dirty games. Don't ask me why. Maybe to prove he doesn't need your connections. Shall we try the neighboring hole before going home? He'll come back when he really wants to."

It was almost nine when they left the second bar. In her kitchen, forgivably bumping into unclosed drawers and dropping an occasional fork, Maud assembled a meal. "May I leave the garlic out of the salad dressing? You know the Italians do, at least the ones in Italy." A Bibb lettuce in each hand, she came to a stop in the middle of the kitchen and there uttered a dreadful sigh.

"Baby!" clucked Elizabeth, "I thought you'd enjoyed yourself tonight." Glass in hand, she was leaning against a varnished-oak counter, swaying dancelike from side to side.

"Yes. But after you've gone—Allan, my friends, they're not like you at all. The future looks, well, uninspiring."

"You have everything you need to be happy. You do know that?"

"Ohhh, happiness . . ."

Maud walked over to the sink. Elizabeth followed her and hugged her from behind. When Maud looked around, Elizabeth kissed her mouth. The lettuces dropped into the sink.

"It's nice of you not to resist."

Maud turned on the cold water. "Don't you think we'd better eat something?"

"I love you, Maud."

"I was having such a good time!"

"You're a *glorious* woman."

"No. I'm not."

"I know. You've lived through forty-nine-and-a-half years of minor disasters. How about joining the party?" Elizabeth held her tight.

Maud kept shaking her head while she plucked a lettuce to tatters. "You're kind, you're a marvelous friend, but you have to accept me the way I am." She looked over her shoulder into Elizabeth's face. "I'd love to love you. It's frightening, though. I've never been with a woman before."

"Look, kissing you was . . . 'I love you' means you inspire me." Maud's subsequent laugh recalled Saint Sebastian at the loosing of the arrows. "Can't you tell I'm happy being with you, 'the way you are'?"

"I have this recurrent impression that I'm a bust."

"No kidding? I admit that sometimes you make me feel sane and efficient, which doesn't happen often. Maybe you could turn into a genuine bust and I'd really be on top of things."

"I'm going on the wagon this second."

"Don't you dare! Anyway, it's too late to start today."

They watched television after dinner. Mandy Rice-Davies followed a newly crowned pope. Elizabeth switched to the Mets, only thirty-two games out of first place and showing progress.

"There goes the Duke."

"He's very graceful. If only I knew what he was doing."

"It doesn't matter. Do you think he could fancy an older woman?"

Maud glanced shyly at Elizabeth and did not answer.

Maud came to like pub-crawling. She enjoyed speculating with Elizabeth about the lives of other patrons. Sometimes, to settle disagreements, the women consulted the patrons themselves, making friends of them for an evening. Maud discovered the easy society flourishing in public places.

One such evening, sitting on a bar-stool next to Maud, Elizabeth said to her, "You know I originally came to see you because you were my lover's wife?"

"Of course."

"I bet you don't know why I liked you right away." Maud

pertly tilted her head. Elizabeth pointed to their reflections in the mirror behind the embottled rear counter. "We have the same nose."

Later that night, the tenth since their meeting, Maud took Elizabeth into the music room, sat her down by the upright piano, and rendered Schumann's *Warum.*

"I haven't played since Priscilla graduated, heaven knows why. I never dared ask you—I've always longed to find somebody to accompany or play four hands with. You don't perchance play anything?"

"Just the one-holed flute, darling."

"Is that the baroque instrument?"

"It is if you treat it right. I'm a musical dunce."

"It really doesn't matter. I like playing alone. Just promise not to listen less than two rooms away."

The Mets tied the record for consecutive losses on the road. An earthquake wrecked Skopje, capital of Macedonia. Arlene Francis was arrested after a car accident. Priscilla called to announce her forthcoming visit.

Still later, Maud asked Elizabeth, "You know my bed's the size of a putting green—would you consider sharing it? It's when I'm drifting off that I recall what it was I wanted to talk about."

"I toss and turn like a seal, I'm told."

"And the morning after, they're vanished. I myself suffer from wakefulness in the dark hours. Can't we try?"

Maud was immediately cured of her insomnia, which Elizabeth immediately acquired. At four o'clock during their first night Maud opened her eyes to see her friend sitting crosslegged at her side. Since her fall in the riding ring, Elizabeth's neck sometimes stiffened painfully when she lay still.

Elizabeth woke up in the morning cradled in Maud's arms. She declared, "I need to get laid."

"I wish there was more I could do."

After breakfast Elizabeth made two phone calls. She told Maud she would be spending the next day and night in the city.

In the afternoon, while Maud was hoeing her herb garden (a task she delegated to no one), Elizabeth's voice streamed through opened windows into the steamy air:

> But this is wine that's all too strange and strong.
> I'm full of foolish song,
> And out my song must pour.
> So please forgive this helpless haze I'm in,
> I've really never been
> In love before.
> Ba ba doobie,
> Ba ba doobie,
> Ba ba doobie
> Ah bah.

Her clear tones had a seductive faint breathiness.

Maud told Elizabeth over dinner, "You could sing opera. Or at least operetta."

"Theater! Music! How I'd love it! Honey, I'm strictly bathwater pops."

For Maud, the following day bristled with event. Up with the sun, in the garden by seven, she drove Elizabeth to the bus station to catch the ten-o'clock southbound and came home in time for Allan's call. He confessed his role in insuring the lately destroyed gelding. Maud could not grasp the facts of his story, even after he repeated it, and she concluded by saying, "What a depressing business! Why tell *me* about it?"

(Allan drew two small consolations from talking to her. She did not mention the portrait, which two nights before he had shamefully surrendered to Owen Lewison. By confirming Elizabeth's presence, she lessened his pain at not being asked back.)

Soon afterwards Priscilla arrived. Maud then learned of

Allan's night with Pauline. She fought with her daughter. Torn between anger and remorse, she decided to give Pauline the money she had intended for Priscilla. At three in the afternoon Walter Trale called to tell her that the "Portrait of Elizabeth" she had bought was a copy. There had been a string of crazy misunderstandings. . . .

Maud believed him. Human communication was going to the bow-wows. Why today of all days had Elizabeth abandoned her? She thought of telling Allan about the painting, then remembered his fling with Pauline. She drove to the Boots 'n' Saddles. Finding the place empty in mid-afternoon, she drank two more solitary chartreuses. At home she was given a message from Elizabeth, with a number to call in the city, of which she did not avail herself.

The next day, Elizabeth arrived earlier than expected. In time for another free lunch, Maud told herself. She had difficulty responding to her boarder's embrace. Elizabeth seemed not to notice.

"Nice enough," she replied to Maud's polite inquiry. "I feel sort of dumb missing a day here."

"It's sweet of you to say so," Maud said, staring into her coffee cup.

" 'Sweet'? Hey—this is *me.*"

Maud pursed her lips. "I've been thinking there's something we really ought to discuss. It's been marvelous having you here, and I want it to go on being marvelous. So don't you think— don't you think it might be better if we decided exactly how long it is you expect to stay? Open-ended arrangements are so awfully . . ."

Unable to go on, Maud shut her eyes. Sneaking up on her, Elizabeth slid fingers under her dirty-blonde curls and took an emphatic grip on her ears. Maud was immobilized. Elizabeth said to her, "Little girl, you're jealous."

"Oh, really? Jealous of what? Of you?"

"It won't hurt to say so."

Maud began to cry. "You move in and take over as though you'd been here all your life. All I know about you is that you spent a week putting out for my husband—"

Elizabeth squeezed Maud's ears to shut her up. "I implore you to forgive me. I'm an unfeeling jerk—"

"Everything's easy for you. You don't have a family to worry about. You don't have any money problems—you don't even have any money."

"My beloved, listen, please, I promise you that starting right now I will never again do *anything* without you—" She let go of Maud's ears.

"If you knew what I've gone through since you left!"

"I'll arrange something right now," Elizabeth said, walking across the veranda towards the front parlor. At the door she turned: "Think of it—our first double date!"

Maud, still snuffling, at these words looked up in astonishment. "What do you mean?"

"I'll find you somebody delectable."

"Elizabeth, stop it! That's not what I meant. I'm past fifty."

From the gloom beyond the door Elizabeth replied, "I'd never have guessed it. But you'll see: at our age, it's a picnic."

Over lunch Maud begged Elizabeth to revoke her good deed. Elizabeth could then play the offended party: "I got three dates broken to make sure you'd have the best." She ended the discussion by saying, "If you don't like him, you say no." Maud consented and began a recapitulation of the previous day.

In the afternoon they went for a ride, starting from a horse farm to the west of the house. Instead of climbing into the foothills as they had planned, they kept to the unpaved roads that ran between level fields of blossoming potatoes and newly harvested corn. Elizabeth questioned Maud about Pauline, and Maud told her about their childhood years, her foster-motherhood, the bitter falling-out over Pauline's engagement to